Things
unspoken

ANITRA SHEEN

Things
unspoken

CHRONICLE BOOKS
SAN FRANCISCO

Library of Congress Cataloging-in-Publication Data:

Things unspoken : a novel / Anitra Sheen
      p.   cm.
ISBN 0-8118-2355-5
I. Title.
PS3569.H392169G76   1999   98-39552
813'.54—dc21

Printed in the United States of America

Cover photos: Gladys Galperin (top) and Frankie Frankeny
Designed by Anne Galperin

Distributed in Canada by Raincoast Books
8680 Cambie Street
Vancouver, British Columbia V6P 6M9

10 9 8 7 6 5 4 3 2 1

Chronicle Books
85 Second Street
San Francisco, California 94105

www.chroniclebooks.com

*I*N MEMORY OF my mother, my father,
Vati, Mavis, Mary, and Peter. The lights still shine.

've come back to Los Angeles on a rare day, when the air doesn't obscure the view. The white letters of the Hollywood sign stand out in contrast to the marbled olive and brown of the foothills, and palm trees raise their shaggy fists into a stark blue sky. There were many days like this when I was growing up here: clear air spreading into tree-lined spaces. Wild poppies growing in vacant lots. But then, there were not so many cars and tall buildings and not so many bars on the windows.

Instinctively, I look up to the hills. We used to see our house from the freeway, its tall Moorish form perched high and white against the mountain. You had to look at just the right time, at just the right spot, or you would miss it as you drove by. As I wind my way through our old neighborhood into the foothills, the familiar canyons come alive with sounds and echoes and I see again my father's roses planted among the chaparral, wild and fragrant and full of thorns.

As I drive downtown, I miss the turnoff. I've forgotten what it's like to drive the freeways in L.A. One distracted moment and you find yourself in the wrong lane, peeling off in the wrong direction, a Jeep tailing eight inches from your bumper. I head south on the 710 Freeway, looking for a good place to exit and get my bearings. A large green sign ahead. How could I have gotten so far off? I take Imperial Highway and veer eastward into Downey, not far from where the Rio Hondo flows into the Los Angeles River. A few modern commercial streets fade into the old residential suburb, which for years consisted of dairy farms and only a few clusters of postwar bungalows. The smell of cows still permeates the air.

Passing the streets that branch off from the highway, I read the names: Esperanza. Consuelo. Via Amorita. Hope. Consola- *tion. A Way of Love. The air seems heavy and I'm conscious of the effort of breathing in and blowing out. I hear the sounds of breathing, a rushing deep against the membrane of my ear. It is an old sound, an old record dropped onto a turntable, the first gravelly scratches as the needle is set down. Then I see the sign on the grass, in front of the old hospital building. I know it now.*

PART ONE

*T*HE GRASS WAS GREEN that summer, so green I remember it first. I remember hot colored flowers too, but the marigolds, zinnias, and the whiteflies that swarm above them are all tinged with green; I look back on that time as if peering through blades of grass.

Every Saturday my brothers and I sat, lay, and rolled on this lawn, waiting. Alex and Jimmy were six and five; I was just under four. At that age, waiting was a fidgety game. We opened our boxes of Cracker Jacks, fingers rummaging for the surprise toy inside. It was the toy, not the caramel corn, we were after. We saved these toys as gifts for my mother, so it was important to have just the right one. If we wanted someone else's toy, we traded. The Cracker Jack negotiations were tense, especially between the boys, who were drawn to the same diminutive planes and trucks and would have fought over them if my father hadn't said it was wrong to bring a gift wrapped in bad feelings. Sometimes I would give up my toy to settle the argument and would gladly pluck a yellow dandelion from the grass instead. To me, a dandelion was also a gift. We ate our Cracker Jacks, then brushed off our grass-dented knees and watched for my father to call us into the sprawling building of Rancho Los Amigos Hospital. Inside, my mother lay paralyzed, waiting for the death that had already reached her neck to claim the rest of her.

Rancho Los Amigos was the largest hospital in the country for patients with poliomyelitis during the sweeping epidemics of the late forties and early fifties. Thousands of people, mostly young, were brought in with various degrees of paralysis. Some left with braces and crutches, some were released in wheelchairs, many never left at all. Every Saturday we walked down the polished corridors. The pattering of our feet mingled with the hushed voices of shell-shocked families and the tidal rhythm of bellows. There were many children. Small heads pressed into the plump white of pillows. Small faces followed us with their eyes as we passed. Some had adults beside them, talking softly or stroking their arms. Some were alone, limp as rag dolls, their chests raised and lowered by positive pressure machines and mechanical rocking beds. Dink respirators, "iron lungs" they were called in those times, were lined up like a fleet of submarines. Rows of cylinders riveted and shining breathed slowly like fish. Quickly we zigzagged through them; we knew our way.

From the side, my mother's respirator was like all the rest: a gleaming metal cylinder, flanked by small portholes, just big enough for an arm, hinged and tightly fastened. Her head emerged from a latched opening, and rested heavily on a white pillow. One could only imagine the body within. But the front end of our mother's respirator was distinctly her own; it was decorated with Cracker Jack surprises from Saturdays past. A rocking horse, a goat, a tiny fold-out beach ball, dried-up dandelions, a cutout of Jack the sailor with his black-eared dog, a miniature book, trucks and cars of various kinds were taped in an arch above her face. Lying there, she could watch the changing constellation of Cracker Jack toys marking the passage of Saturdays: her private zodiac. "Mummy, I brought you the truck, remember?" said Alex. "No, me," Jimmy insisted. They looked up into her reflection and waited for the machine to breathe so she could speak.

From my height it was difficult to see my mother's face reflected in the small rectangular mirror mounted above her. It was even more difficult to hear her voice. The words floated up and away, above the relentless wheezes that flowed from the machine like a pulsing current. I soon grew restless. I played with my shoelaces; I bent my knees and hopped like a bunny; I picked my nose. I tried to imagine where her hand would be and touched that steel cold spot. After a while the boys grew restless, too. My father lifted each of us up to kiss her good-bye. We walked out over the grass, the pungent green in our nostrils, the spongy green under our feet. The green seeped into our bones, silent and indelible.

*M*Y MOTHER DIED IN late September, as the green drained from the leaves in the hot sun. And as the days became shorter, time itself seemed to be shrinking and dark. In the evenings, I waited at the window, staring out into the fading light until I saw the headlights of my father's car beam against the garage door. I knew now that it was possible for a parent to leave, never to return, and in spite of my father's reassurances I worried that one evening there would be no headlights and I would be left alone in the darkness.

My father was starting a medical practice at this time, so he didn't spend much time with us during the week, but he made Sunday mornings a special occasion by cooking breakfast: burnt bacon, buckwheat cakes the size of a skillet and soggy with corn syrup, oatmeal thick and lumpy. "This will stick to your ribs," he'd say. So it did. All day and all night. Sometimes even the following day it was difficult to lift my ribs away from the bog my stomach had become.

He had no facility for what he considered woman's work; it didn't interest or concern him. He figured as long as he could lasso a female for hire now and then, the affairs of the house would be sufficiently taken care of. Since our mother's death he had received an abundance of casseroles from hovering ladies and even more advice. One of the hovering ladies, an elderly neighbor, would occasionally come over with cookies or just to say hello when we were playing outside, but when my father was home, he clearly avoided her. Soon, she stopped coming over, but would nod and smile when she caught my eye. The number of casseroles gradually dwindled, but the advice kept pouring in. My father considered this advice to be trivial female meddling and a nuisance. Consequently he set his mind against all such outside advice, which, since there were no insiders, freed him from meddling altogether. For we had no female relative who might have been moved by duty or sentiment to take charge of the domestic needs of a widower and three small children.

There were some women in my father's life, though not in ours. Traces of women. They left their tracks around the periphery of our life: an earring, a perfumed scarf, a lipstick-smudged cigarette. We found these tracks in my father's office or in his car, never in the house. There were a lot of tracks to be found. But there was no woman in our house to set schedules, to define rules by which we would order our lives. As my father said, no woman could lay claim to us. We were free.

Intermittently, there were other women, cleaning women paid by the hour or full-time housekeepers. They were the ones relegated to the hand-chapping, dirt-pushing chores of the house. Some of them were kind and others were not. It didn't matter; they never lasted long. Well, sometimes it did matter. It mattered, for example, the time I became the victim of an oversight. I coughed and choked and vomited, my eyes and nose drained constantly, high-pitched jungle sounds flew from my lips. I had whooping cough. By then there was a vaccine against pertussis, but like the proverbial shoemaker's child, I, the daughter of a physician, had not been vaccinated. Our housekeeper Melba enjoyed repeating this fact to me and anyone else who would listen. "Can you beat that," she cackled. "Not vaccinated? A doctor's kid!" Somehow I thought it was my fault, not directly, but that I deserved to be sick. This feeling Melba seemed to confirm.

"You can stay in my room, Jorie," my father said as he carried me in the morning from my small rumpled bed into his sunlit bedroom. He propped me up against stacked pillows to ease my breathing, gave me some syrupy medicine in a spoon, then placed the bottle by the bedside. He told me to drink lots of water and gently touched the back of his hand to my cheek.

"It makes me vomate," I said.

"Vomate!" he laughed. "Yes, and throw up, too. That's why you have to drink water. Just try. That's a good girl. I won't be too late. But if you need anything, Melba's here. Okay?" I nodded.

Every morning my father carried me tenderly into his room, washed my face, gave me medicine, and left for work. And every morning, as soon as he was gone, Melba pulled me out of his bed and sent me back to my own room.

"Well I never!" she said. Her hand pushed between my shoulder blades. "What does he think I am anyway, a nurse-maid? If he thinks I'm gonna change these sheets every day, he's got another thing coming. Now you get into your own bed and stay there! And take off those peejays, I'm not gonna wash them either." Then, leaving me in my cotton underwear, she put my pajamas aside, so I could put them back on before my father got home.

When I was back in my own room, Melba spread newspapers on top of the bed and on the floor. In a few minutes she was back with sheets of plastic that had been covering bicycles in the garage. The plastic went under my head and over my chest. My bed smelled of garage, dusty and metallic. When I inhaled the oily dust, I turned over on my side and gagged. Throwing up made her angry so I avoided drinking water, even though I knew I was supposed to.

I knew Melba best from behind. I knew the back of her hair, flattened from sleep, the branching blue veins behind her knees, the crusty bumps on her heels and elbows, the broad shelf of her buttocks, the hem of her dress curving up in the middle. I knew her back, like a closed door. She always rushed from the room mumbling to herself. I never heard the last of what she said; she took it with her when she left.

Once, when my brother Alex came to check on me as he always did when he got home from school, he took the plastic off the bed. "She was hot," he said when Melba stormed into the room. "I'll hot you," she said. "It stays until I take it off. If you touch it again, you'll know what hot is!" Alex stepped onto the crumpled sheet of plastic with both feet and stayed there.

"She's too hot," he insisted.

To pay for my mother's final hospital expenses, my father took on a second job as an assistant to an established doctor in the Wilshire district, whose practice he would later assume. Every evening and every weekend he was on call, which meant that most days he would have just enough time for a nap and a shower before the phone rang and he was off again. We were happy when he was home. We liked to have him put us to bed at night. We liked to hear his wilderness tales and the stories of his own childhood in the high prairie of northwest Canada. He told us about the hardships of frontier life, how he took care of himself, attended school in a one-room schoolhouse, worked hard, and froze. Our life seemed easy and luxurious by comparison. We loved to hear his atonal version of "On Top of Old Smoky," second only to a flat but lilting rendition of "I'm

Forever Blowing Bubbles." Then we would sing the only song we knew, *The worms crawl in, the worms crawl out, the worms play pinochle on your snout* . . . When it was time to tuck us in, we tried to stall by being as uncooperative as possible. Now, since my illness had forced me into an unusual state of compliance, I slipped into bed without complaint, but as soon as my father tucked the boys in, they were out again, jumping on the beds or slithering under them. And when finally we were settled, he would say, "Now I don't want to hear another peep out of you." Then he would shut the door, ignoring the inevitable Peep! Peep! Peep! that rang out in the dark.

Every evening when my father came in to see me, he asked why I hadn't stayed in his room. "I wanted to come back to my own bed," I explained. Melba never told me to say that, but for some reason, I felt compelled to protect her. It was as if I alone could understand the righteousness of her intentions, as if she and I both knew I got what I deserved.

"Melba told me you didn't eat," my father said in a concerned voice. "You weren't hungry?" I shook my head. The truth was Melba never brought me anything to eat. "Want some soft-boiled eggs?" she'd offer dutifully, her large form filling the door frame. She knew I didn't like soft-boiled eggs and I could see the amusement in her face. "No," I'd say. I remember how she would raise her large shoulders in an exaggerated shrug. "It's up to you," she said. "Last chance." After that, she would leave me alone. So I could honestly tell my father that I wouldn't eat of my own accord and that I was left alone by my own choice, not hers.

During the first stages of my illness I was too sick to walk around. But in time I began to feel stronger and would creep from the inferno of my bed to cooler climes. Once Melba found me on the bathroom floor, my face pressed against the cool white tiles. She wasn't angry. In fact, she laughed and said I reminded her of a dog. I took that as a compliment. The only time she got really angry was when she caught me spying on her in the kitchen. Then she threw a drinking glass at me; it shattered near my feet. Other than that, she rarely crossed the threshold of grumbling irritation. With me.

She didn't like the boys.

One day during my recovery my father brought home a present. He came into the room with it hidden behind his back. "Look," he said as he placed a night light on the bedside table and stooped down to plug it in. It was an underwater scene sealed between two thick panes of glass. A tube light within the wooden base cast a glow like a candle flame up through the glass water. There was a graceful sprig of sea grass too sparkling to be real, and a seahorse that was real, and a small school of iridescent fish, some painted on the inside of the glass, some on the outside, which gave the scene a surprising dimension, considering it was flat. I thought this night light was the most beautiful thing I had ever seen. I never tired of looking at it. And during the long, fitful descent into sleep, I would gaze at the waffled body of the seahorse and follow the curve and spiral of its tail. When my sinking eyelids would spring open with a paroxysm of coughing, the seahorse would still be there, friendly, suspended in light.

Melba liked the night light too. She said it was peaceful. Sometimes she borrowed it during the day; she liked to have it on when she was in the kitchen having her Ovaltine. I didn't mind. When I would spy on her, I could see how she was affected by it, how her pinched eyes grew wide and her brows unfrowned. The peaceful light was good for her.

They said my mother was at peace. Sometimes they added "at last." I wasn't entirely sure what they meant. Peace was something that apparently everyone wanted, but they were sorry when someone got it, at last. My father said our mother went on to a better life and we should be happy for her. To me that meant that she would be happier without us, that being at peace meant she wouldn't miss us, and that made me acutely sad.

That's how it seemed at first. Even though she hadn't been with us for months, I felt my mother's absence in a way I hadn't felt it when she was in the hospital. When she was alive, I always had a sense of her presence. She was a song that replayed in my mind. And this song accompanied me like my own thoughts. I recalled our visits in the hospital, how she asked us what we did during the day so she could imagine it when she was alone and that would make her happy. Of course Jimmy and Alex, being older than I, could recount the details of our life better than I could, but I took comfort in thinking of her thinking of me. Then she was at peace and no longer cared whether we drank our milk, or washed our hands, or played in the fresh air, or were, as I had been, terribly sick.

Now I couldn't recall the song that had been so familiar. The voice that had accompanied the strong slender arms became increasingly vague and faint and I could not picture her fair, angular face. I couldn't recall her eyes, although I was told they were a remarkable green. Even her coppery hair began to elude me. It seemed to me then that death had left nothing of my mother, except her silence.

In a couple of weeks I started to feel better. I went to the refrigerator and poured myself grape juice from a small glass bottle. I ate Zwieback toast. I napped when I was tired and walked around the house when I wanted to. Melba didn't mind so long as I threw up on the newspapers and stayed out of her way. I still coughed, but vomited less. She didn't cover my bed with plastic anymore. I started looking for things to do.

One afternoon Jimmy gave me crayons, but forgot to give me paper. Within minutes, my bedroom wall was brightly scrawled in loops of red, blue, and orange. Purple crayons of various hues fell from the box to the carpet and I stepped on them. When Alex and Jimmy saw my work, they got washcloths from the bathroom and frantically tried to clean the wall, but only managed to smear the cheerful, fine-lined loops into large, messy blotches of color that I didn't like the look of.

We had never heard the words that Melba screamed.

Behind our house was a little fenced-in yard with a lawn gone mostly to crabgrass, a large jade plant and a few bottlebrush shrubs. When a branch of the bottlebrush is stripped of its leaves and bristles, it makes an excellent switch. It is thin, strong, and flexible. The sharp end can be flicked like a whip. It cuts the air like a whip with the same whhzz sound, but strikes with a snap rather than a crack.

Melba used a new switch every time. She liked us to watch her stripping off the leaves. She did it slowly, her fat, hooded eyes teasing as she waved the bare tip in front of Alex's face. And when he didn't move, she'd laugh. The boys were brave, but I couldn't help it, I cried. On the day of the crayon incident, when Melba saw that crying made me cough, she sent me inside, but ordered Jimmy and Alex to stay put. When she caught me spying through the screen, she pushed me inside and slammed the back door. Even then I could hear the whhzz snap whhzz snap. From the boys I heard nothing.

It was hot the next Sunday. My father attached a portable sprinkler to the hose so the boys could play in the water as they usually loved to do. "No," they said. They weren't hot. They said they wanted to play inside, in their long pants. "What's wrong with you guys?" he asked. "Wouldn't you like to cool off?" Jimmy dumped his Tinker Toy set on the floor and absently stirred the pieces. Alex lay in front of the small, flickering television screen and cracked his knuckles. I lay on the floor gazing into my night light, which I held in front of me with both hands. Then, as always, being too exhausted and too distracted to notice that something was bothering us, my father used the opportunity to sleep.

I thought about what Melba had often told me. He'd be better off without us, she'd said. A young man saddled with three brats! We were nothing but a burden, a load strapped to his back. And when I watched her scrub the crayon from my bedroom wall I knew she was right: we were more trouble than we were worth.

Later that week I was sitting in the front yard making mud pies, each one topped with a dark red berry, when Mrs. Bailey, our next door neighbor, shuffled up the walk. Perhaps because I had taken the berries from her bush, she felt bold enough to risk intruding. She handed me a fistful of berries and smiled. "My, those pies look good enough to eat!" she said. She was an ancient woman with a braid of yellow-white hair wrapped around her head and swollen ankles that spilled over the tops of her sturdy black shoes. "You're still coughing," she said. "You shouldn't be outside. Don't you have someone taking care of you?" Actually, I wasn't coughing very much now. My condition was much improved, a fact that was confirmed when Melba no longer spared me the lick of the bottlebrush tree. Mrs. Bailey looked over at the front door as if trying to decide something, then back at me. "Look now, you're all wet," she said. "Stand up." I pulled my skirt down, but it was too late, she must have spotted the red streaks on the back of my leg. She walked with me up the front steps.

"I'm Mrs. Bailey. I've come to visit the children," the old woman said to Melba when she opened the front door. She kept her hand on my shoulder; I could feel it shaking.

"The father don't allow visitors," Melba said. But Mrs. Bailey, attached to my shoulder, advanced through the door as if she hadn't heard. "Find your brothers, dear," she said to me, releasing my shoulder with a little pat.

"They're playing Indians," Melba said.

"We were playing Indians," Melba firmly repeated as she untied them.

Mrs. Bailey sat with her rattling cup of Ovaltine balanced on her lap. She was taking a long time to drink it, carefully lifting it to her lips, not spilling a drop. She talked to the boys in a casual manner and encouraged them to come closer, because she was hard of hearing, she said. Closer still, she wanted to see if their eyes were blue or green. "My, what beautiful red hair," she said to Alex. Did they watch Kukla, Fran, and Ollie? And the Lone Ranger? She hadn't seen them playing outside for awhile. Her gentle, tremulous voice put us at ease. She nodded and laughed a little at our responses, not too much. In a short while, even Alex, usually unfriendly with strangers, looked up from his lap to answer her.

"Come, sit here," she said to me, patting the seat next to her. She was pleasant to Melba too, remarking about the change in weather, that we could use the rain. "Oh, just look at your trailing philodendron," she said. "I can never get mine to grow like that." Melba, who at first had stood stiffly by the door when the old woman sat down, now smiled and leaned back into her chair, stretching her legs out in front of her. You could see the tops of her stockings rolled down below her knees.

It was like the nicest of tea parties. Maybe our neighbor hadn't noticed the red marks on my legs when she saw me outside; she was very old, after all.

Melba told her the story of my not being vaccinated. "Can you beat that?" she said, slapping her knee. "Well, I nursed her back to health. You can see she's much better."

I showed Mrs. Bailey my night light and delighted when she took it in her hands, her pale eyes examining it closely. "How lovely!" she said. "How perfectly wonderful!" It was nice to have a visitor.

Mrs. Bailey looked solemn when she got up to leave. She patted each one of us on the head as she said good-bye. "Everything will be all right," she said. My father marched in at four o'clock that afternoon, an hour at which he was never home. "Come with me," he said to the boys. "I want to have a look at you."

Soon I could hear Jimmy and Alex crying as they came with him back into the room. Then I started to cry too. Melba chewed her lower lip and told me to shut up.

"Get out," my father said to Melba as he drew me back. "Get out, right now."

Then all three of us were crying, "She didn't do it! She didn't do anything!" But he wouldn't listen. His anger was un-tethered; it flew wildly around the room. I felt it everywhere. It bounced off the walls and buzzed around us in frenzied flight. "I said, GET OUT," he repeated. I had never heard my father raise his voice, and as I watched his face flush red, I could feel the fear rising within me.

"Kids know what's good for them," Melba said.

The pulse in my ears grew louder and louder. My tongue felt thick in my mouth, but I could still get out the words I had to say: "She didn't do it. She didn't."

Within the hour, Melba was gone.

My father painted the deeper cuts with Mercurochrome, then painted some little mice on my legs as well. Some of them had long whiskers and corkscrew tails. "I'm sorry," he said. "I should have known . . ."

The next day my father brought home a tiny kitten. She was completely black except for one white dot on her cheek, a beauty spot in reverse. He called her Jetsam. I knew she was a kind of offering so I took her ceremoniously and held her against my chest. That night the kitten settled down on my pillow and purred into my face. When I turned over, she would move to the other side because she liked to sleep nose to nose. Now when I woke in the middle of the night, I would watch the gentle face of the seahorse and feel the soft, rhythmic breath of the kitten on my pillow.

Mrs. Bailey would stop by for a visit on the days she felt well enough. Then she would read to me from Kipling's *Just So Stories.* I loved to hear how the leopard got his spots and I believed her when she said the story was true. She also said that my mother was in a place called Heaven and that she and some angels watched over us. I supposed it was the same kind of call arrangement that my father had: when one was busy, the others would cover.

Then for the first time, my mother visited me while I was asleep. At first I was angry at her for staying away so long. Why didn't she visit me before? I thought she was gone forever and that I wouldn't be able to remember her. But when my anger subsided I told her about all that had happened: that I had been sick but now I was better, that we had a kitten named Jetsam, and that I knew how the leopard got his spots.

"Tell me everything," she said.

I wanted to tell Mrs. Bailey about my mother's visit and waited faithfully for her every day, with Jetsam and the *Just So Stories* in my lap. After many days of waiting, I began to think she'd forgotten me, but then my father told me she had died. I asked him if the angels would make her take call.

After Mrs. Bailey died, I would talk to her from time to time, addressing the air. But then I gave it up because I felt alone again and thought she must be too far away to hear me. Mrs. Bailey had told me that the dead don't forget you, and although she didn't visit, I liked to think of her remembering me and I wanted my father to remember me too, even though he was not dead and didn't exchange call with angels.

A YEAR AFTER I had recovered from whooping cough, in the dense fog of a June twilight, my father was abducted by gangsters. It happened on an evening when his office clinic was open late. They must have parked outside, waiting for the last patient and the nurse to leave, because just as he was locking up, two men walked in. One was short, with spit-polished shoes and a light gray hat and tie; the other was what my father described as a goon in a suit, a huge man with scarred knuckles and a simian face. Later, when we watched reruns of the Kefauver Committee crime hearings on television, we would point to Frank Costello or Joe Adonis, saying, "Did he look like that, Dad? Did he look like that?"

My father loved to tell us this story. He told it vividly, like a tall tale, each character speaking in his own particular voice. There was something about the incident that amused him and that appealed to a side of him that at that time we rarely saw. It wasn't until much later that such predilections were to surface. He told it like this: The short one took off his hat. "Doc Mackinnon, you're comin' wit us," he said. "We're askin' ya nice ... By the way, you'll need your bag. Max here will help you get it."

Max followed my father into his office. Before he could open his black bag, Max peered inside, handed it back to him, then waited, patient and slack-jawed, as my father added some instruments and bandages. "Rather like a St. Bernard," my father described him.

Outside, a driver was sitting in a brand-new Cadillac, the motor running. Pio, the short man, got in first, then my father, then Max. The driver laid rubber. "Take it easy," Pio said. "We don't want to attract no cops."

As soon as they crossed Hollywood Boulevard, going north, Max slipped a blindfold over my father's eyes. After about ten minutes driving on winding roads, the car passed through a creaking gate and wound its way up a steep driveway, then stopped. They walked across some gravel, up a few stairs, down a hallway, then through a door which was locked behind them.

"Da Boss is in here," Max said, removing the blindfold. "He got hit."

"Thanks for comin', Doc," said the man lying on a leather sofa. My father said he looked like a boss, even lying down.

"You mean I had a choice?" my father said. He reclaimed his bag from Max.

"No, but thanks anyway. It don't feel too bad."

The wound looked worse than it was. The bullet had tunneled through his side and exited from his back without hitting anything important.

"Lucky you're fat," my father said. "I don't get to say that very often."

The Boss grabbed his side as he started to laugh; blood ran through his fingers.

"I have to clean this up," my father said. "I'll give you something for pain."

"No, I can take it. Besides, I don't trust that stuff. Nothing personal, Doc."

"It's up to you," my father said. "Then we'll just have a little chat. It'll take your mind off what I'm doing."

"Fine. Okay. But I'll ask the questions. You got family, Doc?"

"Yes. Two boys and a girl."

"A little girl, huh. I got a soft spot for little girls. I bet she's cute. How old?"

"Six. She's a little monkey."

"She's a tomboy?" he asked, disappointed.

"No, I wouldn't say that. Not a tomboy. They're all a little wild, I guess, since their mother died . . ."

"Ah, tough break."

"Yes, but they're flourishing," he said. That's what he always said: *flourishing*. After the dressing was applied, Max replaced the blindfold and my father was driven back to his office, unharmed and somewhat richer. But that wasn't the reason he didn't call the police. He liked the Boss, he said, and he didn't like the police. Police were necessary, but we didn't have to like them.

I wasn't sure what a gangster was, but from the excited looks on my brothers' faces, I guessed it was something wonderful. For several days, Alex ran around yelling, "Rata-tat-tat! Tat-tat-tat! Okay, youse guys. Shut up yur ugly mugs or you'll be swimming in cement boots!" Jimmy yelled, "Pow! Pow! Pay up or we'll turn ya into Swiss cheese!" After a while I guessed that gangsters killed people. I didn't see what was so great about that.

The next Sunday morning, my father recounted his adventure with the gangsters as we drove up the Pacific Coast

Highway to Zuma, a remote and, at the time, undiscovered beach north of Los Angeles. Driving up the coast was my father's favorite Sunday outing. We walked along the sand and stood sideways in the surf, our rolled-up pant legs wet and clinging. Then we sat for a while on the shore watching the pelicans scan the water. There were no toys, no buckets or balls, nothing to distract us from the nature of things, from the sense of our flyspeck selves at the brink of a vast unfathomable deep.

We walked again while the winding peninsula dissolved into a fog bank and a distant rock became a lone fisherman sitting forward on the sand.

"Catching anything?" my father asked him. The boys ran over to look in his bucket.

"Nothing much," the fisherman answered as he stood up to check his line. "Rock cod, mostly." They stood together in the man space that spontaneously arises on such occasions, their man faces looking parallel out to sea. They spoke about sinkers and test weights, about boats and rigs and ultimately, the War.

". . . Naw, not fishing," I heard the man answer. "I lost these two fingers in Iwo Jima. Shrapnel flying everywhere. I guess I was lucky I didn't lose more than that." My father smiled knowingly.

"Where were you?" the man asked. "China," my father said, "Shanghai, Nanjing. I was there during the Japanese invasion of '37. But I was wounded and had to come back before the end of the war."

"You look fine now," the man said, glancing down at his own mangled hand.

"Yes, I came through it okay," he said. "Except for a few dings that don't show." During his time in China, my father had suffered several wounds, including the loss of three toes and most of one lung, but the public parts of him were the picture of health. His clear, florid complexion set off pale gray eyes and dark bushy eyebrows, making his face a distinctive palate of contrasting hues. Such vigorous good looks and a tall, straight stature belied the heavy toll taken by an inclement youth and the years spent at sea and in the War.

As they talked, a strong breeze blew the sand into little rifts against the kelp that had washed up on the beach. Our light clothes flapped. My father's tee shirt blew tight against his back, sinking in below the shoulder where flesh and bone had been blown from his body. The two men continued to talk with a familiarity to which their scars entitled them. The War. It was beyond my imagining: a collective phenomenon, male, terrible, and glorious. When my father spoke of the War, his face took on a particular look of excitement. His cheek muscles grew taut and his eyes widened, revealing an enlivened gray. His eyes glowed with the same strange excitement every time he told us about the gangsters.

"Tell us the story again about when you were kidnapped," we asked my father as we sat leeward of some large rocks that trailed down into the surf. We could never tire of Pio, Max, and da Boss, of their starched collars and polished shoes, of their scars and bulging jackets, and their funny grammar. Jimmy and Alex, who were then seven and eight, always wanted to hear about the guns. The first version of the story had no guns, but with time, a few guns appeared, in shoulder holsters and on the table. The boys were thrilled, especially Jimmy who reveled in tales of adventure, often dressing up in makeshift costumes, transforming himself into a changing array of characters. Even out of costume, Jimmy was usually to be seen with some kind of weapon in a holster or a pocket. Soon the story of the gangsters took its place among the other stories: of hungry wolves in the Canadian winter, of sailing around the world on a merchant ship, and the War. More than anything we loved the telling of these stories, this folklore that was ours alone.

"Gangsters are bad men," I said.

"Of course," said Jimmy.

"But we like them anyway, right?"

"Right."

"Of course we like them," Alex agreed, but looked down unsurely.

I looked over at my father, hoping he might explain why we liked gangsters. But it was obvious he hadn't been listening. He was watching the pelicans glide over the waves. I could see his eyes drop each time a bird suddenly plunged down and disappeared.

As we drove home along the coast, my father took the turn I always dreaded. Sometimes he would stop on the way, sometimes on the way back, but he always took the turn, even though I prayed that just once, he would forget and drive past it. He turned up a steep, precarious one-lane road cut into the cliff-side that joined the coast highway to the overlooking bluff. It was an old unpaved road, leading up to a cleared lot that was never built on. Erosion had taken its toll; it bit into the road's edge, which was slanted and crumbling. The disintegrating road slanting from the side of the hill was frightening enough, but once we got to the top, it was terrifying.

At the top the ground was flat, swept down to granite by unrelenting wind.

My father wouldn't stop the car until it reached the very edge of the cliff, until I could see nothing but air in front of the hood. I asked him to please let me out at the bottom of the road, or to let me out when we reached the top, or at the very least, before he parked. But he wouldn't. He said he could see the edge, even though I couldn't.

As soon as the car was parked, the boys and I jumped out. My father liked to sit on the hood with his feet resting on the chrome bumper that jutted out like a sulking lower lip. On a clear day, we could see Catalina Island, about thirty-five miles southwest, and the Channel Islands, about the same distance north. On other days, we watched cloud banks roll in over calm silver water. Behind the sheer cliff where the car was parked was a canyon filled with wild grasses, prickly pear cactus, and the rusted wreck of an old car. The boys rushed down the hillside to play in the car. I avoided the rusty carcass; I knew it had fallen from the cliff where we parked. Jimmy poked out from the glassless window. "Rata-tat-tat!" he shouted, pointing his arms at me. "You're dead!"

"I am not!"

"You are too. I rubbed you out. You're dead."

"Am not," I said under my breath.

Alex had started to hike back up the slope. "Will you walk down the road with me?" I asked. "I don't want to go in the car."

Alex shook his head. "Dad will know you're afraid," he said. "Don't be such a girl." My father never said it in words, but one thing he wouldn't tolerate was fear. Fear was a kind of weakness, and it was unmanly. The fact that I was a girl could be overlooked as long as I was brave. "Just close your eyes. That's what I do," Alex whispered in passing. It hadn't occurred to me that boys could be afraid too. The important thing was not to show it. When the car lurched forward as my father clutched into reverse, we all laughed, Alex most of all. Several times on the way home, Alex burst out laughing. My father asked where he got that laugh; it sounded like a chicken cackling. "That was so funny!" he said, gasping and gulping air. "I can't stop laughing."

I didn't sleep well as a child. The night was full of dreams. And the dreams were full of images that my waking self would have snapped her fingers at. My waking self would hold a tarantula or a snake if her brothers dared her, or crawl under a dark, deserted house. Nothing was too dark or too high, or too strange that I would not have faced it in the light of day, scared yes, but without complaint. But zombies slithering in darkness visited me in sleep; these I couldn't face. They kept coming, through closed windows, through locked doors, no matter how I hit them, or shot them, or stabbed them, they came at me until I sat up, silently screaming, and flung open my eyes. And after waking, startled and sweat-soaked in the middle of the night, I would stand in the corner of my room, willing myself awake. Some nights, I wouldn't go to bed at all, but would stand fully dressed, in the corner, fighting off sleep.

It was just such a night when I heard a car pull up in the driveway, followed by men's voices trailing down the hall to my father's study.

" . . . just fine, since you patched me up," a voice said. It was a soft voice, not unlike my father's, but fast-paced and breathy, flute-like. "I got another problem I want you to take care of. A drink? Sure, thanks . . . Max doesn't . . ." The conversation was hard to follow; words popped out at random from an ongoing hum. I dozed off. My head was bobbing from side to side when I was jarred fully awake by voices raised in excitement.

" . . . I was there too! In '35? Well I'll be damned. You must have known . . ." I couldn't hear much of what my father said, but I could feel the lift in his voice and the harmony of the other voice, the words coming fast and punctuated with laughter.

By now I had guessed who these visitors were. I'd heard the name Max and although I didn't hear his voice, I knew he was there. And as I was slouched in the corner I was thinking I should see for myself who was sitting in my father's study, where no stranger ever sat—who it was who filled the air with noxious smoke. A visitor was a curious thing, a rare thing in our house.

At the end of the hall, a slant of light crossed the floor in front of my father's study. With my toes gripping the carpet runner, I crept toward it. When the voices stopped, I stopped. When they continued, so did I. Now down on my knees, I crawled up to the open doorway. And there I was, face to foot, with Max. To my relief, he didn't look down.

Quickly, I backed up. From that position I could barely see the far corner of the room, and a man sitting there. Fat fingers around a fat cigar. "I think we can do cash business, Doc . . ." he was saying.

My father said, "Well, I'll think about it," which I knew meant No. At least that's what it meant when he said it to us. I wondered if the man knew what my father meant, if he might get it wrong.

The man, who I now guessed was da Boss, replied by sucking in his cheeks while the end of his cigar flared up. Maybe that meant something; I don't know. "Do that," he said. "Think about it."

When he tapped the disk of ash from the end of his cigar into the ashtray, I noticed that his fingernails were clean, even shiny. His white shirt was clean, too, and stuck with a tie pin to a dark blue tie. I watched the way he leaned back into the chair, his big belly jiggling, and the friendly way he nodded in agreement when my father spoke. "Ah, those were the days," he said nostalgically. "They ran everything from girls to opium, right under their noses . . ." This was no growling Edward G. Robinson, or sneering James Cagney. I knew the Hollywood image of gangsters, so popular with my brothers. This was no angry movie killer with steely eyes and curling lip. But there was something disturbing in this, in the fact that a killer could be so clean and jovial and friendly, so unlike what you'd expect. I wanted to see what a gangster looked like, but what I saw was just a regular man.

He must have caught the movement of my head in the doorway because suddenly he was looking straight at me. It was unmistakable, pupil to pupil. I'm sure my eyes were wide as saucers, but without even blinking he continued his sentence. Not even the slightest movement betrayed me. I waited a moment, paralyzed, wondering what he would do. Then I saw him roll the cigar from one side of his mouth to the other, mutter soft words, straighten his tie, sip from his drink, all the while looking directly into my eyes without a flicker of recognition and at once I realized that a gangster was not in fact a regular man. A regular man shows himself in his face. Even my father, the ultimate practitioner of subtle expression, showed himself in his face.

And now these eyes that were not eyes at all but just dark openings, were peering at me from behind a jovial face. The cheeks that faced my father bulged with good-fellowship. This to me seemed more dangerous than any blowing rage.

One evening, a few weeks later, we were waiting for my father in his office as we often did, before hospital rounds and house calls. Alex sat in my father's chair, nose down, in an anatomy book. He held the book up slightly, to prevent us from seeing what he was seeing. Jimmy, rummaging through my father's black bag, had his own concerns. "Do you think Dad keeps a gun in here? Just look at all this mean stuff!" He had hung the stethoscope around his neck and was playing with a mask made of wire mesh. He placed it over his nose and mouth, crossed his eyes and pretended to pass out. With no one laughing, he sat up and sighed. "What's taking Dad so long?" He took out a scissor-handled instrument with long jaws and interlocking teeth. Jimmy was always into something, led by a puppyish curiosity. And unlike Alex, he was never cautious. He grabbed first and checked later. "I wonder what this is for?" he said.

"Get out of there," Alex said, trying for some authority. As usual, it didn't work. Jimmy looked over at Alex, eyelids lowered in his usual contempt. "Suck eggs, splatter-face," he said.

"Dad doesn't want you going through his bag."

Jimmy tried the instrument on the bottom of his shirt. "Since when do you know what Dad wants? You're not exactly on his A list."

"Shut up," Alex said, picking up the book again with feigned interest. I noticed it was upside down.

It seemed to be taking an unusually long time for my father to lock up. Hazel, the office nurse, had long since poked her head in the door to say good night. Alex was still looking at books, while Jimmy, bent over a rolling stool, was propelling himself up and down the side hallway. I wandered back toward the lab in search of cookies. As I turned down the hall, I saw my father step out of a room with two men in dark suits. The larger man put on his hat and smiled.

"Jorie, you know where you're supposed to wait," my father said to me as I stood, frozen in my tracks. It wasn't the two men who alarmed me; they could have been anybody. It was the look of alarm on my father's face when he saw me: it told me who they were; it told me that he didn't want me to know they were there. It wasn't that I cared about who they were, but I was dismayed at the thought that he would keep secrets from me. For at that time I was exorbitantly possessive. I felt I had proprietary rights when it came to my father, that I had a right to know where he went, whom he was with and what he did, that loyalty allowed no secrets. But with this chance encounter with secret friends came my first inkling that he wasn't faithful to us. Jealous and angry, I disappeared around the corner and retreated back to his office. I felt betrayed.

"What took you so long?" Jimmy whined when my father walked into his office. "We've been waiting for *hours.*"

"It hasn't been that long," said Alex who was still sitting at the desk. My father paused for a moment, as if surveying the room. I could feel him looking at me as I stood, silent, by the window.

"Jorie's pouting again," Alex said.

"Who cares," said Jimmy. "Can we just go now? I'm starved."

"Hold your horses, son," my father said. "We're going." He pulled open his black bag and shook his head at the obvious intrusion of little hands. "Okay, who was in here?" he asked rhetorically. He knew there would be silent shrugs and know-nothing eyes. My father picked up the stethoscope and placed it in his black bag. Then we followed him, like ducks in a row, out to the street, where his old Kaiser waited solemnly under a streetlight.

The next day a messenger arrived, carrying a large box wrapped in plain brown paper. It was addressed to my father, but an attached card read: *For your little girl.* It wasn't signed. Under my father's eye, I opened it slowly, pulling out layers of crumpled tissue paper, until I saw a small pink hand. After removing several more layers of paper, I saw all of what I had unshrouded: a very large doll, beautiful and lifelike. Undoubtedly, it was expensive and the latest thing. The skin was softly textured and the hair was rooted, platinum blond extruding in neat rows and curling around her heart-shaped face. Eyelids fringed with glossy black lashes slid closed when she lay down and retracted over her eyes when she was upright. Below her eyes, the lashes were painted on. The inner corners were dabbed with red. The eyes themselves were blue glass, with dark lines radiating around the pupils. Her rose-red lips parted slightly, revealing little teeth. She was luxuriously dressed in a necklace with a gold locket, a frilly dress, coat and hat, socks and patent leather shoes.

"This is from da Boss," my father said to me as he lifted the doll from the large box.

"What for?" I asked.

My father thought a moment. "For being a little girl," he said. "Isn't she a beauty?"

I didn't see her as a beauty. Like the jovial mask of the man who sent her, her vapid pink face sent shivers up my spine.

The only doll I had was one my mother had given me as a baby. It was a small wooden doll with its hair and face painted on. It never had any clothes that I can recall. I rarely played with it, preferring instead a stuffed rabbit that was attached to its own satin pillow.

Surprised by my apparent lack of interest, my father made a point of explaining how special the doll was and how lucky I was to get such a remarkable gift. Other little girls would be jumping up and down. What was the matter with me?

The first thing I did when I was alone with the doll was to pull out her eyelashes. Then using a spoon from the kitchen, I pried her teeth loose and knocked them back into her mouth in an attempt to push them down her throat, but she didn't have a real throat, so I had to settle for the teeth rattling around in her head. When I yanked on a lock of hair, it wouldn't come out, but I soon discovered that if I separated the hair, it would pull out easily, a hole at a time. This was time-consuming work, but I was patient.

I was less patient with her fingers, which, though separate, would neither twist nor smash with the spoon. So I bit them off, one by one.

Next I pulled off her arm. I did this by twisting the arm around and around, rocking it back and forth until the plastic bar that held the arm hook was sufficiently weakened to release the arm with one determined pull. A few days later, this severed arm, taken into the living room by Jetsam the cat, alerted my father to my secret mission.

"Jorie, why did you do this?" he asked, after discovering

the remains. The doll looked pitiful in his hands: her scalp a colander, her mouth dark as a cave.

"I don't know."

"You must have had a reason."

I stared down at the floor, avoiding the sight of the doll, who was still too much intact as far as I was concerned. I had an urge to finish her off.

My father looked at me kindly. "I'm not going to punish you," he said. "But I'm going to put the doll away until you're old enough to appreciate it." I nodded solemnly with a look of repentance I didn't feel. He placed the doll on a top shelf in the hall closet and shut the door.

I was often alone in the house. There were gaps between the times when the "day woman" was there, the boys were home from school, and my father was home from work. On fine days, I roamed the streets on my tricycle, but on this day, as soon as I got the chance, I scaled the closet. First I stacked two kitchen chairs, using a third chair to climb on, but that wasn't tall enough. Then I dragged in an old tin wash tub, overturned it, then stacked the chairs on top of that. With the addition of a phone book and a coat hanger, I was able to push the doll off the shelf with a shaking reach that sent us both tumbling to the floor. For a moment I was stunned, my hand pressed to a fast-forming egg on my forehead. But as soon as I saw that staring blue lashless eye, I knew what I would do.

In school I spent much of my time as the other children did, painting. But I didn't paint lollipop trees and peaked houses as they did. I painted only one thing: a large tree, thick-trunked in brown or black, with long spiky branches. Sometimes, I would hang a bright yellow moon in its branches. My teacher thought it was grapefruit. She would give me flesh-colored paint for people and blue for sky, but I wouldn't use them. I wanted to paint this tree, nothing else.

So this day I was painting the tree, but the doll was on my mind. Her remains were still in the house, scattered and well hidden, but still there. I started to paint her under the tree, a recumbent flesh-colored tube with a circular head, arachnid legs, and arms sticking straight up.

"Oh how nice," my teacher said. "Is it a baby?"

"Yes, Mrs. Zuk," I nodded, forcing the corners of my mouth up.

"Is she taking a nap under the tree?" Gravely, I moved my chin up and down. When she passed on to the next easel, I took the paint and started to cover her legs in large brown brush-strokes. The gold locket dangled from its chain around my wrist. Mrs. Zuk glanced back. "Oh, you're covering her with a blanket. How sweet. When your picture is finished, you can take it home to your father; I'm sure he'll like it very much. It's nice that you're painting something new, Marjorie."

No one called me Marjorie. Mrs. Zuk had called me Marjorie from the beginning, but I never said anything for fear of inviting questions about myself. I waited until Mrs. Zuk had moved across the room before I filled the doll full of brown holes. When the holes were dry, I completely covered her with thick brown streaks, and added black splotches, which drifted down to the bottom of the paper. Except for these splotches, the painting now looked like all my other paintings. The doll it had swallowed had disappeared, like a victim in the East River, wherever that was.

*F*OR SOME TIME I felt proprietary about my father. This was especially true during the years close to my mother's death. Whose lipstick was this, I wanted to know, as I sacked his desk drawer. Who made the cookies he brought home from the office? "Someone nice" was not a good enough answer. "Who exactly?" I demanded. "What is her name?" My father was not amused. He would not be possessed; not by me, not by anyone else. But I felt that his attention was scarce, that it had to be won and jealously guarded. Of course I was terrified of losing him; he was all that I had. There were times, though, when events conspired to reassure me, like the time shortly after we moved into our new house. A saleswoman, Miss Wyler, had come from Carpet Town to "assist in the selection of beautiful carpeting in the privacy of your own home," just like it said in the ad.

"Let your daddy look," she said as she straightened the skirt of her black and white checked suit. Several times she had tried to take the carpet sample book away from my brothers, but she couldn't get around their hunched backs as they flipped through the squares of carpet, Alex yanking each page from under Jimmy's elbow. "It's all right," my father said. "The children can choose the colors for their own rooms."

We had been living in our new house for over a month, but our beds, the piano, and my father's eroded reading chair were still the only pieces of furniture in all of the rooms. And, of that scarce bit of furniture, only my father's bed and the chair were being used. The boys and I slept in sleeping bags on the floor of my father's bedroom. We started the night out in our own beds, but one by one we would creep down the dark stairway to his room, leaving the large, cold, creaking, unfamiliar spaces empty in the night.

Not only our beds, but the piano, too, was little used since we had moved to the new house. Our piano lessons had been disrupted because our teacher, Mrs. Baumberger, who lived within walking distance of our old house, didn't drive. Mrs. Baumberger cried when we left. "Your mother wanted you to play the piano," she told us. "She was a wonderful musician. Promise me you will keep playing, no matter what."

"Who's going to be our teacher now?" Alex asked.

Mrs. Baumberger sniffled into the handkerchief she always kept stuffed in her sleeve. "I don't know," she said. "I don't know what will happen to you now. God knows, with that father of yours . . . Oh, I shouldn't say anything; after all, he is your father."

I missed Mrs. Baumberger, but I didn't miss having to practice. But we still played games on the piano. Our favorite was to pick out songs about a designated topic. We would just call out topics until one "took." For instance, if we all agreed on "house," we would play "My Old Kentucky Home," "This

Old House," "Home on the Range," "Mansion in the Sky," and
so on, until we ran out of songs. Jimmy preferred playing these
games to playing the piano, but Alex and I did miss our lessons.
My father did not miss Mrs. Baumberger. She couldn't stop
herself from giving him advice. He seemed glad to be rid of
another "meddling female."

I was happy in our new house, and relieved. I had left behind
an excruciating year in school in which I had been suddenly
placed in an alien world of mothered children my own age. I
already knew how to read and write and count, having picked it
up from my brothers, but otherwise I understood little about
the games and occupations of other children. Most of the time
I had been disoriented and bored.

But worst of all, I had earned the irreparable and well-
deserved reputation of being a liar. I couldn't help it; lying was
as involuntary as hiccups. Lying was an urge inseparable from
its action. It was never premeditated.

"How many children went to church on Sunday?" Mrs.
Zuk, my first-grade teacher, asked on Monday morning. I
raised my hand with the others.

"And how many children went to synagogue?" I raised my
hand with the rest.

"Marjorie, stand up. You're lying again. Did you or did you
not worship last weekend?"

Slowly I pulled myself up from the chair, my heart gallop-
ing, and stood in front of Mrs. Zuk and the whole ogling class.
I had never been to a church or a synagogue, nor had I any idea
of what people did there. But it seemed to be the thing to do, so
I raised my hand.

Mrs. Zuk's chest lifted with one long, wheezy breath. "No
one LIKES a liar," she said. Her cameo brooch shimmied on
the exhale. "No one TRUSTS a liar. No, Marjorie, don't sit
down yet . . . Class, what is the rule?"

The rule rang out: NEVER TELL A LIE.

"Remember that, Marjorie," she said. "You may sit down now."

I did remember it, but that was not enough to make me stop. When we lived in our old house, I rode my tricycle up and down the residential streets down to the crowded traffic of Wilshire Boulevard and pedaled fast along the wide, long blocks. One evening, a woman stopped me at a corner as I was waiting for a light. "Does your mother know you're riding here alone?" she asked me.

"Of course," I said. "She said I could."

I had done it again, without thinking. For one thing, lying was so much easier than explaining. It was simpler to give people the answers they expected. It should have been the truth anyway, I thought. I could say: Yes I ate my vegetables last night at dinner. Yes I helped my mother with the dishes. Yes I went with my family to Palm Springs for the weekend, just like the girl sitting next to me.

"Marjorie, you are still a liar! Stand up." Mrs. Zuk's eyes converged on my burning face. "You did not go to Palm Springs. Your brother told me."

"I did," I said weakly. "He didn't."

"I don't believe you," she said as her mouth disappeared into her face. "We can't believe anything you say. I don't believe that you're moving away either. Are you or are you not moving to another home?"

"No," I said. "We're not moving." I was lying. My father had bought a house in the Hollywood Hills, overlooking the city. We were going to move during the summer. I wondered how Mrs. Zuk had found out. I had confidentially told only one person, Debby Blatt, who always gave me the hard-boiled egg her mother put in her lunch pail.

"Ugh," she said as she watched me eat it. "How can you eat that?" That was when I told her I was moving.

Now I knew my suspicion was right: you can't trust anyone with the truth. A lie, on the other hand, is public domain.

That was a few months earlier, a lifetime. I would never have to see Mrs. Zuk or anyone from my old school again. I had resolved never to tell another lie. And I believed absolutely that I never would. There was something in the emptiness of our new house, its blank walls and vacant floors, that affirmed my resolve. Partly, there may have been absolution in a clean slate, but also, I detected a certain propitiousness in the unfilled space. It was as if by leaving our old house behind I could also leave behind the parts of myself that I didn't like, the parts that shamed me. In our new house I would be a new person, a better person. And I would be undisputed queen.

"But Dr. Mackinnon," said Miss Wyler. "Surely you're working with a color scheme." She looked around the room, at the blank walls, the ceiling, the stairway leading to the next floor with its white columned arches leading up to unadorned space. After twisting this way and that, she seemed satisfied that no real colors were in evidence and faced forward again, straightening her skirt. My father looked at her knees and smiled faintly. "Naturally," she said, adjusting the dark seam running up the back of her calf, "the colors in the house should coordinate . . . Have you decided on your colors?"

My father's eyes followed the path of her fingers as they made their way up the soft curve of her stocking. She moved forward in the chair, pulling the hem of her skirt with her. Then she pushed back a curl that had slipped onto her temple. I was intrigued with her hair. It was curly on the sides and straight on top, short, shiny, and of a color I had never seen on a real person: pinkish beige. I wondered if my father thought she was pretty.

"I thought that's what we're doing now," he said. "Deciding."

"Oh, that's not what I meant," she said. "I thought you might have already given it some thought. Most people think about these things in advance. After all, it is a large investment and you'll live with this carpet for years. Most people think that's important." She was fingering the small pearl button at the top of her suit. I had never seen anyone so uneasy about her clothes. It was as if they would come apart at any moment.

My father watched her fingers with an amused smile. "We're not most people," he said. I had noticed that he had an unsettling effect on women. Nurses blushed and dropped things in his presence. Waitresses gripped their pencils.

"This is it!" Alex interrupted, holding up the sample book by its large metal ring.

"It's exactly the color of dirt!" Jimmy said excitedly. "Wait, let's make sure." The boys jumped to their feet and ran from the room, arms pumping at their sides. Miss Wyler picked up the book from the floor where Alex had dropped it and passed it to my father, slowly. It seemed funny that she didn't hand it over right away, but my father didn't seem to mind.

"Perhaps the lady of the house would like to look at it too?" she said tentatively.

My father smiled in my direction and pointed with the palm of his hand upturned. "This is the lady of the house," he said. "But she won't mind if I look first. Would you, Jorie?" I nodded my consent.

He looked through each sample, giving each an equal amount of time, not seeming to favor one over another. Miss Wyler licked her lips. I licked mine too. I had never seen anyone do that before and I wanted to try it out. I had the habit of studying women as if they were exotic birds. The way they moved, their gestures, the sounds they made, were all so different from the males in my household. I found them fascinating. Miss Wyler saw me watching her and adjusted the strand of small pearls that closely encircled her neck.

My father turned back to a carpet sample; he remembered the exact page. "I'll take this one," he announced. The color was a soft, pale green, the color of celery, or of shallow water suffused with sunlight. He looked pleased.

"It'll be a difficult color to match," Miss Wyler said.

"Match?" he said. "Match to what?"

"The colors you'll be using in the house. Furniture. Drapery. Accessories. The colors have to complement each other." Miss Wyler surveyed the empty room. She looked directly into my father's eyes as if she had known him a long time. I felt my teeth press together.

"Dr. Mackinnon, I think you need someone to help you." she said. "This is a very large house. There are so many decisions to be made . . ."

"I've decided on this one." he said. "I like this green; it suits me just fine. Why would I need help?"

"If you say so," she said in a voice full of warning. Miss Wyler adjusted her suit jacket with a tug and said under her breath: "It's certainly different working with a man."

Something in the way Miss Wyler said *If you say so* seemed also to say *You're making a mistake.* And something in the way my father said *This green suits me just fine* seemed also to say *I'll do what I please, regardless of what you think.* I rarely saw my father with a woman who was not employed by him or who was, in some other way, his subordinate. But with a woman independent of him, it was always the same—the silent push and pull, the tension. I couldn't decide if they liked each other or not.

"Perfect!" Jimmy said as he dropped a fistful of dirt onto the carpet sample. The small brown pile was filled with ivy roots and something else that seemed to be crawling. "Yup, you'll never see it."

"We've decided on this one," said Alex as he unhooked the window screen and tapped the carpet square on the window sill. The dirt fell to the stairs below.

"Jorie's turn," Alex said as he handed me the sample book. Alex was always careful about whose turn it was; he had an acute sense of justice. I could hardly hold the sample book; so heavy was the weight of making a wish. I had never had the responsibility of a purchase of any consequence, or any purchase for that matter. By the look on Miss Wyler's face, I knew this was not the regular purview of a six-year-old. My father and the boys watched as I slowly turned the pages. My father raised his finger to Jimmy when he started to make suggestions. "No coaching from the wings," he said. Then, turning to me he said, "Take your time, Jorie."

The colors were all so beautiful, I didn't think I would be able to choose between them. But as soon as I saw it I knew. Red. The reddest red I had ever seen: clear, brilliant, eye-rubbing red. Scarlet it was called on the label. Miss Wyler gasped. "You realize the entire floor will be covered in that color?" she said sharply.

At that point I hadn't pictured the color beyond the square in my hands; it sang to me like a Chinese poppy. But at her suggestion I envisioned a whole floor, vibrating red, startling as blood. It made me smile.

"Now here's a beautiful color," said Miss Wyler, resuming a condescending tone. "Paradise Sand. Any little girl would love to have this in her room. It's so light and pretty, and it goes with everything . . . perhaps a canopy bed?" She held the carpet sample up for my father to see and winked at him conspiratorially. Then she turned it for me to see. "With ruffled pillows and a white eyelet cover?"

"That's a nice color too," he agreed. "What do you think; wouldn't you like this better?"

"Much more appropriate for a little girl," she interjected.

"Think about it, Jorie, this would be very nice in your room," he said.

Miss Wyler pulled at the sleeve of her jacket and smiled.

I didn't like it. I didn't like the insipid color, and worse, I didn't like the feeling that my father was conspiring with this woman. He was being taken in by a stranger when he should have been loyal to me. I looked up at my brothers who were now kneeling beside me on the floor.

"Do half and half," Jimmy said.

"Nah, I don't like those colors," said Alex. "Do blue."

I didn't like their suggestions either. I picked up the square of carpet I had chosen and rubbed my fingers back and forth over the bright red loops. I liked the way the color changed with each stroke: red, redder, red, redder. I could feel my father watching me and saw Miss Wyler watching him. "I'll just put down Paradise Sand," she said triumphantly, as she started to write. "I assure you that you'll be very happy with it."

"Jorie?" my father said.

Back and forth I stroked the carpet. The red loops glowed beneath my fingers. I looked up at my father with all the earnestness I could muster, so he could read my face.

"Scarlet it is," he said.

Miss Wyler clicked and unclicked her ballpoint pen. "Really, I think you should consider—"

"Scarlet it is," he repeated, with an unwavering glare. His voice was firm.

I couldn't help but smile.

"Very well," Miss Wyler said archly, copying down the number. As she did this, my father excused himself to answer the telephone. She cocked her chin and looked at me downways.

Suddenly I was overtaken by the old urge. I had vowed never to lie again, but it was irresistible. "My mother would love this color," I said quietly. "She loves red."

"Your mother?"

"Yes, I know what she likes."

"Your mother? I thought—"

"My mother is famous. She's touring the world."

My father came back in a rush. "Sorry, Miss Wyler," he said as he headed for the doorway. "I have to leave now. An emergency call. But I think it's all decided. The green, the brown, the red. You have all the information, don't you? If not, please call me. At the office."

"You know all sales are final," she said, bristling.

He looked at her with a puzzled expression. The spell was broken. "I would expect so," he said. She had been dismissed.

Miss Wyler continued to fill out the order. I wanted her to look up from her notebook. I wanted her to see the corners of my mouth, turned up just enough. I wanted her to see my face, which, at that moment, was only for her.

ITHIN A FEW MONTHS of moving into the new house, we had settled down comfortably on our bright-hued carpets and lived an untamed life. The periods of time between housekeepers grew longer, but the duration of their employ was shorter, as we could generally dispatch a new one within a day or two. It became a point of pride to dispatch one quickly and cleanly, a kind of surgical strike, as it were. It had been six months since the last one left, so I thought we might get by that summer. Without a housekeeper, our domestic life foundered from neglect, but at least then my father was compelled to spend more time with us, and when he was home, we would gather around him like scouts at a campfire, unkempt but happy.

But my father got optimistic in July; he said he'd found someone for the house. When we asked him about who she was and what she was like, he just said: I'm optimistic. An answer like that meant he didn't want to discuss it further. Some things were up for discussion and others weren't. We usually knew the difference. We could discuss a lot of things, like how penicillin works and the war in Korea. My father especially liked to talk about science. The objective quality of subjects such as the exosphere or blood plasma allowed for comfortable conversation, that is, he would talk about these subjects, and only these, with an ease and volubility that made us savor what might have been heavy fare for many children our age. Not up for discussion were the many nights he didn't come home until long after we had fallen asleep, often in chairs or on the floor, where we had tried so hard to wait up for him. Nor did we discuss the times when he didn't come home at all, the times he would telephone to say to call his answering service if we needed anything really important. He said he trusted us to use common sense.

My father was what some people call an old-fashioned G.P. That means he delivered babies, bottled and dispensed pills for such things as urinary infections, made house calls, and often exchanged his fees for services, like house painting or tuning up the old Kaiser. What it meant to us was that we hardly saw him, except on Sundays.

Sometimes he would bring us to his office where we got to know some of his regular patients, like Elizabeth Bingham, an elderly woman who was one of his favorites. "They'll grow up to be criminals!" is what she used to say. "You need a woman in the house."

"I suppose you're right, Elizabeth," he'd say. "Too bad you're not younger."

"It's been years since your wife died. Look at this girl," she said, shaking her brown hand in my direction. "She's growing up wild."

"So what's wrong with being wild?" I said. I was thinking of lupines and poppies and the lantana that stretched its purple blossoms along the side of our road, and wild cherry cough drops, and *The Call of the Wild,* and the raccoons that raided our garbage cans. I loved wild things.

"Wild Indians!" Elizabeth Bingham said to my father, now shaking her hand at my brothers who were pitching emesis basins down the corridor.

"Don't worry, Elizabeth," he said. "A new housekeeper is coming next week." Overhearing this, Alex and Jimmy stopped their game and we stood, sentenced, in a stiff and silent row. My father smiled affectionately at the heavyset woman. "The lineup," he said.

"She's here!" Alex called from his lookout post as Jimmy and I peered down from the patio. The taxi door opened, revealing first a sensible shoe, then a woman to match, plain and neat in a shirtmaker dress. Her hair was short and fell close to her head, the bangs so straight they could have been painted on. Squinting, she looked up at our house, which loomed white and towerlike from the road below.

"Welcome to the house of stairs," Jimmy said at the first landing, grabbing the handle of her suitcase. "No," she said, tightening her grip. "That's too heavy for you. James, is it?"

"Jimmy," he said, correcting her, still pulling the handle, pinching her hand until her grasp loosened and the suitcase went crashing down into the street. He shrugged. "I was just trying to help," he said. Jimmy offered an unconcerned smile. He expected to be forgiven. Of the three of us, Jimmy had the most charm. He had a cherubic look about him, with his mass of golden brown curls and dimples embedded in both pink cheeks. He knew that adults found him appealing and used it to advantage. It was not lost on me that Jimmy's dimples had spared him not a little trouble, while Alex's red hair and freckles also had some charm, but to lesser effect. I, on the other hand, having neither dimples nor freckles, but only a pale and subtle face, had no charm at all.

"I can do it! I can do it!" Jimmy said, now making another pass at the fallen suitcase, but the woman waved him off.

"I'll manage," she said firmly. Suitcase in tow, the woman made her way up the two flights of stairs, taking slower and slower sideways steps, finally reaching the front door, panting. I was sitting on the top step in my hand-me-down tee shirt and rolled up dungarees. I must have looked wild as a musk ox, my hair frizzy and tangled. "Hello, Jorie," the woman said.

"Hello, JoBeth," I replied, picking foxtails from the curly strands.

"Well, you know my name!"

"Well, and you know mine," I said, without looking up.

JoBeth paused to catch her breath. "What a big girl for seven," she said.

"I'm almost eight. And I know how old you are. You're thirty-nine . . . and trying out," I added. As if she didn't quite know what to say, JoBeth looked relieved when the front door suddenly swung open. Alex, then a lanky, scrawny boy, stood in the doorway. His red hair was fierce as he silently inspected the new housekeeper.

"This is Alex the Hun," I said.

"Hello, Alex," JoBeth said, extending her hand. "Can't you say hello?"

"You're number nine," he said at last, glowering at her retreating hand.

"She is not. She's number eleven," I said.

"You can't count the ones who didn't last a whole day."

"I count everyone who tries out."

We took JoBeth into the living room for observation. There was plenty of room to circle around and the light was good. Her looks were rather disappointing. She had a nice toasty look: nut brown hair and eyes, and a brownish complexion. But she had nothing special like some of the other housekeepers: a chin covered by a web of burn scars (number six), or an enormous bosom that merged in the middle (number ten). We watched for signs like crescents of perspiration under the arms, facial twitches (number seven had a tic of her left eye-lid), any spasm or quiver that might reveal a certain weakness. This one was composed; as we looked at her, she looked around. Our living room, which took up the entire first floor, was empty except for four unmatched chairs in front of the fireplace and my mother's grand piano. Books and sheets of music were strewn about the room, carpeted in my father's favorite green. Jetsam slept in a patch of sun filtered through a dust-spattered window.

In the boys' bedroom, two flights up, the mattresses were bare, with army surplus sleeping bags crumpled on top. "We're not interested in sheets," they told our father. What they really were not interested in was washing the sheets and putting them on the bed. Dusty blue jeans, old jockey shorts, pellet guns with ammo scattered about, Franco-American spaghetti cans, notebooks, old socks, chess pieces and inside-out shirts littered my brothers' wisely chosen brown carpet. JoBeth said that living things must be crawling underneath. "Let's tidy up before your father gets home," she said.

"Why should we?" Alex demanded. Not really a question.

JoBeth ignored him. "A clean house is a happy house," she pronounced.

I didn't like being spoken to in slogans, and by the sour looks on the boys' faces, neither did they. With a strengthened tone of resolve, JoBeth then told us that our father would be so proud of us if we cleaned up, and besides, she added, *she* was in charge.

"You don't know anything about what he's proud of," said Alex, turning to leave. "I'm going to practice."

"Not so fast, young man. Come back here," she said. "You listen to me!" JoBeth's voice became louder and louder. The louder her voice became the less we listened. Finally, we stuck our fingers in our ears and walked out. "Come back here right now! All of you!" JoBeth shouted to the empty room.

Soon we could hear Alex practicing, the pounding chords of Rachmaninoff echoing up the stairs. My father said that music was our mother's exclusive gift to us. He had tried to develop an appreciative ear, but the fact is he was tone deaf and didn't have a drop of rhythm in him. Music came naturally to us. I played the piano well, but Alex excelled. Our new teacher, Miss Luvah, was my father's patient. She drove to the house in a large, pink Cadillac, taking up the entire middle of the road as she honked the horn continuously up the winding street. We could hear her a mile away. We liked Miss Luvah, so we practiced, Alex most of all. His long fingers reached more than an octave and his chords were clean and strong and called out in a way his voice never did.

Later that day I watched JoBeth push her straight brown hair away from her face and stare blankly through the dusty kitchen window, as she talked aloud. "They're only children after all," she said to herself. "Children need discipline." Hadn't she read somewhere that children actually liked to have limits set? It made them feel secure. She just needed to assert her authority. She couldn't let them get the upper hand. As I listened to JoBeth's words, a faint hope grew even dimmer. I didn't want a woman in the house, but at the same time I liked the order that a woman brought. If only she would make a different start. If only she could find a different place to put her foot down.

"Hey, Jimmy! We got another one who talks to herself," I said.

He rolled his eyes in mock irritation. "So soon?" he said. "They usually don't start talking to themselves until the third day." Jimmy walked into the kitchen and opened the large, tin-lined bread drawer. He dug through it like a dog in a garden, leaving crumbs scattered behind him on the linoleum.

"Wanna cookie sandwich?" he said to JoBeth, pushing an oatmeal cookie wrapped in bread into her hand.

"No thank you," she said. "What about your dinner?"

"We eat when we're hungry."

"Oh? We'll see about that."

"Let's see what we've got here," JoBeth said, opening the refrigerator. There wasn't much; quart jars of mustard and relish sat on sticky shelves. "Any hot dogs?" she asked.

Jimmy spread peanut butter on a cookie. "Naw, it's Friday. Hot dogs are the first things to go."

"What about milk?"

"We finished that off, too."

"What did you have for lunch?"

"Nothing. I told you, we eat when we're hungry. You can have whatever you want. We don't have regular meals."

JoBeth's voice became measured as she straightened her back. "In the future we shall eat together in the dining room."

"No we won't," I said. "We don't use the dining room that way."

"Oh really? Just how do you use the dining room?"

"See?" I said, leading her into a large room adjacent to the kitchen. The walls were lined with books stacked in freestanding bookshelves of various heights. On the tops of these shelves, books, stacked horizontally, reached the ceiling. More books were stacked on the hardwood floor, some open, some closed with markers sticking out from the pages. "This is where we do research," I explained, waiting to see if JoBeth would look at some of the books, and if she did, which ones. JoBeth didn't look at the books, but fixed her attention on the dining room table on which was a partially assembled skeleton, surrounded by little piles of bones. "We dug up a cat, *Felis domestica*," I said. "The thoracic vertebrae are here, the lumbar here, then the sacral—"

"This is not the kind of thing you do in a dining room. It even smells in here!" She looked slightly dizzy and her skin turned greenish.

"That's just the Drano you smell," Jimmy said. "We had to use it to get the flesh off."

Sinking into a large upholstered chair, JoBeth sat for a moment with her eyes closed.

"You're not allowed to sit in that chair," Alex said accusingly. Slowly she opened her eyes, Alex's hair and face flaming before her. "That's my father's chair. You're not allowed—"

"I heard you, Alex," she said. "I didn't know it was your father's chair."

"If you knew, you wouldn't care. What do you know, what do you know about anything? You don't care. You don't care!" He was shouting now, his narrow chest heaving wildly. He beat the air with his fists and stamped his feet.

I stood close to him, without touching. "It's okay. It's okay," I said. "Calm down. Count to one hundred, remember?"

I was worried about Alex. More and more, it seemed the slightest thing would set him off. And a housekeeper wasn't a slight thing to him. I didn't think this one was mean though, not like number seven, who tied him to the clothesline pole. Alex always got it the worst. When we needed to, Jimmy could charm himself out of situations and I could make myself invisible, but Alex would lose control, throw tantrums, throw anything in sight, and when he did, trouble was sure to follow. When I asked why Alex acted like that, my father said that no one bothered to understand him, that he just needed to let off steam. I wondered why he had so much steam to let off. My father said that when our mother died, Alex lost his best friend, the only one who really understood him. But now she was just bones. He said people stay bones for a long time, then they're dust, depending on the soil.

Putting a skeleton together is very tedious, especially when you don't have the right picture. We couldn't find a picture of the skeletal anatomy of a cat, but we did find one of an extinct horse, *Protohippus*. Close enough, we thought. Just as we were starting on the thorax, JoBeth started racketing around in the kitchen.

"How can I concentrate?" Jimmy said.

"Impossible," I agreed. "We may as well go see what she's doing." Alex didn't want to, but we said, "Come on," so the three of us dragged our chairs into the middle of the kitchen and watched JoBeth clean the refrigerator.

"I hope you're taking notes," she said. She had brought the trash can over, using it to prop the refrigerator door open. A little foot pedal opened the top, which made a loud clang when it closed. Now she was dropping in empty jars and wrappers, blackened tomato paste tubes that had long since spit out their contents, mystery packages thick with frost, and wizened pieces of vegetables in various stages of decay. Clang, clang went the top, until the can was full and she had to press down to close it.

"There. That's how it should look," she said proudly, after washing the inside with baking soda and water. I was dazzled by the shiny whiteness of it. It gave me a good feeling to see something clean and neat, but I would never let on. The show over, we scurried out, leaving the chairs in the middle of the room.

"Come back here, you little twerps," I could hear JoBeth's voice calling behind us.

I remembered my mother's voice. It was a high, laughing voice with a pronounced accent. The accent was Austrian, which is German, only softer. I remembered her humming when she played the piano, her head bowed as her fingers flew over the keys. I was told that she kept me in a basket beside the piano. I remembered her face vaguely, and that her hair was thick and the color of new pennies, but I couldn't describe the color of her eyes. I tried to recall more of her, but that's all I could come up with: the heavy outline of her hair, and the voice. Alex remembered much more.

You could tell when my father was really busy because he spoke like a telegram: *Hi Jorie. Will be late. Primip. Don't wait up. Bye.* Primip is short for *primipara,* a woman bearing her first child, which meant: It'll take all night. At least we were old enough now to be left alone. A few years past, we would sleep in our clothes, ready to be led or carried to the backseat of the car where we would wait, sleepfully, as my father eased one soul out of this world or ushered a new one in.

Sometimes I would wake up in the cold dark of the back seat, forgetting where I was. Or, on a moonlit night, I would wake as if in a dream, my brothers' faces gleaming in the silver light. The chrome horn glowed round like the moon and little pieces of moon reflected off knobs on the dashboard, the lighter, and the choke. I would hold out my arm to the moonlight, gazing at its cold whiteness and I'd think: This is what it looks like to be dead.

The baby's delivery did take most of the night, so JoBeth's first day would go unreported. My father, who did not come home that night or the following night, would hear neither her version nor ours.

On her third day, each of us had plans, all conflicting. Jimmy wanted to go to the beach with a friend, but Alex wanted us to go together to the LaBrea tar pits to look at the bones. I had planned to visit our neighbor Dmitri. Naturally, at the bottom of all our plans was an urgency to get out of the house. No doubt JoBeth had plans for us too.

"The thing to do," Jimmy said in our huddle at the top of the stairs, "is to run down the stairs and out the door as fast as we can, before she can say anything."

"So what if she says anything," said Alex. "This is our house, not hers. Just let her try to say something . . ."

"Don't get mad, Alex. She hasn't even said anything yet. The thing to do," I said, "is to just act serious, like you're late for an important appointment or something. Then, if she says we can't leave, just look at her like she's crazy."

"Yeah," said Jimmy. "Then run out the door as fast as you can." Slowly, quietly we started down the stairs. She mustn't hear us coming; she mustn't be prepared. "Stick together," Jimmy whispered. "We'll be gone before she can say boo." Just then, the back door slammed.

"She's gone outside! Go!" Jimmy shouted, as we scrambled down the stairs and out the front door.

It was a typical Los Angeles spring morning. Clouds hung gray and low over the city and the air was cool and damp. I didn't own a sweater, nor would it have occurred to me that I needed one. Shivering, I walked across the street to be with Dmitri. I didn't say I went to visit him; I would never have disturbed him with conversation. I simply went to watch him work, just to be there. Dmitri was a sculptor, a short, pink-skinned, muscular man from the Caucasus. "The mad Russian," my father called him following those occasions when they would play chess and drink vodka. There was a kind of accord between them: something sly, something to do with women. Once I overheard him say to my father, "Come next weekend. I introduce you to woman you never forget." Dmitri had been married four times. He now lived alone and saw women "strictly for his health," a line my father liked to quote.

The entrance to Dmitri's house was flanked by two man-sized, terra-cotta sculptures, half cherub, half fish, one with a tail that flipped rakishly to the side, the other with a very wicked smile. If his door was locked, I would go away without knocking; if it was unlocked, I would go on in. This was an unspoken understanding between us. In fact, we rarely spoke.

When he was working, he would only occasionally glance over at me, his eyes light and smiling behind thick glasses. I would bask in his presence, admiring the tracks of his wide hands in the clay. At Dmitri's I felt comfortable in a way I rarely felt; not at school, which was an alien land to me, not at home where each day was a blind alley.

Leaning back against a chair, I would sit on the floor, not too close to where he was working. I was careful not to be underfoot when Dmitri was building the armature for a large sculpture. He needed a wide berth for his hammering, sawing and wrapping of wire. I would move from one side to the other, watching him construct the skeleton, then bring it to life with muddy flesh. I watched the concentration on his face, which at times was within just a few inches of the clay. Other times, he would stand across the room to study his work. Then he would rub his head, leaving flecks of clay in the white hair.

The studio was flooded with light. Sunlight rushed through glass panels overhead. Music also flooded the room: Bach, Vivaldi, Corelli, and sometimes Russian songs so sad our eyes would glaze with tears. When he allowed me a request, I always asked for Korsakov's "Suite of the Snow Maiden."

I lost all sense of time when I watched Dmitri work. There was only music. Music and the gray shapes forming under Dmitri's hands. After a while, I slipped, catlike, out the door.

"Where have you been?" JoBeth demanded when I got home. Her face was flushed and I was sure she had been talking to herself.

"Out," I said, challenging.

"Out! You dare answer me that way!"

Gandhi, I remembered. *Meet aggression with will.* My father had told us about Gandhi, about how passive resistance had brought the British to their knees. "Out," I repeated.

I could tell by the way she clenched her hand she wanted to

hit me, but I also knew she wouldn't. She was still trying out. "How do you think I feel?" she said. "Your father called and asked me where you were. And I had to say: 'I don't know. Your children have been gone all day and I don't know where they are. I don't even know when they left!'"

Even while my head was pulsing, I made my face impassive. I thought of Gandhi and glared back at her until she lowered her eyes.

"Look, Jorie," she said. "I want to be your friend. All I ask is that you give me a chance. Let's start over. Now, tell me where you went. I was worried about you, really I was."

I wasn't going to fall into that trap. I was experienced after all; she was number eleven. Ten women just like her had already left us, one by one. I knew that she would leave too. But I couldn't say to her: *I don't want to be your friend. You are a stranger to me and that's the way I want it.* I knew she'd soon be gone like all the rest, but even if she stayed awhile, how could I explain? My life was private. I had been allowed my own territory, free from intrusion, and I was used to it. My father never asked where we were or what we did. We told him what we wanted to, what we thought would interest him. And he accepted that and never asked for more. That seemed perfectly normal to me then. I didn't know yet how other families lived.

When Jimmy came running in, he almost knocked JoBeth off her feet. He continued to run, but she managed to catch him by the back of his tee shirt.

"Hold on, young man," she said. "I want to talk to you."

"Me?" said Jimmy, struggling.

"Yes, you. I told you to pick up your room and you didn't do it. Then you left without saying a word. I didn't even know where you were. This is not the way children should behave."

"Let me go!" Jimmy shouted, squirming in JoBeth's grasp. I walked up behind him and pulled on his ear.

"Remember Gandhi," I whispered.

Jimmy stopped struggling and turned to face her. She let go.

"And where were you today?" she asked.

"None of your beeswax," he said, giggling. He had gone too far. She grabbed him by the hair. Then, turning on her sensible heel, she marched him upstairs, passing Alex on the way. We pattered up after them.

Jimmy watched in silence as JoBeth grabbed old underwear, shoes, and books from the floor, collecting them in her arms. Then, dashing over to the open window, she tossed them all out. We could hear the shoes, bouncing down the cement stairs, two floors below. Back and forth she ran, hurling armfuls of my brothers' accumulations out of the upstairs window. Alex and Jimmy looked at each other, their eyes wide and knowing. Jimmy poked me in the back. Within minutes, she looked up wildly from an empty floor.

"Now!" she shouted. "Go pick it up. All of it. And put it away."

"No," said Alex.

"I won't," said Jimmy.

"They're not my things," I said. "But if they were, I wouldn't pick them up either."

Later that night, my father stepped over piles of clothes and rubble as he climbed to the front door. "Who did this?" he asked, his voice soft as usual.

"I did," JoBeth answered.

"Well, pick it up then," he said.

"I told the children to pick up their things and put them away."

His voice became softer. "If you threw it there, you pick it up."

Jimmy and Alex stood shoulder to shoulder, their faces exultant with victory. With my feeling of victory came a twinge of regret. I imagined the refrigerator, now so white and gleaming, lapse into sticky neglect.

JoBeth stiffened. "Dr. Mackinnon, these children must learn!"

"I will decide what they learn," he said. His voice was almost inaudible, weary. His weariness fell on us like rain as we stood in silence, careful to look only at each other's shoes.

The next morning, Jimmy and I watched the back of a shirtmaker dress descend down the stairs and disappear into a waiting taxi. We had dispatched number eleven and we expected our father to come home, mildly exasperated, to attend to us, to ply us with patient complaints. But he did not come home that night or the next. We debated whether to call him at the office, but decided against it, since we were not supposed to call, except for urgent matters. We agreed that we were in enough hot water as it was. For three days we waited, humbled by an empty victory. Alex played Chopin on the piano, fast and furious.

*A*FTER JOBETH LEFT, my father's optimism turned to impatience. During this time, he would often come home just long enough to shower and change. If I hurried up, he would allow me to choose his tie. Then he would leave again, wearing a dark blue suit and smelling of English Leather. It was clear he was annoyed that we couldn't keep someone in the house. I had to look up the word *incorrigible*. I wanted to ask him: What have we done? What have we not done? Why don't you want to be with us? I wanted to say we'd try harder, if only we didn't have to have more housekeepers. The boys and I pleaded that we didn't want any more of these women in the house; we just wanted him.

"One more try," he insisted. It was necessary.

A few days later, Kitty arrived at four-thirty in the afternoon, exactly seven and a half hours late. This was to be her first day on the job, but by the time she arrived, the bloodthirsty excitement with which we always met a new housekeeper had all but petered out. After much peering out windows and running up and down flights of stairs, we greeted her with a worn but still skeptical calm. She drove up in an old, dilapidated flatbed truck with a steamer trunk fastened with chains to the wood planks in the back. Truck and trunk looked as if they might have been abandoned by the railroad tracks. Kitty did too. Below a striped gypsy skirt, her long, thin legs stretched into bony ankles and bare feet, black between the toes. She wore a turban like Carmen Miranda, but except for that, she was not like anyone I had ever seen before. The boys made her park the truck again, closer to the curb with the tires facing out, so it wouldn't roll down the hill. Then we put wood blocks behind the back tires, just to make sure. Jimmy insisted on being in the cab to give directions. Then he insisted on turning the wheel himself when she backed it up. The truck was a big hit.

"How are we going to get my trunk up all those stairs?" Kitty asked.

Alex eyed her dubiously. "Just leave it there," he said. "Who knows, maybe you won't have to carry it up after all."

She turned to Alex and smiled. "So, trying to get rid of me already!" she said. Now she was grinning, a cartoon strip of straight square teeth. "Well, it won't be that easy. And after you kids help me carry up that trunk, it'll be a long time before you'll want to carry it down again. But wait until you see what's inside. Treasures of the world!"

Kitty herself was more intriguing than the contents of any trunk and we brazenly stared at her. "Well, now what?" she said, as she sat down on the front steps, her skirt spread out in front of her like a doll on a shelf. I sat down beside her and stared at her feet. Beneath the dust there was some chipped nail polish, bubble gum pink; she wiggled her toes.

Sitting close to her, I noticed she wasn't terribly old, thirty maybe, and she smelled like ripe fruit. She closed her eyes briefly as if making a wish. When she opened them again I could see they were tea-colored and glazed like carnival glass. I asked her where she was from.

"Philadelphia," she said.

Kitty wasn't like the others. She laughed; she played ball with us in the house and in the street, never mind the windows or the cars; she ate ice cream for breakfast; she lay naked on the sun porch; she drank. We loved her.

We loved the way she swerved her flatbed truck down the hill, us hanging on to the rusty rear posts, swinging our feet out around the corners. We loved sitting scrunched between her and the truck door, steering; she let us take turns. Sometimes she took her hands off the wheel and as we rolled down the canyon road around the blind curves she would lay on the horn. "Let them watch out!" she'd laugh. We loved going to the Yee Fong Cafe late at night, Kitty in her nightgown under a fold-up plastic raincoat. "Yoo-goo-gai, moo-goo, woo-goo-mai-pan," she ordered. We giggled wildly, shouting out our own versions of the syllables. "And sweet and sour shlimp!" she added, brandishing her chopsticks. She ordered more tea and added to it from a bottle in her purse.

Some nights she took us to a Brazilian restaurant where they served *feijoada* with manioc root and real pigs' ears. It was in a part of town we had never been, southeast of Chinatown, off an alley. When we arrived, a dark man would come out of the shadows to sit in the truck, filling it with the mulchy smell of beer and cigarillos, until we returned. Twice he drove us home while Kitty, passed out in the back, snored loudly. He never said a word, but smoked fiercely, drawing hard on the thin dark cigar until the end flashed orange and the smoke descended from his nostrils in dense white columns. On these two occasions, my father had been called out and was not home when we got there. "I have a guardian angel," Kitty said in the morning.

Kitty liked to go to interesting places and didn't mind

taking us with her. Like the time she drove us down to San Diego to watch a naval ship come in, only it was a school day and I was a little nervous about that.

"Well, this is educational," she said as we watched the majestic gray bow, banners flying, cutting through water toward the dock. "Besides, your grade isn't important."

I didn't want to remind her that Jimmy and Alex were also away from school. I liked the feeling of her arm around my shoulder.

Occasionally she took me to an Indian restaurant that featured vegetarian dishes. Above the door, the words *Self Realization* were printed in gilded letters. It was the owner of this restaurant, Mr. Baniyankar, whose black eyes glistened when Kitty appeared and who supplied her with brightly colored saris. He was the thinnest man I had ever seen. His dark skin sank into valleys between prominent bones. He didn't strike me as handsome, but Kitty said he was exotic, which, according to her, was even better. Sometimes Kitty and Mr. Baniyankar would disappear into a back room while I ate yogurt whipped with prunes. Once, after I had waited a long time and had eaten as much yogurt and as many carrots as I could endure, I watched Mr. Baniyankar ceremoniously unwrap pieces of folded fabric, and let them spill over his arm in delicious shades of orange, blue, and gold. He motioned with his hand for Kitty to choose. It was a graceful motion, dancelike, the brown back of his hand rolling over to a cupped palm and fingertips holding the silk like living tissue. She said the tangerine-colored sari was her favorite.

The next day Kitty carefully pleated and tucked the skirt before she tossed the gold-bordered fabric over her shoulder. "This goes well with Alex's hair, don't you think?" she said. Since she had dyed her hair the same color as Alex's cherry wood red—in fact, had dragged him down to the hairdresser for an exact match—she no longer referred to her hair as her own.

Alex had gone with her grumbling and growling as usual, but I could tell his heart wasn't in it; he was secretly pleased. She would wear "Alex's hair" braided in a pigtail when she wore the bright silk happy coat she bought in Chinatown, or she would set "Alex's hair" in waves when she wore her green velvet flapper dress with two rows of fringe on the bottom. These clothes, interspersed with other treasures like shadow puppets from Bali, ancient Chinese bronze mirrors, and Cherokee peace pipes, Kitty would draw from her steamer trunk like scarves from a magician's hat.

I imagined Philadelphia was a wonderful place. Kitty laughed when I told her. Her parents were still there, she said. She hadn't seen them in a long time. When I asked her why not, she said they'd never change, only now they'd be old. She said if a fiery sun were poised on the horizon, her parents would not have watched it, for fear of being late for dinner.

"What were they afraid of? What would happen to them?" I asked.

"Oh, nothing. It's just that they're afraid of everything," she said.

"Like what?"

"Like being late, being out of style, being criticized." She laughed. "Heaven forbid!"

It was hard to imagine Kitty being afraid of anything like that, certainly not of being late. She was late all the time. For her, time was irrelevant, that is, the kind of time that divides life into precise slots of minutes, hours. But she could tell you when the moon would be full or when the tides would ebb. She knew when the wildflowers bloomed in the desert, when the grunion ran, when the carp spawned in Lake Arrowhead.

On the other hand, she didn't know how to keep appointments, which didn't matter to us since we didn't have any, or what time food should be served, which also didn't matter since we got our own. A meal for us was, more often than not, just a cookie and a jar of peanut butter held between the knees. Also, Kitty didn't seem to have any idea of what time we should be in bed. This was a relief, since bedtime was often the first issue of contention we had with housekeepers. For Kitty, sleep was not scheduled. When you were tired, you slept, anytime anywhere.

In short, Kitty was one of us, which is why I trusted her about the birthday party. I had never had a birthday party, nor had I ever been to one. They were as mysterious to me as Eskimo gatherings, and as remote. Until the day Kitty said, "You're going to Sandra Chaffey's birthday party."

"What!" I said. "I am not." My stomach folded on itself. "How do you know about Sandra's birthday party?" I said. Kitty had a playful way of pressing her lips together when she was harboring a secret. It made you ache to know. But how long she held out depended on how much she had to drink; the drunker she was, the faster she let the secret out.

"I know you're invited and I'm going to take you," she said. "And, we're going to get you a special dress, just for the occasion. What do you think of that?"

I didn't know what to think. I still couldn't figure out how she knew about the party. I never knew about a party in advance. I knew only what I overheard at school, usually days after the event. I knew other kids went to parties and did things together outside of school, but I didn't know how these things were arranged. I pictured all the kids in my class together, going wild, with no teacher.

"I don't want to go," I said.

Kitty frowned. "Why not?" she said.

"Because I don't want to. Besides, I don't know anybody."

"Sure you do," she said, regaining her grin. "You see these kids every day. It's time you get to know them outside of school." Kitty looked at me as if she were cold sober. "Come on, it'll be fun. I promise."

I thought about a special dress, my first. I imagined it pink with a full skirt and a sash that tied in back. "Will you go with me?" I asked. Her eyes opened wide with exasperation, but warm and teasing at the same time. "Of course I will," she said.

That was a relief. It couldn't be so bad if Kitty were with me. "Oh," she added, "you have to bring a birthday present."

"What should we get?" I asked.

Kitty thought for a moment. "I think the very best present is one you make yourself," she said. "It shows imagination and effort. And it's always more appreciated than just something you buy. Anybody can buy something. All that takes is boring money." Since I didn't have any boring money, making the present sounded like a good idea. I asked her what I should make, but she said we had lots of time to think about it; the very best present is thoughtful.

After school the next day, I walked so fast up the hill that the back of my legs hurt. We were supposed to go shopping for my special dress. But when I got home I saw that it was one of those days when Kitty had locked herself in her room. I could hear her knocking things over, then throwing them against the wall. I heard the soft thud of her body when she fell down. She was talking to herself and weeping.

At first we were alarmed when Kitty had her binges and tried to coax her out of her room, but during these drinking bouts, she would not be coaxed. My father told us to leave her alone, that she would come out when she was ready. But he would coax her out after we left. I would sometimes hear their voices in the kitchen late at night, Kitty whimpering like a wounded animal, my father gently scolding. The next day Kitty would usually announce that she was "on the wagon." This meant that she would be more subdued than usual and would place bottles of vodka behind the encyclopedias and in the bottom of the laundry basket. This also meant that her morning glass of milk would smell of whiskey.

But this time, it was two days before she came out. I was getting worried about my dress. "Can we go tomorrow for sure?" I asked.

"For sure," Kitty said. Her face was the color of putty. Her eyes sank deep in potholes of shadow. Her hair hung limp around her sunken face, uncombed and greasy. Tomorrow was doubtful.

The next morning I brought Kitty a cup of coffee. I had put in an extra heaping spoonful to help wake her up. "Thank you," she said, taking a sip and wincing. "Just leave it there, on the bedstand . . . I want to drink it slowly." She lay back on her pillow and put her hands over her eyes. She had a headache, she said. She lay there without moving, exhaling long, pungent breaths. "Are you getting up?" I asked. Kitty rubbed her eyes. "No," she said.

"You said today—"

"I know," she said. "I'm sorry." She took my hand.

It felt awkward, my arm pulled out like that, but I locked my fingers in between hers and moved closer so she wouldn't sense that it was awkward and let go. I couldn't remember anyone holding my hand before. Oh, I suppose my father took my hand when I was very little, crossing the street, but I didn't remember it like this—the softness, the slight contractions of the fingers, the spreading warmth. "It's okay," I said. "It doesn't have to be today."

Then she was sleeping, her mouth slightly open and her eyes moving a little behind her pale eyelids. She patted my hand gently when I started to withdraw it, then turned over, pulling the sheet up over her head, hair trailing on the pillow, red and tangled.

On the day before the party I knocked on Kitty's door. It was locked.

"Kitty, what about my dress?" I said. "I have nothing to wear." I tapped on the door. "Kitty . . . Kitty, it's me." I could hear her coughing, deep and wet, and the rustling of material. She must have been wearing the silk robe that went whoosh against her legs.

"Kitty, what about the birthday present? I don't know what to make. Tomorrow's the party and I don't have anything."

The quiet was broken with another cough. I stood at the door and continued to knock gently. "Kitty," I said. "Please."

Footsteps, muffled and uneven, padded across the floor, the sound of silk against her legs. Then a cough; a clearing of the throat. The heavy rubbing of her forehead against the door. "Don't be mad at me, baby," she said at last. I could hear her breathing through the door, long pulling breaths, followed by a soft whine.

"Please come out, Kitty," I said. "I'm not mad at you. I'll make you some coffee, anything you want. Kitty?"

She said nothing else.

The day of the birthday party was bright and sunny. I wasn't. Kitty had broken her promise. I should have known better than to trust her. Early in the morning I went out for a hike in the foothills around our house. Jetsam followed along. I didn't care about the new dress, I told her, wondering if cats could tell when you were lying. And I didn't care about going to a birthday party. In fact, I was glad I wasn't going. That was only half a lie. I scratched behind her black, tattered ear. The cat stared at me blankly.

When Jetsam and I got back, Kitty was standing in the kitchen. I fell into my sulkiest face and marched past her without saying a word. Noisily, I stomped up the stairs to my room, expecting to throw myself on the bed in a huff, making the most of my bad humor.

But there on the bed was a ruffled pink dress and not only that, but white socks and shoes with straps like the ones other girls had. Until then I'd had only brown and white Oxfords, which I hated beyond description. Scooping the dress into my arms, I ran downstairs to the kitchen. "You got it! You got it!" I said excitedly. "When did you get it? How did you get it? "

Kitty pressed her lips together. "I'll never tell," she said. "My secret."

"Thank you," I said. "It's beautiful. But Kitty, what about the present?"

"I can't think about that now," she said, pressing her hand to her forehead. "Don't worry, just make something simple. Make a card like you made for your father's birthday; that'll be fine." Now she was pressing both hands to her temples. She said, "I want to rest before the party."

After making the card, I placed it in a shoe box and tied a curling ribbon around it so it would look like a present. Then I washed the glue from my hands and put on my new outfit, piece by piece, standing in front of the mirror.

After I was dressed, I went down the stairs to my own treasure chest in the basement of our house. It was a box containing items that belonged to my mother, photographs mostly, and some letters in German, but there was some jewelry too, which I would occasionally take out and wear in my bedroom. This being a special occasion, I removed a garnet necklace and put it on under the dress. It felt cold against my skin, then warm. It gave me courage.

On the way to Sandra's house, I rode inside the truck with Kitty so I wouldn't get dirty. It wasn't until she said, "I'm not going in with you," that I noticed she wasn't dressed up. She was wearing her old toreador pants and white tabbies. Her hair was tied up in a scarf. "I can't," she said. "I'm sick."

"Then I can't go either," I said petulantly. "I'm sick too." I really did feel sick. My heart was pounding fast and hard and the dress felt like sandpaper against my skin. "I can't go either," I repeated. But I could see in her face that she would not turn back.

By the time we got to Sandra Chaffey's I was breathing fast and inside my head was throbbing. I started to protest, but Kitty had already climbed out of the truck and opened my door. "You'll have a good time," she said. Her face was so pale I was afraid to upset her. I knew she couldn't come in with me. Some other children were coming in late too, so I melted into this little group as they walked into the house and hoped I was invisible.

Inside, children were yelling, laughing, jumping, running from room to room. I couldn't make sense of all the noise; at home we never screamed like that for no reason. I had never seen so many children in one place outside of school. A fat boy who had a handkerchief tied over his eyes was stumbling around, his arms forward, holding a long piece of paper in his hand. Each time he staggered near them, kids would either dart away or push him, sending him spinning. For some reason, this brought on screeches of laughter, except from the boy, whose guppy mouth quivered below his blindfold. What were they doing? Whatever it was, it was not at all funny. Then I was struck by a terrible thought: What if they did this to me? I imagined being blindfolded, maybe tied up, not knowing what to do. The children laughing.

I dashed into the next room, a kind of den, and slipped behind a heavy drape. It smelled of dust and old smoke and I had to rub my nose to keep from sneezing. I flattened myself out against the window and didn't move; I hardly breathed. After a while, my feet got pins and needles. The screaming and laughing went on and on. I could hear the stampede of footsteps moving from one place to another. Then I heard the children sing Happy Birthday, followed by laughter and clapping. My legs started to ache from standing so straight for so long, but I was afraid to sit down in case someone could see a bulge behind the drape. Finally, I slid to the floor and lay on my side, my ear resting on my upstretched arm, the back of my new dress pressed against the wall. I stayed like that for a while then stood up again. Unable to stay there any longer, I decided to make a run for it. Slowly I crept out from behind the drape, my knees tingling and my back hunched. I tiptoed into the hallway. I had almost reached the door when Mrs. Chaffey appeared out of nowhere.

"My goodness!" she exclaimed when she saw me. "Where did you come from?"

I stood stock still, the shoe box under my arm.

Sandra walked in behind her mother, looking surprised. "Were you here?" she said. "I didn't see you before."

I tried not to look at her.

"Well, you're just in time for opening the presents," Mrs. Chaffey said as she herded me into the next room with her hand on my back. Sandra sat down among the brightly wrapped boxes and expertly slipped the ribbons off the corners, one by one. From whispering white tissue emerged dolls' clothes, socks, books, and a miniature four-poster bed for her doll house. I noted with alarm that nothing was handmade.

Mrs. Chaffey slipped the shoe box from my grasp. "This is from—" I stood frozen. Sandra looked up. "Jorie," she said. She lifted the card from the box. HAPPY BIRTHDAY SANDRA! I had printed on the front. Inside was a glued arrangement of pressed wildflowers—a sprig of lupine, another of wild mustard. She started to smile, but the curve of her mouth quickly reversed itself as she let out a rattling scream. The card and the shoe box went flying from her lap as she jumped to her feet. Then, the other children were jumping just like Sandra, hopping from one foot to the other. No one but Sandra had seen the card, but a chain reaction had been set in motion, the screams electrifying each child in succession. Piercing cries filled the air, soon joined by Mrs. Chaffey's screams of *What happened! What happened!* Then some of the children shook their hands in a strange kind of palsied dance. Dumbfounded,

I bent down to pick up the card. The pressed flowers were still in place, but the large pressed grasshopper had come loose. It was hanging from its still-attached head. It was my best grasshopper so far: *Melanoplus differentialis.* None of its legs were broken and it had stayed in a nice position, its back legs at perfect angles, exactly as I had found it on a twig. The body was still greenish. And, not too much brown stuff had squished out in the pressing. For a fleeting moment, I wanted to take it back. But I left it in the box and looked for a way of escape, not knowing what else to do amidst all the noise and commotion.

"Thank you for a nice time," I said to Mrs. Chaffey as Kitty had coached me, and scrambled out the front door.

I ran as fast as I could away from the house until I no longer knew where I was. I took several wrong turns leading into blind cul-de-sacs, then finally happened onto a street that curved down toward the city. Like a beacon, the spire of the Capitol Record Building came into view. I walked down Franklin Avenue in the twilight and called Kitty from Victor's Market. She told me she had fallen asleep. I waited for what seemed to be a long time in the dark until Kitty picked me up. In the car I wouldn't talk to her. When we got home, I went to my room and locked the door. Later, when Kitty knocked, I refused to answer.

"I'm sorry, Jorie," she said. "Come on, open up." She stood there for a long time, gently knocking now and then. Finally, she went away. Just before bedtime, Kitty came back to my door. "I brought you some hot chocolate." I heard the thump of a tray against the door. "Please talk to me, baby," she said. "I'm really sorry."

I sat on my bed in silence, staring at the doorknob. I knew how to sulk. The silence, the cast-down eyes, the taut lips— these I fell into naturally. What I didn't know was how to stop sulking; that did not come naturally. When the silent anger drained away, I didn't know how to get back to where I had been. I felt stranded, shipwrecked.

The next day Kitty stayed in her room with the door locked. I wanted to knock on her door, but something prevented me. The feeling of being wronged had lasted through the night; I woke up with it still there, lingering and sore.

"Not again," Jimmy said as he passed by me standing outside Kitty's room. "I wonder how long it'll last this time. Should we call Dad? Tell him she's on another binge?" I shook my head. Jimmy shrugged. "Well, I guess we should just leave her alone. She'll come out when she's ready; she always does." Jimmy was losing patience with Kitty; the novelty had worn off. She had disappointed him a couple of times, but he carried no grudge. "I don't need her to take me to a ball game," he'd said. Unlike me, Jimmy relinquished hope easily and with grace; it was one thing he learned before I did. Taking a flying leap, he jumped onto the banister, pivoting with his right hand. "See ya, old girl," he called as he slid out of sight.

After Jimmy left, I listened for the sounds of Kitty's footsteps, but there were none. I told myself it was her own fault if she was drunk; she should feel bad. After all, she didn't deserve to be trusted. I sat down outside Kitty's door and stayed there all day, not speaking or knocking but wanting to, pinned by the weight of forgiveness withheld.

The next evening was windy and cold. The wind came in gusts with long hushed pauses in between. The eucalyptus trees rustled and rested, the pines sang out and fell silent. We could hear the siren getting closer and closer until we saw the red light flashing around the corner, then the ambulance itself coming around the flashing bend and stopping abruptly in front of Kitty's truck. Two men slid a stretcher out of the back, looked up at the three flights of stairs, hesitated, then started to climb, the man in front climbing backwards, step by step. Kitty still lay on the floor of her room, beyond the broken door, my father bent over her, supporting her head. She was less blue now and had started to gasp and sputter in response to something he had given her. He checked her blood pressure and pulse and nodded to the attendant next to him. The men placed the stretcher on the floor, then slid her onto it, tucking her arms under the sheet and buckling the straps over her chest and legs. As they lifted her, wheels dropped down and locked in place. I came up beside her. "Kitty, Kitty," I said. "It's me." But her face was turned away from me. I touched her hand through the sheet. Then my father pulled me back, out of the way.

We watched the ambulance turn around, its light flashing in the dark as it started down the hill. I remembered that first day, watching for Kitty and finally seeing her flatbed truck winding up the road. By this time, I'd watched so many come and go. But now, as the siren began to wail, I was stricken by loss and unmade peace and I could not even pretend it didn't hurt. From the upper floor the ambulance looked like a large box and I thought of Kitty's trunk with its treasures of the world.

*O*VER A YEAR HAD passed since Kitty was carried out of our house and now we had returned to an insular life. There were no more attempts at parties or to draw us out into the larger world. Jimmy and I leaned back on our heels and watched the whirling red vinyl as voices floated mysteriously from our portable record player and scratched their way through the air.

"Snooks, you must never be a sloop," her father says.

"What's a sloop, Daddy?" Baby Snooks says coyly. We knew that she already knows what a sloop is, that she's asking not for the answer, but just for the pleasure in the answer.

"A sloop is someone who slurps his soup," her father says in his announcer's voice. Snooks giggles. "I know that, Daddy."

We already knew that too. But every time we heard it we laughed; the word still tickled us. Even Alex laughed, but added, "That's dumb."

"Bluurrrrrg . . . bluurrrrg . . . bluurrrrg . . ."
"Snooks, what are you doing?"
"Nothing, Daddy."
"You are too! You're blowing bubbles in your milk!"
"I am?"
"You are. How many times have I told you? You must NEVER blow bubbles in your milk." At this point, as if on cue, we raced out to the kitchen. Ceremoniously we brought back glasses of milk in which to blow noisy trills as we sat around the record player.

"I love Baby Snooks," I said under my white moustache.

My father, sitting in his reading chair, looked over at us and smiled. "She's an inspiration," he said.

We spent a lot of time listening to our Baby Snooks record; it was a touchstone for the world of families outside our own. At home and on outings Snooks was taught the practical and moral lessons of daily life, such as table manners, looking both ways before crossing the street, and telling the truth. Most of the time the father of Snooks gave warnings—Snooks, don't tease the animals at the zoo—unlike my father who, during our trip to the zoo, had calmly watched a lion pee on Jimmy as he was rattling the bars of the lion's cage. In response to my brother's furious sobs, my father had simply shrugged and walked on. I gently patted Jimmy on his one dry shoulder. "That lion must have thought you were a tree," I said.

Unlike my father, the father of Snooks laid down rules. He would say: "Don't cross the street on a red light." My father would simply say: "If you cross in front of traffic, you'll be squashed flat as a pancake." My father didn't like to give directives, didn't really believe in them. Nor did he believe in maps, fences, beacons, or buoys. He believed in an inner voice and trusted us to find it.

Also, my father did not believe in answering certain kinds
of questions. He had no reluctance in discussing the technical
aspects of sex, birth, death, the nature of time, or any questions relating to the objective or contextual worlds. But he
made it understood that feelings were not to be expressed—his
or ours. When our mother died, he explained that the polio
virus attacks the central nervous system, that if it takes hold
high on the spinal column, the victims are completely paralyzed, unable to move or breathe on their own. They are placed
in a respirator. The muscles atrophy. They die. Inevitable. He
did not want to discuss the consequences of this inevitable
death on those of us left living, nor how we felt about it. Did we
have any questions relating to the polio virus? No? No more
questions.

"But I have another question," Alex said. "Well?" said my
father, stiffening.

"What does *inevitable* mean?"

My father's eyes did not move from his hands, which were
folded tightly on the table. "*Inevitable* means," he said, "you
must accept it." That was the only time I can recall my father
giving a definition. When we didn't know the meaning of a
word, he always told us, "Look it up." When we had questions,
he directed us to the encyclopedia. I was later to discover there
were questions that could not be looked up. But these were
precisely the questions my father wouldn't answer. I also
learned that he often linked these kinds of questions to the
nature of being female. He implied that men didn't bring up
uncomfortable questions, only women did. But once, a couple
of years earlier, before I knew better, I'd made the mistake of
asking my father, "Do you love me?"

His face and neck flushed red. "Why do women always ask
that question!" he said. "Your mother used to ask the same
question. All women do. I don't understand it. Don't I take
care of you? Don't I treat you well? Do you have food in your

stomach? Have I ever hit you?" Methodically he filled his pipe, pushing down strands of mud-colored tobacco with his finger. "Actions are what matters. Love is just a word. Overused, at that."

"I know," I said. "But, do you?"

"You should know the answer," he said. "I shouldn't have to tell you."

"Just once. Just tell me once and I'll never ask again. I promise."

"Women always promise, but they keep asking. No, don't ask me again. This is the one place I'm free from that nonsense. Don't you start now." He turned his back to me then, and walked away.

But by this time, I had learned to keep these taboo, feminine questions in check. I had learned that my father's predictable response was to turn away and I was afraid that I would drive him away entirely, that one day he would look at me with no love in his eyes and simply not come back. So I learned to ask about planetary orbits, the growth of an embryo, or the circulation of blood. In this way, I tried to earn his interest and pride, but also, the answers were genuinely interesting to me and at times I even shared my father's relief that my mind had not been sullied by a woman's touch. Conversations between girls at school were completely foreign to me and I found their concerns puzzling, but I also recognized that there was a whole sphere of common knowledge, passed from mothers to daughters, from women to girls, from which I was excluded. Among other things, this sphere contained the conventions of social decorum, matters of taste, manners, grooming, acceptable euphemisms, acceptable questions, how to behave with men. Quite simply, girls with mothers knew things I didn't know.

Our most sustained contact with a woman had been with our second piano teacher, Miss Luvah. I suspect she had known my mother, as had Mrs. Baumberger, our first, but she never spoke of it. Perhaps I believe this because of her tenacity, her insistence that we carry out our mother's wish for us to make music. Although she was working off her medical bill with my father by trading piano lessons for ultrasound treatments, her interest seemed more than just financial. Sometimes she would take me to her house for homemade plum dumplings, which she said no one in the world seemed to enjoy more than I did. But after contending with teaching "wild kits" as she called us, no doubt she wondered whether hers was the short end of the bargain. Coping with bursitis might have been less troublesome than coping with us. For Alex was irritable and moody, Jimmy refused to practice, and I refused to read music. While I knew the rudiments of music, mostly I played by ear. Patient soul that she was, Miss Luvah played each piece for me, first all the way through, then measure by measure. Once I knew the notes and fingering, we worked on the dynamics by imagining visual images, making each piece a kind of story. From Miss Luvah, I learned that music has an inner life. But outside of music, Miss Luvah was unable to guide me, she herself being a refugee from a small attic room on a bleak street in Labunowo.

One day my father said out of the blue, "We're going to visit Errol Flynn." The famous actor was a patient and friend of my father's, but I had never met him. It was unusual for us to be included in any part of my father's life outside the tiny domestic realm that the four of us occupied. Other than our neighbor Dmitri's rare visits, he never invited anyone to our house, even casually. Never. Perhaps Errol Flynn had insisted that he bring us for dinner; perhaps my father couldn't find a convincing enough excuse. Nevertheless, when the announcement was made that we were going to Mr. Flynn's house, I was both excited and fearful. I knew certain things would be expected, but I didn't know what they were exactly. I could only hope that I would guess them before I brought shame on myself.

My first obstacle was that I had practically nothing to wear. The party dress Kitty bought me had been destroyed in the wash. I had outgrown the shoes. Now my wardrobe consisted of faded tee shirts, old dungarees, and one dress that was too small and cut me under the armpits. My socks had disintegrated. Our clothes were in an especially bad state by that time because we were finished with housekeepers. Estelle, the one following Kitty and the last one ever, was fired. This was unusual since they usually quit before my father had a chance to fire them. When Estelle left, she had taken things out of the house, mostly electrical appliances, including the toaster and the iron. "Good riddance to scorched shirts," my father said. "Good riddance to burnt toast!" the boys chimed in. "Good riddance to housekeepers forever!"

I didn't think she was too bad, considering the others. We had reached a mutually satisfying relationship: we ignored each other. But there was one thing I admired about her and that was her "invisible" hair net.

My second obstacle was my hair. How could I go to Errol Flynn's house with hair like this? It looked like a rat's nest. I had never seen a rat's nest, but it must have looked like one because that's the first term that spontaneously came to people's lips when they saw it. But fortunately I had tucked away an invisible hair net, which I had talked Estelle into giving me after pointing out a small hole in it. Naturally I did not point out that I was the one who made the hole.

I tried to gather my hair into the net, but it was long and heavy and slipped out of one side, then the other. Finally, I managed to get all the hair encased in the net which then draped along the side of my neck like a fat sausage. From the hole in the net at the top of my head, a loop of hair herniated out. Thus, with my hair sufficiently neat, wearing the short-waisted dress and brown Oxfords with no socks, I presented myself at the front door, ready for visiting. My father and the boys looked a little startled at first, seeing me so fixed up. Noticing their double-take, I felt a little burst of pride.

You couldn't tell from looking at his children, but my father had impeccable taste. All of his suits were tailor-made, either here or in Europe, where he vacationed every year. He chose only the finest wool or silk. He never spoke about these things, nor did they seem important to him. Dressing well was merely something he did. This was the year, 1953, that he brought home the Mercedes-Benz from Germany, a moss green 300 Coupe convertible. It came with a full set of pigskin luggage in the trunk. I thought it was the strangest car I had ever seen. I was used to the old black Kaiser. It was so rare to see a Mercedes in Los Angeles in those days that drivers would stop on the road and the men would get out and circle round, patting and exclaiming as if inspecting fine livestock. My father always wore leather driving gloves which he tossed over his shoulder onto the seat when he left the car. He frequently wore a hat pulled down at an angle over his bushy eyebrows. What children wore was inconsequential. Children were to be unencumbered by such material concerns. They were not to be distracted from their solitary metamorphosis from little undifferentiated beings to mature individuals. Being covered up was enough. And so we went to Errol Flynn's house covered up, nothing more.

The butler answered the door. He was dressed in a plain dark suit, but the maid was in full uniform, just like in the movies. She wore a gray dress with a starched white apron, ruffled along the top. The apron did not have straps and I wondered how it stayed up. She seemed to have a muffin cup on her head, but on closer inspection, I saw it was a little pleated hat. After my father and Errol Flynn had drinks, we followed this dovelike maid into the dining room.

The dining table, covered with white damask, was long and narrow. The three of us were seated together, facing the men. The edge of the table was about at the level of my chest which allowed me to unobtrusively tug at my armholes. During the salad I gazed at Errol Flynn, dressing him in my imagination. First he was Robin Hood, all in green, a jaunty feather in his hat. I had seen *Robin Hood* several times when we walked down to Hollywood Boulevard for the matinee every Saturday. I especially liked the grand theaters, the Pantages and the Egyptian, but we usually went to the smaller theaters like the Paramount, where the management was more lenient. The boys liked to sit in the front row and throw popcorn at the screen. But that was too distracting for me. I liked to sit farther back, to be swept up in the story, as I was now swept up, gazing at Errol Flynn across the table. Then he coughed, and Robin Hood was transformed into Major Vickers of the 27th Lancers, riding in the Sahara. Clouds of dust billowed up around him but never marred the starched white of his uniform. So gallant, even though Olivia de Havilland didn't love him. So gallant, even so. Then he was Captain Blood, sheathing his sword, taking great masculine strides in his black pirate boots. He smiled at me, a pirate's smile. Unlike my father's low murmurous voice, his voice was loud and resonant and made me jump each time he spoke. His accent was crisp and lyrical. People thought he was Irish, but he was Tasmanian.

"Have you heard of Tasmania?" he asked.

"Of course," Alex said.

"And Tasmanian devils," I added.

"Ha! Ha!" he laughed, his puffy eyelids bulging like dough. "So you think I'm a devil?" The drink splashed in his hand.

"I don't know," I said. "But I meant Tasmanian devils. You know, the marsupial mammals related to kangaroos. I read about them in the encyclopedia. Did you ever see one?"

"Sure, lots of 'em—"

"Where?" I was not convinced. Because of the rakish characters he played—pirates and muskateers—I thought he would be an adventurer, someone with a vast experience of the world, but now I had my doubts. He looked so different, an older, bloated version of the dashing buccaneer of the movies. "Where did you see them and when? How many were there?"

My father set his fork down with a subtle clank. "Jorie, that's enough of this subject," he said.

My skin tingled under his reproof. Such stern words were hardly necessary, as the slightest elevation of my father's eyebrows was enough to undo me. Now with everyone looking at me, I just wanted to evaporate, to disappear from sight. But I was saved when Errol Flynn stood up at the sound of approaching footsteps and all eyes were averted toward the door.

"I have a surprise!" he said. "My daughter is visiting me from Paris. Hello! In here!" he bellowed.

"Good evening, Papa," she said, handing her brass-buttoned coat to her waiting governess. "We had a wonderful time at the ballet. Toumanova was *magnifique*."

"Darling, I'd like you to meet Dr. Mackinnon and his children."

"*Enchantée, Monsieur le Docteur,*" she said, crossing her delicate foot behind her, bending her knees. She curtsied. She actually curtsied!

My father's face filled with enchantment. Even the boys picked up their chins. Her smile was easy, warm and wide, flanked by a dimple deep in her rosy cheek. She bowed sweetly to Alex and Jimmy. Why was she bowing to them? She must have been about their age, even a little older. Her shining hair was pulled back from her face and caught in a bow (too big, I thought) and hung down her back in bouncing ringlets. I thought I saw my father's eyes glow. By the time she looked in my direction her sweetness had begun to wane. She looked at me with arched eyebrows. Could it be my invisible hair net?

"Do you study ballet?" she asked.

"No," I said.

"Modern dance?"

"No."

"Tap, perhaps?"

"No."

"Oh well, do you speak French?"

I looked at Jimmy for help. "Are you kidding?" he answered.

Alex leaned forward in his chair as if he were on to something. "Do you play the piano?" he asked her.

"Mais oui," she said, smiling. "I study with Madame LeJurre in Paris. And I also study with Madame Renault in Montmartre; she is teaching me the harpsichord."

"Oh," said Alex.

"I don't want to play the harpsichord," I said and glanced across the table at my father. He was not looking at Mademoiselle Flynn as I thought he would be; he was looking at me. It was a familiar look, intense, removed, that I didn't understand at the time. I now realize it was the look of an observer. My father observed his children with curious detachment, as a spirit might observe those living out their karma.

I couldn't help looking back at Errol Flynn's daughter, buffed-up and radiant. She was comfortably settled in the attention of everyone at the table. The wide lace collar of her dress rose and fell; she purred. I hated every perfect ringlet on her head. But there was nothing I could do except scrape my bare ankles together. I shivered in the chill wind of my father's judgment.

Then came the clams. We had never seen a clam before, at least not without some seagull pecking at it. The bowls were deep and steaming, brimming with shells, a choir of open mouths choking on their tongues. I didn't know what to do. After watching my father, I put one in my mouth and held it there, unable to swallow. I could see that Jimmy and Alex had done the same thing. Alex pointed down, the signal for a conference under the table. Careful to stay in our chairs, we bent down, ducking our heads under the tablecloth. We spit the clams out into the palms of our hands.

"Barf-O," said Jimmy.

Alex held the clam between his thumb and index finger. "They use these for bait," he said.

"I think I taste sand," I said. My face was getting hot from being upside down. "What should we do?"

Jimmy stuffed his clam in his napkin.

"No, you can't do that. They're cloth," I said. "They don't get thrown away."

"Here, do this," Alex said, stuffing the clam in his pocket.

Jimmy stuffed the clam into the pocket of his plaid flannel shirt.

Errol Flynn's voice vibrated across the table. "Where are your children, Doc? Did they leave?"

"No, they're just having a conference."

"That's my kind of business, eh Doc? Under the table. Ha!" With that he slapped his hand on top of the table, rattling the glasses and silverware.

We popped up in our seats, feeling dizzy as the blood drained from our heads. Alex looked like a ripe tomato, his red hair and face flaming.

For a while I watched the boys furtively spit the clams into their hands then slip them into their pockets. I had collected as many clams as my left hand could hold. Errol Flynn's daughter was delicately chewing as she extracted another clam, without so much as a click from the shells or a drop of broth on her fingers. With my right hand I pointed down for another conference.

"I don't have pockets," I said to Alex's reddening face. "Can I use yours?"

"I don't have room," he said.

"Me neither," said Jimmy. "You'll have to think of something else. And take that thing off your head. You look bizarre!" *Bizarre* was Jimmy's word for the week. Every Sunday my father gave each of us a new word. We had to look it up then use it in a sentence.

"I can't take it off now; it's making my hair neat," I said. But my confidence in the invisible hair net had been shattered. Did everyone else think I looked bizarre? Desperate, I stuffed the clams into my underpants.

The vague thing I feared had started to take shape. It's not that I thought I did something bad, it's just that I wasn't guessing things right. I was failing somehow. Why did I have to have clams in my pants? Is that the best I could do? I looked at my father across the table; he was talking to Errol Flynn's daughter about her school in Paris. She touched her dimple when she smiled, in case he hadn't noticed it. I reached in my underpants to retrieve a clam that had drifted seatward.

It's not that I was afraid my father would get angry about the clams. He had never shown anger with us. He showed disappointment; he showed something verging on disgust. "I'm going to trade you in," he would say when I behaved badly. "I'm going to get myself another little girl. I'm going to get myself a little black girl. Her skin will shine like ebony and her eyes will sparkle like jet. She'll laugh and sing and the house will light up with her cheerfulness." Or another time he'd say, "I'm going to get myself a little blond girl. Her hair will be like spun gold. Her cheeks will be the color of roses and her sweetness will waft in the air." I didn't know if he would carry through with this threat. But I looked at my unblack, unblond, uncheerful self and knew that I could easily be replaced.

After the clams, the dinner improved. We had Salisbury steak, and ice cream for dessert with chocolate sauce, which all three of us dripped on the tablecloth. The men had espresso coffee and cognac. Errol Flynn's daughter had a red drink with a cherry; I wouldn't chance it.

By nine o'clock we were led into a brightly lit den that was quite modern. Inset into white painted walls were cabinets filled with records and radio equipment which my father referred to as Hi-Fi. To the left of a gleaming piano was a small tweed couch which my brothers and I quickly piled onto. Mademoiselle Flynn stood demurely by the piano.

"Darling," Errol Flynn said to his daughter, "would you play something for us?"

"Oh, Papa, I don't really think . . ." Her hand pressed against her chest, she looked back and forth between her father and the piano, torn between dutiful love and gripping modesty. Alex rolled his eyes. "Well," she said, "if Dr. Mackinnon wants me to?"

"Of course," my father said. "We would like to hear you play. Please play."

"Well, just for you," she said. "Mozart. Sonata Number Three." Following a dramatic pause, she bent her head back, eyes closed, then dropped her face downward in passionate concentration. Her delicately arched fingers played out the first few measures. Ignoring my brothers' elbow jabs, I sat rigid as a broom, overwhelmed and astonished at the sheer ineptitude of her playing. She was terrible! "Lower the curtain," Jimmy whispered. As I listened to this piece of music that I knew well, reduced to a series of drudging, half-speed scales, an electric feeling came over me. There was the purring princess, oblivious to the awkward hesitations, to every missed note that caused Alex to wince, recklessly playing on, her back turned. I sensed the kill.

We clapped wildly with relief at the end of the first movement. Alex and I looked at each other. I knew he could dazzle the room with a Chopin polonaise; he played much better than

I. But how much sweeter it would be if I could be the one. I stood up. "I can play the second movement," I said.

"Yes! Play the second movement, Jorie," the boys said gleefully.

Errol Flynn's daughter rose reluctantly from the piano bench. My heart pounding with expectation, I stepped forward. Then my father rose, his towering height unfolding, and gave me a look that would stop a bullet. I sat back down. "Thank you," he said to her. "That was very good, a perfect ending to a fine evening. But it's late and we must go."

The moon was low over the Hollywood hills that night as we drove home over the narrow winding roads. Its light was cold and cast ghostly shadows among the eucalyptus branches that swayed in the wind. I sat in the back seat against the door, as far away from everyone as I could and still be in the car. I reeked of clams. The hole in the invisible hair net had enlarged, resulting in a massive eruption of hair. My dress finally gave way and opened up along the seam. I didn't care.

"Great dinner, huh, Dad?" Jimmy said tentatively.

"You liked it, son?"

"Yeah, great . . . Only, his daughter, well, she's extra *girlish*, don't you think?"

"Yes, I know. She's going to be a real heartbreaker."

I sank down in the seat, huddled against the cold night air. A heartbreaker? And what am I going to be? I wondered. My father looked at me curiously in the rearview mirror, then looked away in silence.

I HAD PLACED A MARKER in the encyclopedia volume that included marsupial mammals, so I could easily find it again. Tasmanian devil: *Sarcophilus harrisii,* voracious marsupial, a relative of the koala, bandicoot, and kangaroo. I was fascinated by marsupials and I liked the picture of the little joey in its mother's pouch. My interest had shamed me at the house of Errol Flynn, but I continued to read about marsupials; they became part of the ramblings of my mind. Marsupial mammals have primitive reproductive systems; infants are only partially developed at birth. The kangaroo fetus is blind and only three-quarters of an inch long when it is born, and weighs only 1/30,000th of its mother's weight. But it must make the long journey to its mother's pouch unassisted. Under the indifferent eye of its parent, it must climb unerringly, hand over fist, or die.

This time I'd left the encyclopedia in the dining room, next to my father's chair, on a stack of old magazines and newspapers. As I reached for it, an envelope caught my eye. It was filled with a jumble of loose photographs. One was a snapshot of my father. He was sitting at a table with Errol Flynn, each with a well-dressed and beautiful woman at his side. They were in a booth, apparently at a restaurant. There was a mural of palm trees in the background. One palm frond hung like a fan above their heads. In the black-and-white photograph, the dark hair of my father's companion blended with the tufted leather behind them, bringing her pale face forward in glowing contrast. Her eyes were sultry, like Greta Garbo's, and looked into the camera lens as if she had something to prove. Her long fingers rested on my father's arm, while the other hand, braceleted, was wrapped around a glass. I looked closely at the woman's face, trying to place her in some dim memory—a patient, a nurse—had I ever seen her? No, I would have remembered. I didn't recognize the other woman either; she was blond and slightly chubby, with a short neck and a deeply scooped dress. Then there were other photographs that showed my father with people I didn't recognize, strangers in strange houses with strange children, my father in a backyard swimming pool with an unknown toddler on his back, even a cat that was not our cat. There were a few pictures of us as well: a blurry snapshot of three ragamuffins, squinting into the sun, another snapshot of the same three ragamuffins, pant legs rolled up, at the beach. I couldn't remember him taking a photograph of us, ever. He didn't even own a camera, that I knew of. The last photographs were brown-toned and wrinkled. They were slightly stuck together, separate from the rest.

In one photograph, there was a foreign street filled with bodies, women and children lying helter skelter in pools of blood. In another, there was a Chinese woman in a dark padded coat. The coat had long sleeves that covered her hands; it made her look like a child.

I looked at the photographs for a long time, putting them

back in the envelope, then taking them out again, to make sure I remembered every detail. I examined the brown envelope and the backs of the pictures for identifying marks, but there were none. Pictures in, pictures out. It was as if by looking at them over and over I would finally recognize someone, or discover what they meant. My father had saved these photographs for some reason, and had been looking at them for some reason. Not having the slightest idea why, I buried the envelope under the pile of papers and magazines where I'd found it. From then on, I could not think of marsupials without thinking of the photographs. And I could not think about the photographs without associating them with marsupials. I returned to the envelope twice, then it was no longer there.

I knew better than to ask my father about the pictures. It was one of those unaskable questions, something not to be acknowledged, like a conversation you should not have overheard. The images, however, never left me. I would retrieve them from my memory many years later as answers to questions I would finally dare to raise.

Months after I stumbled upon the photographs, as I helped my father plant an old tea rose beside a hillside path, he talked about his life in China. This was the way he revealed himself to us. Unasked, in a serendipitous moment, he would give us a glimpse of a scene from his childhood: frost on the bedroom wall, bathing in a tin tub in a warmed kitchen. Or a glimpse of a later time: a burial at sea of a fellow merchant marine, the swathed body sliding into the water. We were well aware that we had no right to these revelations; they were gifts.

"This is an old species, from the family *Chinensis*," he began. "The Chinese have been cultivating roses for centuries. When I lived in China, I learned about roses from my wife." Without looking up, he continued to dig in the dry dirt. "I never told you I was married, before your mother—"

"No," I said, dumbstruck.

"She was Chinese and Portuguese, from the island of Macao."

I thought of the picture of the woman in the padded coat, but couldn't admit that I had seen it. "What was her name?" I dared ask.

"Her name was Li-hwa," he said. "She was killed by the Japanese, at the beginning of the war."

"That's terrible," I said. "She must have been very young."

With his foot, he tamped down the soil around the bush. "Very young," he said, "but she knew about roses." Then he wiped his hands on the sides of his pants, gave me the look that said Subject Closed, then walked away.

This was my dream: I'm following a woman in a dark coat, but she's walking so fast it's hard to keep up with her. Finally, she turns around. Her coat is open, exposing an abdominal pouch with a joey in it. The joey has the woman's Chinese face. They are both very beautiful. I'm just about to speak to her when gunfire erupts. Machine guns and loud explosions. There is blood everywhere and people are falling down and crying. They are the people in the photographs—my father, the woman in the restaurant, children I don't know.

*J*UST THINK," JIMMY SAID. "It could have been right here, this exact spot, where they set up camp. He probably rode his horse up the back trail and saw this nice hill where our house is now, then rode back down to where Vine Street is and told the others to bring the wagon. His tent could've been right here and the camp fire right there."

I looked at the table where he was pointing. On it a library book lay face down. I imagined a camp fire smoldering there under a blackened tin pot. Chunks of firewood glowed red and crackled as they broke apart. "Gosh," I said.

"I'll bet it was! No, I'm sure of it. I'm positive. This was the place all right; he described it perfectly." The "he" Jimmy was referring to was William Brewer, a member of a team sent in 1860 by Yale University to make a geological survey of California. Brewer was the subject of Jimmy's sixth-grade report on California history.

Jimmy picked up the book. "'Camped at Los Angeles, December seventh,'" he read. "'We are camped on a hill near the town . . . Here is a great plain from the ocean to the mountains. Over the level plain to the southwest lies the Pacific, blue in the distance; to the north are the mountains of the Sierra Santa Monica; to the south lies the picturesque town with its flat roofs; the fertile plains and vineyards stretching away to a great distance; to the east are some mountains without name, their sides abrupt and broken, still above them are the snow-covered peaks of San Bernardino. . .'"

"You're right," I said. "This must be the exact place. Just think, this was all vineyards and fertile stuff . . ."

"Amazing," Jimmy said, shaking his head as if he couldn't quite believe it himself.

I tried to think of Hollywood as it was then: before the railroad linked up to southern California, before droves of sunseekers migrated from the east, before land speculators divided the sprawling ranchos into small square promises. It wasn't hard to imagine because the hillside where we lived was still as it was in those days: manzanita, buckthorn, and greasewood still filled the canyons, and clematis and mountain mahogany trusted their seeds to the wind just as they did before the first brown foot climbed up to take advantage of the view.

In the early fifties much of Los Angeles was still green and dappled with vacant lots. Houses like ours with their backs buried in the mountain were separated by enough space so that a home came with a sense of territory. Above the slope in back of our house, a twelve-acre plateau overlooked the city. It had been cleared at one time, but had long since been reclaimed by its roots. Wild grasses and shrubs turned green and brown in their cycles and gave way only to the worn paths of children. In this Hollywood Jimmy developed a taste for the rural life.

At least that's how I explain why he wanted more than anything in the world to own a Golden Eagle. The Golden Eagle wasn't just any air gun, he explained. It had a pistol grip, a two-power factory-mounted scope with two lens caps, a ramp-style front sight, a combination peep and open rear, and a gold-decorated barrel and receiver. He said it looked exactly like a real hunting rifle.

Jimmy picked up the book from the table. "It was just a cow town when Brewer was here," he continued, flipping the pages to a pen-and-ink illustration of the original pueblo. "General Figueroa and José Sepulveda hunted deer and elk, even antelope, right here in these hills. And there were Indians and ex-slaves and lots of outlaws. Everyone was scared, even the geologists." Jimmy closed the book with a sigh. "If only I could have been there," he said.

I thought for a moment about a cold, smelly tent filled with loaded guns and decided that I wouldn't want to have been there. "Not me," I said. "I'd go on the survey expeditions, but then I'd go to a motel."

"They didn't have motels in those days. They didn't even have cars," Jimmy said. *"Mo* stands for *motor.* Mo-hotel; everyone knows that."

I didn't know it. He could have been making it up. "All motors aren't cars, you know," I said triumphantly.

"What! You think it means boats?" he said.

I knew I'd taken a wrong turn; I'd have to think fast to stay in the game. "Just because you say *mo* stands for *motor* doesn't mean it does," I said. *"Mo* could stand for *Morris,* the inventor of the small hotel." I made it up. "And, I happen to know that Morris lived in 1860 . . . and traveled West."

Jimmy crossed his eyes.

"They'll stick," I said.

On an occasional Sunday, my father liked to putter in the garden. It was expected at these times that we work in the garden too. We didn't object because we wanted to please him and were afraid to jeopardize the only day he spent with us. We'd do whatever was necessary to keep him at home. Since our yard was a mostly wild affair, it seemed to make little difference whether we pulled the lantana from the ivy geraniums or cut the wild anise that poked its feathered fingers through the rock wall. By the next week whatever we had cut seemed to magically reappear, smug in the face of our futility. But as much as we said we didn't like it, there was something wholesome about working in the yard, some deep satisfaction in inhaling the fragrance of earth as you wrenched up a plexus of roots, some sense of wonder at the nursery of sow bugs unearthed by your spade.

On this Sunday however, Jimmy could not keep to his gardening tasks and badgered my father with questions about guns alternating with facts about the Old West. My father smiled patiently and said as he handed him a shovel, "It's possible to work and talk at the same time." It was possible for us, but Alex now kept out of talking distance, keeping to his own corner of the yard as he grudgingly pulled weeds from the reluctant dirt. My father looked down at Jimmy, a reduced image of himself. Like him, the boys were long and lean in the body, their wavy hair insistent on standing away from the head. Jimmy stuck the shovel in the ground and rested his foot on it.

"I need a Golden Eagle, Dad. It's a necessity," he said with an earnest face. "You never know when you have to stop something bad from happening, like a coyote going after the cat, or a hawk swooping down on one of the kittens, or a rattlesnake." His face lit up with sudden inspiration. "Yeah, a rattler about to bite Jorie."

"Come on!" my father said with a burst of laughter. "I can see you hitting a rattlesnake with an air gun. Besides, Jorie would bite it back before you could line up your sights."

"Nu-uh," Jimmy protested. "I'll practice. I'll be quick. And deadly. Men have always carried guns in these hills, even Brewer. And he was a scientist."

"I'll tell you what," my father said after a pause. "You may have a Golden Eagle if you earn the money to pay for it. But, now listen: BUT, you have to learn the rules of gun safety. And, you have to learn how to take care of a gun. And, stop jumping and listen, it's a man's responsibility. You understand?"

"Yes!" he said. "Like the back of my hand."

"That's not right," I said. "You don't *understand* the back of your hand."

Jimmy looked at me and frowned. "I know what I understand," he said. Jimmy was finishing his report on William Brewer, the focus of which had slipped from trails forged through granite hills to encounters with *desperados*. Jimmy ceremoniously placed his pen on the report. "There!" he said. "Finished."

"Did you finish with the part about the shotguns?" I asked.

"Of course," he said. "That's the interesting part."

Jimmy was still so excited that evening, I wondered when the obvious problem would finally hit him. "Boy oh boy!" he said, aiming his arm at the light bulb. "Ping!"

"Ping!" he said as he squinted over his outstretched arm toward the round Venetian glass window. "Ping! Ping!" He stalked the cat. "Come here, little Jetsam," Jimmy said with his arm behind his back.

"How could you!" I said, scooping the cat up into my arms. She quickly jumped down and shook her back at both of us. Jimmy said, "Ping!"

I watched him take aim. "You don't have it yet," I said.

"I know that."

"Well?"

"Well, what?"

"How much does it cost?"

Jimmy held out his hands about a foot apart, as if he were holding a real Golden Eagle, then dropped them to his sides. "About fifteen dollars," he said. "The leather BB loader is extra."

Fifteen dollars. I knew it wasn't really a lot of money, if you had it. I also knew he didn't have it. Neither did I. Our small allowance vaporized in Jimmy's hands. In mine, it broke down into miserly aliquots: a dime spent, a dime saved, a dime for things that come up unexpectedly. Jimmy knew I was always good for a loan, but not this time; it was too much money. He sat down to think.

It came to him on the radio. KMX was offering a five-dollar prize each week for the best jingle advertising Ennd-O, a product containing the wonder of the age: chlorophyll. In those days chlorophyll was added to toothpaste and tooth powder, roll-on deodorant, mouthwash, soap, cough drops, and gum. It was even added to dog food. Ennd-O, "high potency" chlorophyll tablets, promised freedom from all personal odor offense. It was a natural.

"Swallow green, smell clean!" Jimmy said.

We were sitting at the table with our pencils and paper, squeezing out finger-tip dollops of Chlorodent toothpaste and eating it, for inspiration.

"Smell fresh as a daisy, inside out!" I said.

"No, no . . ." Jimmy said, crossing out words.

"Make friend-Os with Ennd-Os! Why let odors stand in the way?"

"Go on," Jimmy said. "It needs more. It has to rhyme."

My father, who had been sitting with his feet up in his reading chair close to the window, looked up from his book and after a long pause said, matter-of-factly, "Chlorophyll doesn't work."

We didn't want to hear that. We were just hitting our stride.

"Think about cows," he said.

"What about cows?" said Jimmy.

"Well," my father said thoughtfully. "Cows graze on chlorophyll all day long, and they still smell pretty bad."

I put down my pencil, thinking he had a point. When I

picked it up again, I realized that I had lost faith in chlorophyll. And with it, any jingly ideas I may have had. While Jimmy continued trying out words that rhymed with green, I looked out the window and erased the city spread below it, and put in its place a gentle green slope reaching out to the ocean.

I thought about the Golden Eagle. I wanted Jimmy to have it. He was lucky to want something like that, its steel and wood so real in your hand. Something you could earn and pay for. Something you could carry. I thought about the Brewer expedition and how things were then and whether people felt the same way inside, whether they wanted the same things. I glanced over at Jimmy. He was singing to the tune of Yankee Doodle, "Your breath stays clean with Ennd-O green . . ."

On that Thursday afternoon, I was playing the piano. When I was alone in the house, I carried the dynamics of the music to ridiculous extremes. The *fortissimo* of the Warsaw Concerto reverberated through the house. The sounds of the bass chords were rich and mellow, the lower register of the old Hoffmann piano being a better survivor of the Atlantic crossing than the upper. I had the top propped all the way open for maximum volume, so when Jimmy came in yelling, "Quick! Turn it on!" I could barely hear him.

"Hurry!" he shouted. "They're announcing it!" He ran to the radio and switched it on. The dial was already on KMX. "In just a minute," the announcer was saying, "we'll announce the winner of this week's jingle contest. But first, a word from Ennd-O."

We sat on the floor, looking up at the mesh behind the diamond pattern on the front of the radio. Jimmy was smiling as if he had already won.

"Yes, with Ennd-O tablets you never have to worry about embarrassing odors again and remember, if you want to enter our weekly contest, you have to be over eighteen and only one entry allowed, per contestant. All you have to do is give us a jingle!"

"Did you know that?" I said.

"Yup," Jimmy said.

We could hear the shuffling of papers behind the mesh. "And this week's winner is—James Brodnapov!"

"Brodnapov!" I said. "You used Dmitri's name."

"James Brodnapov," the announcer repeated. "Mr. Brodnapov is a geologist from Hollywood, California. Congratulations, James. And here's your jingle—"

"Yahoo!" Jimmy yelled, jumping to his feet. "Five dollars down, ten to go!"

"Subtracting the $2.75 we paid to get the box top," I reminded him.

Jimmy won the contest the next week too. He wrote on the entry form that he was James Dewey, an ex-con, trying to turn over a new leaf. He said he had a thing about bad smells, that he took Ennd-O three times a day. He said he was renting a room from Hazel Walker, my father's nurse, until he was back on his feet; they could leave a message for him at her number.

The following week Jimmy submitted another jingle using my father's name and office number, but my father made him retract it. He said that would constitute a medical endorsement, and besides, he didn't think a jingle dealing with flatulence had a chance of winning.

Jimmy worked for two months to get the rest of the money. He washed cars, collected newspapers and Coke bottles, and, hardest of all, he posed for Dmitri for a sculpture entitled "Choirboy." His jaw was sore for a week.

Finally the day came when I watched Jimmy hold the long-dreamed-of Golden Eagle in his lap, stroking its narrow spine as if it were warmed by blood. He cupped a palmful of BBs, then, tipping his hand, let them slide into the magazine barrel in a copper stream, slowly slowly, careful not to spill. So this is what it's like, I thought. You want something, you know what it costs, you do what is necessary to pay for it. And eventually, when you've done what is necessary, you hold it in your lap, looking at it in awe and wonder.

"That's it?" I said.

"Yup," Jimmy said. "Nice, huh?"

"I guess."

"You guess! It's the best air rifle ever. It's the best thing I've ever had in my whole life!" With one hand he picked up the round tin of BBs, with the other he gripped the wooden stock. "Come on," he said. "I'll show you how to shoot."

We picked out some empty cans from the trash and spaced them in a row along a ledge. He showed me how to cock the rifle by pulling the cocking lever down and how to aim. When I got a can in my sights, I was to squeeze the trigger. The first can went down. Five shots, five cans. "Cans are no challenge," said Jimmy. "You need a moving target."

"Not something alive," I said.

"I didn't say alive," Jimmy said. He turned slowly, scanning the hillside, the pink oleander bushes, the trees, the side of the house. He scanned the dirt and kicked a rock. I went back inside.

For several weeks, he carried the Golden Eagle slung over his shoulder, looking for whatever there was to be shot—cans, street signs, flowers, seed pods. Long stretches of afternoons would be punctuated with pops and pings. But more and more, he traced invisible quarry in the air and gripped the stock with a restless urgency. Then there were times he would just sit with the gun lying heavily across his knees and sigh. I wondered if actually having a Golden Eagle was as much fun as writing the jingles to pay for it.

On a Friday afternoon Jimmy appeared in the doorway of my room with his Golden Eagle hanging from a shoulder strap and a rolled-up sleeping bag under his arm. He told me he was going on an expedition, that he couldn't find a buddy to go with him, at least a buddy whose parents would allow him to go, but that he was going anyway, alone.

"I'll go!" I said. I would have been happier to go on a short hike, not having to carry anything, and getting home before the mosquitoes were out in force, but I didn't want to miss the chance to be a buddy. I felt I still had a chance with Jimmy. With Alex, it was too late. By this time, Alex had already started to withdraw from us. I think of him during that time as a kind of fierce archangel, a kind of self-appointed protector, who kept himself at a vigilant distance. But it was a thankless job and he would soon give it up. Now, seizing this opportunity to prove myself, I was determined to convince Jimmy to take me.

"I'm going way up in the hills," he said. "Brewer's trail. Not where we usually go. It isn't a hike for shrimpy girls."

"I'm not a shrimpy girl," I protested. "I can keep up with you any day."

"Hah. Even if you weren't a shrimp, you're still a girl and that's bad enough. This is a man's expedition."

"What does that mean—a man's expedition? Why can't a girl go on an expedition?"

"Too much trouble, for one thing. I'd have to be watching out for you all the time."

"I won't be any trouble," I said. "I promise. And I can watch out for myself. You won't even know I'm there. Come on, I'll be the rear guard."

"I don't need a rear guard."

"Okay. I'll be the front guard."

"I don't need a front guard."

"Then I'll be the scout."

With a quick dipping motion Jimmy hoisted the sleeping bag onto his shoulder, bending and unbending his knees until it was balanced. He looked at me with eyes full of doubt. "You have to carry your own gear," he said.

The hills we hiked to were in back of our house, which at first didn't seem like much of an expedition, but with the added weight of our provisions and the knowledge that we wouldn't be going home as the sun went down, our hike soon took on a seriousness lacking in our usual forays in the same terrain. Besides, we had never camped out all night before and it was clear that Jimmy intended to explore beyond our usual boundaries. "We've never been on that hill over there," he said, pointing to the hill across a broad ravine. "That would be a great lookout place."

"I can't carry this stuff all the way over there," I said, adjusting my blanket roll. "Can't we find a closer place to make camp?"

"All right, in a little while," Jimmy said. I could tell he was sorry he'd brought me.

The sun, already low, glared in reddish reflection over the brush-covered slope. I thought of Brewer and his team, with their pickaxes and satchels for collecting rock specimens, watching the same sun descending over this same hill, with the same sight of a red-tailed hawk, a *Buteo jamaicensis*, circling overhead on the rising thermals, stopping suddenly to tread the air, then floating away. It had been ninety years since Brewer saw what we were seeing, but it could have been ninety days, or even ninety minutes. This is what it means when time stands still, I almost said but stopped myself. I realized even then that my thoughts tended to be overblown. A procession of quail with chicks scurried across the trail in front of us, a large black-faced male standing at the rear and calling a shrill alarm. Before Jimmy had the gun off his shoulder, the quail disappeared in the dry grass. "Ping!" he said while aiming halfheartedly, but added, "I wouldn't have done it."

We continued farther along the trail leading to the ravine, but even in the slow darkening of May, he must have realized that we could not have made it to the other side before night set in. We headed back toward the plateau. Jimmy walked fast along the trail, his head down as if he were concentrating on the ground, looking for spoor. He seemed to sense that I wanted to talk, so he kept ahead of me, well out of talking distance.

Finally he slowed so we were walking side by side when we came upon a man lying near the low brush beside the path. I presumed he was a man by his size. I couldn't see his head or his feet. There was a tattered, Indian-patterned poncho draped over his shoulders and a remnant of camouflage material wound around his neck. He looked like a heap of rags. "Do you think he's dead?" I whispered.

Jimmy shrugged and took a step closer. "If you think he's dead, why are you whispering?" he said. The man was facing away from us, lying on his side with his knees pulled up. We made a wide circle so we could see what he looked like. This day the sky was sliding directly from blue to purple and cast a cool light over the man's pale matted hair. His face was covered with short reddish whiskers flecked with white. He looked like an unshaven patient in the charity ward where my father sometimes made rounds. A stream of drool had formed a dried rivulet descending from the corner of his mouth, down to the stubbled curve of his jaw. When I stepped closer to see if he was breathing, I could smell a pungent odor rising from his body; it had an underlying sweet note, like ripe fruit. I looked for a bottle. And there it was, at the end of his arm, square and empty, one dirt-caked finger hooked around its neck. The man's own neck, long and ringed with mud-filled creases, stretched awkwardly to one side like the neck of a game bird laid out on a table.

"He's out like a light," Jimmy said. "Boy, could he use Ennd-O!"

"Do you think he's a hobo?" I asked, looking at the hole in the side of his shoe.

"Nah, he's not a hobo," Jimmy said. "He's just a bum."

Then some imperceptible movement must have occurred, some slight change in breathing that attracted our attention to the man's abdomen. Our eyes fell on his belt.

"Look, a Bowie knife!" Jimmy said.

"Is it really?" I asked.

"Positive."

Bowie or not, it was a big knife, large-handled, in a long leather sheath. For a moment I stood looking at the knife but not thinking about it, thinking rather about what had changed about the man since we first came upon him. For one thing, his mouth had closed. He had somehow moved without my seeing him move. Just as I noticed the man's lips pulled taut, his arm shot out as if on a spring. A large hand gripped my ankle. My voice fled with a yelp. I pulled my leg and kicked but his grip only tightened and it was all I could do to keep my balance. The man's eyes had scrunched closed as if clinging to breath but it escaped through his teeth in a hiss. Around my ankle a circle of pain grew deep under his fingers; below the circle, my foot was getting numb. I struggled and kicked at his free hand which grabbed at my other leg. Whichever way I turned, the man's hand was there, while the other hand tightened its grasp. As hard as I tried, I could not free myself. I could see Jimmy beside me dodging my flailing arms, trying to get in closer. He was holding the gun by the barrel. Even in that moment of terror I remember thinking how strange that was, that he should be holding the gun that way instead of holding it by the grip and stock, then taking aim, then pulling the trigger: that's the way to use a gun. For what couldn't have been a long time but seemed so, I felt removed from the action, from pain and struggling and fear and felt only a languorous, musing curiosity at the sight of my brother holding the barrel of a gun aimed at himself. Then I could see Jimmy's body twisting, winding up, taking a full swing with the gun like a baseball bat, the blur of it forming a ring around him like Saturn. The wooden stock hit the man square in the face. There was a loud crack, then blood gushed from his nose. Blood spurted from both nostrils and sputtered from his mouth through smashed lips. His teeth were slimy with it. He fell back with a thud on the dirt.

We ran. We ran over our own fresh tracks in the soft dirt and tumbled down to the lower trail that led to the narrow road winding its way to the Hollywood Reservoir. At the reservoir we sat down, panting, and stared at the water until we caught our breath. The Golden Eagle was in two pieces. The stock was cracked in several places and had broken away from the barrel. Jimmy held a piece in each hand and looked from one to the other.

"Can you find your way home?" he asked after a long silence. "I don't want to go back yet."

"No," I said. "It's too dark."

I looked over at him. Jimmy stared right past me and heaved a great, disgusted sigh. He ran his fingers along a splintered piece of stock and turned it until the ragged edge matched the other piece then let both pieces drop to the ground. The barrel lay powerless across his knees.

"I'm sorry your gun broke," I said quietly. I was sorry, but more than sorry, I felt guilty and I wanted him to say that it wasn't my fault, either mine in particular or girls' in general. I wanted to be absolved. "It was his fault," I said.

"He wouldn't have done anything if you hadn't been there," he said.

I said nothing; I didn't want it to be my fault.

Jimmy was now just a silhouette against the shimmering expanse of water, black outlined against black. The cement embankment was dark in shadow. Far away on the other side of the reservoir a light came on in the small watchtower. Jimmy picked up the broken carcass of the Golden Eagle and sighed.

"You're okay," he said, turning toward me in the dark. "So don't say anything, to anybody. Ever. Nothing happened."

He didn't have to tell me not to say anything. A code of silence was understood in our family. I had learned how to keep quiet. Since I wasn't hurt and we had managed without help, there was no point in making a fuss like a baby, in shaming myself by admitting fear. This is what I repeated to myself as the fear retreated slowly from my limbs, centered in my throat, then sank to a place visited only in dreams. What followed was numb relief. It was as if I had just fallen from a very tall building, had helplessly watched the street swirl closer and closer, people scattering, and finally hit the ground quite miraculously, without dying, without so much as a broken bone or even a scratched elbow, with only the fear knocked down my throat. I got up and brushed the dust off my knees.

I was disturbed by the thought of the man bleeding there as we left him. It occurred to me that he might bleed to death, which would mean that we killed him, both of us, Jimmy directly; me indirectly. It occurred to me that someone would find him and we would have to confess. Then I told myself it was just a broken nose; people don't die from that. "Do you think he's okay?" I said into the dark.

"He's okay," Jimmy said. "He was drunk; he won't even remember what happened."

"You said nothing happened."

Jimmy leaned toward the water, dark and featureless. "That's right," he said. "We won't talk about it again, starting now."

I didn't see him the following day, which was not unusual for a Saturday. But on Sunday morning he poured Shredded Wheat into his cereal bowl just the same as on any Sunday. My father peered at him over the editorial page of the Sunday *Times*. He had lowered the paper just enough so that it buckled along the crease. Even in the silence of the room he seemed to have heard something. He had this uncanny sense of knowing when something was up. I was sure my father could sense a ripple in the universe.

"So, Ennd-O man," he said. "Did you get your Brewer report back?"

"Yup," Jimmy said with exaggerated casualness. "I got an A."

"That's good. So, where's your side arm?"

Jimmy reached for the milk without looking up. He quickly filled his mouth and shrugged.

"Out of ammunition?" my father said and waited for him to swallow.

"No," Jimmy said, "I've got ammo."

"Out of targets?"

"No, I've got stuff to shoot at."

My father noisily turned the page of his paper, but Jimmy didn't look up. He looked at Jimmy with a bemused smile. "Who could ask for anything more?" he said. When Jimmy filled his mouth again, my father did what he always did when he sensed something was up, he made space. He took off his glasses and put down his paper and waited. But he never forced it. I think he trusted whatever he should know to make itself known, in its own way and its own time. Several minutes passed. He held his paper without reading it, Jimmy played with the rest of his cereal without eating it, no one spoke. And when Jimmy left the table with his cheeks bulging with the impression that there was more food in his mouth than there really was, my father put on his glasses and picked up his paper and looked at Jimmy with inscrutable patience, then looked at me and it was all I could do to keep from blurting out the whole story, that we saw a man on the hill and he was drunk and he had a knife and grabbed me and Jimmy hit him with his gun and broke his nose! And now his gun is broken! But I could see the resolution on Jimmy's face and felt a sudden need for air.

Avoiding my father's gaze, I took my faltering silence and left
the room. I went to a window and breathed in long drafts of air
until I could feel the silence grow calm around me. With the
silence quelled I became aware of the light that radiated over
the canyon in gold spokes that cut across trees and trails and
roads and the shadows that fell between. You couldn't see the
city from there, only the hills that had always been there, that
Brewer had seen, and the green that had nothing to do with
chlorophyll tablets or jingles or odors or money or guns.

"Before you go, son," I heard my father say, "I don't have
to know what happened to your gun."

"Nothing happened," Jimmy said. "Really, Dad."

"Yes, it's all right," he said. "A good man keeps his own
counsel."

*O*NE SUMMER MY FATHER decided to return to the home he ran away from when he was a boy. He had never been back. We couldn't believe he was going to take off a whole month to spend with us. Our excitement was unbounded.

I remember waking to the whine of mosquitoes in a strange room, my traveling clothes draped over an unopened suitcase, one arm numb beneath my chest, and the other arm already stinging with a dozen swollen bites. I had no idea what time it was or how long I had slept. We had been traveling for two days to get there: from Los Angeles to Salt Lake City on a DC-8, a trip so rough that even the stewardess got airsick; from Salt Lake City to White Fish; on to Edmonton on a small, smelly, single-prop plane; then driving northwest along the old fur trading route, into the wheat fields of the high prairie, through the Peace River country, approaching the Northwest Territories. This is where my father was born.

He was born in 1910, only five years after Alberta had joined the Confederation and four years before the Dingman oil well would blow the province into the twentieth century. My father's parents were among the first European settlers north of the Peace River. Before then, the inhabitants of the area were Crees, Athapaskans, fur traders, and itinerant dreamers trailing the golden promises of the Klondike.

My grandparents were Scottish immigrants who had found the richest, harshest, most remote part of the Canadian landscape in which to settle and farm. Being Scots, they could not pass up the Homestead price of ten dollars for 160 acres. And being Scots, they were rugged enough to survive on those acres. Of nine Mackinnon children, only six lived to assume farm responsibilities—the value by which they were measured, so my father had explained. When my uncle James was killed at age fifteen and my father ran away for good two years later, that left only four children, three of whom were girls, not worth much for working purposes. "Your grandfather is not a forgiving man," my father had said. "He crossed my name out of the family Bible when I left. And I'll bet he's still spitting mad; that's how I remember him. He could make the Angel of Death shake in his boots."

We didn't know then, in the summer of '55, whether my grandfather was still living. But my father said if he were still kicking, we would find him.

Outside, it was already light. I wandered out, still dazed from sleep and rubbing my arm. "What time is it?" I asked my father, who was standing by the porch railing of our guest lodgings.

"It's only four o'clock," he said. "This far north, you don't get much darkness during the summer nights."

"I can't believe we're here," I said.

"Nor can I, Jorie," he said. "Nor can I. I haven't seen this place since I was a kid, but I remember it so clearly. I suppose I'll find changes—nothing stays the same. As they say: You can't go home again."

"Who said that?"

"I don't remember. It's the title of a book."

But is it really true, I wondered, that there's no going home? What was it then that I saw in my father's face, flickering recognition like some distant light? And what were the scenes and voices that played back in the muscles of his face, when I saw only wheat fields in the morning silence? Was this not coming home? From the look on his face, I could tell he was not seeing what I was seeing. He was home and I was not.

After a while, he asked if the boys were awake. I said I didn't think so, but I was willing to check. In fact, Alex and Jimmy were awake and cranky, slapping at mosquitoes on their crumpled beds.

We dressed and rode into town on a dirt road. "Well, they finally paved it!" my father exclaimed when we drove onto the only paved street, which bisected a small collection of one- and two-story, wood-frame buildings that stood shoulder to shoulder. The buildings themselves were small, mostly unpainted, and opened onto sidewalks made of wooden planks, elevated about two feet above the ground. The effect was that of a movie set, only not as quaint. Several unpaved streets intersected the main street, where we parked; some of these were covered with gravel, some were not. Except for a Baptist church with a rather threatening spire, most of the town's attractions seemed to be on this main road, optimistically called 500th Street.

Looking for a place to eat, we walked past a dry goods store, an outpost of the Hudson Bay Company, a gunsmith and armory, and finally, the only coffee shop in town, the Rising Up Cafe. But my father wouldn't go in. "I want to see if I can find something," he said. "A little bakery. What was her name?" he repeated to himself.

At last, Alex spotted a little shop with gingham curtains and loaves of bread in the window. "Is that it?" he said.

"Even if it isn't, I'm going in," said Jimmy. "I'm starving." As the yeasty aroma curled toward us, we picked up our pace.

"Charge!" Jimmy yelled, disappearing through the open bakery door. He was already devouring a biscuit when we got there, standing in front of a middle-aged woman in a white apron, obviously amused.

"Lindsay! That's it, Mrs. Lindsay," my father said, looking at the woman with surprise.

"That was my mother," she said. "I'm Maggie Cronin. And you're a Mackinnon, aren't you?" She was neither friendly nor unfriendly. She was as plain in her manner as in her appearance, which could only be described as worn but tidy. "You're all Mackinnons, eh? I can see it right off."

"I remember a Tim Cronin," my father said. "His family lived in Grand Prairie."

"Tim was my husband; he was killed in the war," she said.

My father nodded his understanding; it was common news in those days.

"I'm looking for my father, Ewan Mackinnon," he said as we sat down at the corner table with a basket of biscuits and oatcakes. Maggie poured coffee, but did not sit down. "The farm is sold, you know. Quite a long time now, since the last girl died. He was alone there and couldn't keep it up. Too bad, eh?"

"Where is he now?" my father said, drinking his coffee in short steaming sips.

"You'll find him at the far west side of town, a little place called Perkins Camp; he lives there."

With a bag of hard rolls as provisions, we made our way back to the car, onto the dusty roadway, and headed in the opposite direction of Perkins Camp.

"We're going to find the old homestead," my father said as he stepped on the accelerator. He said we'd better start off early since it was probably going to be a long drive. Most likely we wouldn't have time for anything else, he further explained, as if to himself. Besides, he added, he didn't know if he'd have trouble finding the farm after so many years, things being so changed as they were.

But things were not so changed. Even I recognized this place from the stories he had often told us at bedtime when we were small. In place of fairy tales and Mother Goose, our sleepy heads were filled with tales of grizzly bears and timber wolves, children on wooden skates, speeding down frozen creeks, the ice crackling behind them. Winters at forty degrees below, turning the milk to slush before you could pour it from the pail. Four children to a bed and glad of it when the frost was thick on the walls. No electricity, no running water, moonlight glittering blue on the snow when you made your way, shivering, to the outhouse. And summer, like this, when gold light blew hot and powdery over fields of wheat, and fields of oats bent dreamily under their own ripe weight. And, like now, the length of days stretched northward to midnight.

It was just as my father had said: the prairie shimmering and parted into golden patches, the sky blue, the mountains purple on the horizon.

"What's that yellow stuff?" Jimmy asked, pointing to a field not gold, but the bright yellow of daffodils.

"I don't know," my father said in a puzzled voice. "I don't recognize it—but I do recognize that farm. Yes. That's Smoothy Jackson's place. Well, I don't believe it—the old place is still standing."

"We're going to see Smoothy Jackson!" we said in unison, bouncing on the seats. My father looked uneasy. No, he said, we would visit him later. There were other things to see first. We had lots of time.

We knew all about Smoothy Jackson. It was said that his mother was a full-blooded Cree, but nobody knew for sure since she had died in childbirth. He got the nickname Smoothy when, as a teenager, he failed to grow a beard. His brown, smooth face stood out among the neighboring men who were of a fuzzier race. He lived alone after old Jackson died; no local girl would have married a half-breed.

It was Smoothy who heeded my father's cry for help when his brother James was shot in a hunting accident, who brought back his body—the heart blown right out of the chest—and washed him and wrapped him in a clean shirt before returning both boys to the Mackinnon farm.

It was Smoothy who had sheltered my father when he ran away, had given him a rucksack full of food and all the money he had stashed in an empty coffee can, along with a map and an address in Vancouver. It was he who remained silent when Ewan Mackinnon offered a cash reward for his son's return. "Alive," he had said. "He's of no use dead."

"Can't we see Smoothy now, Dad? Since we're already here?" Alex said. He was probably getting car sick. He always got car sick.

"Yeah, Dad," Jimmy and I said in a round. "Let's go *now.*"

"Stop whining or you'll walk," my father said in his soft, matter-of-fact voice. We stopped. He was not one to issue idle threats.

For the rest of the day, we drove along the dusty roads, adding our tracks to the deeper imprints of tractor treads, the car veering dangerously close to the roadside ditch as my father craned his neck, looking from one field to the next as if in each one he would find a landmark or a clue. Like a man famished, he conjured up morsels from his memory: a smokehouse that was there, by the bend in that creek, a horse path that led all the way into the mountains where hunters had stalked bear and lynx, a small farm where Jean, the schoolteacher, had lived. But all we saw were open fields with ramshackle houses sitting at one end or the other, and the dirt road scarred with the ruts of farm equipment, and more roads, and more fields, and soon, everything looked the same.

We had been there two days, driving around, subsisting on bread and rolls until my father broke from his reverie and seemed ready to face the present. When we got in the car on the third day, we knew even before he touched the steering wheel that we were headed for Perkins Camp.

There was no real sign, just the name Perkins Camp scrawled in uneven letters on the side of an old toolshed now used as a mail depository. To the left of the shed was a wooden shack perched up on cinder blocks, an old geezer sitting in the doorway, his legs outstretched, his gnarled blue-white feet wiggling in the sun.

"Mackinnon?" my father called up to him.

"Eh?"

"Mackinnon!" he repeated, louder this time.

"Eh?" the ancient occupant said again, motioning for us to come nearer. His mouth was caved in from lack of teeth, but his eyes were sharp as he looked us over, pointing first to Alex's red hair, then to a similar shack across the path. That door was closed.

I had never known a relative before, outside of my parents and brothers, who for some reason I didn't count. We didn't have relatives because it seemed the one thing members of our clan had in common was dying young. The idea of relatives—grandparents, aunts, uncles, or cousins—appealed to me, so I had sometimes wished for them. The idea that there were other people derived from the same blueprint made the world seem less lonely. And I liked the idea that love, like the Hapsburg jaw, was genetically shared. Now, here was the test: Would I love my grandfather right away? Would he love me? Or, would it take a little while to break the ice, to get right down to chromosomes? And what would it feel like, this affection in the blood, this unearned love? But now, standing in front of this old shack, splintered and faded in a strange country air, I had no such notions. I had no expectations at all, only blank curiosity.

We watched my father raise his arm against the door, banging against it with the flat of his hand. It was not a tenta-tive sound, but an insistent thud that stopped only when the door swung open. The two men faced each other in silence and unsurprise, as if the intervening thirty years had been just a brief pause.

My grandfather stood taller than my father's six feet, two inches, even though his legs and back were slightly bowed. His white hair was thin, but his eyebrows and beard were bushy and still streaked with remnants of once fiery hair. He held himself straight and silent. My father wasn't speaking either and the long silence strained and frayed like an uncoiling rope.

At last my grandfather spoke. "What's this about, Tom?" he said. He pronounced it "a boot."

At that my father laughed a little. "We've come to visit, father," he said. "I've brought your grandchildren." Gathering us in front of him, he introduced each of us in turn, with a little push on the back. "This is Alex, age twelve; Jimmy, eleven; and Jorie, nine."

"Almost ten," I said, waiting to see if he would take my hand, which he didn't. He glared at us awhile, without smiling. The chromosomal connection was definitely not working.

"They don't look Chinese to me," he said, looking us over once again.

My father shrugged.

"I'd heard you'd got yourself a bit place in China and had taken a Chinese wife."

"Well, that's true," my father said. "But she died; that was a long time ago, twenty years now. These are the children of my last wife, Therese, who also died, six years ago."

"Och ay, and your mother and sisters. All the queans are gone," he said. He looked at me as if it were just a matter of time.

"Well, can we come in?" my father asked.

"No, you can't," my grandfather said directly. "There's bare a stick to sit on, but you can sit out here on the stoop, if you don't like standing about."

The boys and I settled ourselves on the stoop, but my father and grandfather remained standing and faced off.

"And what's become of you then, Tom," my grandfather said. "It's a damned long time since you worked in the field or had a strap to your dowp. You're looking fair prosperous; the cushy life must agree with you." The word *agree* seemed to spin from his mouth, the extra *r*'s and *e*'s quickly unraveling.

Then my father seemed more at ease and half sat on the wood railing. "I'm a doctor now," he said. "After I left China, I went to California to study medicine. There I met the children's mother; she was Austrian."

"Och, a man of the world you'd be," my grandfather said in a mocking voice. "I should have known when always we'd find you with your face in a book, full of whines and plaints about your bit work. And your brother James doing the work of two, so you could go to that teacher quean."

At that my father stiffened, his face darkening.

My grandfather rubbed his beard in satisfaction. "Losh Tom, my memory's too long. No one's memory should be as long as that." Then, to change the subject, he pointed his long arm in our direction, extending a gangling finger from his huge, freckled hand. "So these here are the result of a second wife, eh? Why was she not in her own country? Och, but never mind; I tire of all this talk."

"The story's brief," my father said. "Therese's father was a professor in Vienna and her mother was a concert pianist; they were not friends of Hitler. Therese escaped, but her parents didn't make it."

"Not brief enough," my grandfather said as he turned to go inside. My father invited him to have a meal with us, but he said No.

"Perhaps another time," my father said.

My grandfather just looked at him.

"I'll bring the children back to see you before we leave."

"Not necessary," he said. Then he shut the door without so much as a nod.

I was not optimistic about getting close to my grandfather. Had the family resemblance not been so strong, I might have wondered if we were adopted. For a fleeting moment, on the way to Perkins Camp, I had imagined calling him Gramps. Now, the thought of calling him Gramps seemed quite funny to me, but I decided to try it out anyway. "Good-bye, Gramps," I said into the air. Alex and Jimmy ignited with laughter.

"He was crazy about us," Jimmy said.

"Baloney," Alex replied.

"No, really," Jimmy said. "I can tell. He was crazy about us, especially us guys. I don't know about the *QUAIN* here—she's the kiss of death!" Before I could stop him, Jimmy grabbed me in the crook of his elbow and planted a noisy slobber kiss on my cheek. "Ugh!" I said, wiping my cheek off. Then the three of us waved to the old geezer's door and joined arms as we walked down the path, singing: *I am a happy wan-der-er, beneath the clear blue sky . . . val-der-ree! val-der-ra! val-der-ree! val-der-ra-ha-ha-ha-ha-ha.* With each Ha, Jimmy puffed out his breath, until with the last Ha! he fell to the ground, deflated.

By the time we got to the car, my father was smiling again. "Okay gang, let's get some grub at the Rising Up," he said.

The Rising Up Cafe was not what you would expect of the only restaurant in a little town in the wilds of northwest Canada. It was entirely owned and operated by Chinese. These were descendants of immigrants who had worked as coolies on the Canadian Pacific Railway in the late 1880s and relatives whom they had since brought over. After an exchange of warm and astonished greetings in Nanking dialect, in which my father was fluent, he was whisked away into the kitchen, which soon became a resounding chant of alien syllables and intonations. In a few minutes it quieted down and three white-clad Chinese pushed through the kitchen door and rushed over to our table. Their eyes were filled with delight. They seemed to marvel at the sight of us. "Hollywood," they crooned. "You from Hollywood."

From that moment on, we were celebrities in the Rising Up. We were anointed by the light of stars. I had never thought Hollywood was anything special. I knew that movies were made there and movie stars lived there, but the admiration of the waiters was puzzling. It was as if by touching us, they might pick up some stardust of their own. "Hollywood," they would sigh when I ordered a peanut butter and jelly sandwich. And when they refilled our milk glasses, they would recite names: Laurel and Hardy. Abbott and Costello. Martin and Lewis. Charlie Chan. We nodded. Yes, we knew them; some were patients of my father's. They sent us Mission Packs for Christmas.

After my father's hour of speaking Chinese with the owner of the Rising Up Cafe, he became quiet and pensive. He seemed disturbed that one past should intrude on another. It was as if some dark corner had been unexpectedly lit. "I don't want to talk about it now," he said when we asked him about the conversation in the kitchen. "Today, we're going to find the old schoolhouse," he said.

It was all Alex could do to keep from groaning. More wheat fields and winding dirt roads. He would throw up for sure this time. "Can't we do something else, Dad?" he asked. "Besides driving around, I mean."

"Today we're going to find the schoolhouse," my father repeated as if Alex hadn't heard the first time. The color had already started to drain from Alex's face and he leaned his head out the window to catch the wind.

"Gee, Dad," he said. "Isn't this supposed to be a vacation?"
"No," my father said. "What gave you that idea?"

The schoolhouse, or what was left of it, sat in an open field, not far from Saskatoon Creek, which wound its way through most of the farms in the area, including Smoothy Jackson's, which was to the south, on the other side of the road. Inside, the schoolhouse was only one large room, plus a smaller "mudroom" where the children removed their boots and hung their coats on wooden pegs. My father pointed to where the big, wood-burning stove had been and to where Jean Gordon had taught children in twelve grades at the same time, in this very room. Not always were there twelve grades, however, since many children left school at grade ten because they were needed on the farms. So no one gave it a thought when my grandfather forbade my father to return to school when he was fourteen. No one except my father, that is.

We spent a lot of time at the schoolhouse. It was shabby and dirty, but it was better than riding in the car. We tried to find all the names and initials that were carved in secret places and to find the earliest and latest dates. Alex found the earliest—1915, carved under a windowsill; I found the latest—1942, finely etched on the side of a wooden coat peg. My father was looking for something too. Then he found it, carved under the bench in the mudroom: James Mackinnon 1920. When we saw what he had found, we just stood quietly and waited. The story was always the same. My uncle James, who was two years older than my father, was strong as a full-grown man, and smart. *Clever* was the word my father liked to use because James had that kind of mind. He invented things, like traps for marauding wolves and a little guard plate that kept the field mice from gumming up the reaper. He had an instinct about how things worked and could fix almost anything or would rig up a new mechanism that worked even better. My father had shown us the notebook he kept, filled with drawings and sketches for various devices, including a new kind of grain elevator. I preferred the more fanciful ones, with things flying through the air. I didn't want to know how they worked.

James had an instinct about fishing, too, and could cast a fly as skillfully as many old-timers. With perfect rhythm, he would cast out so that the fly and leader were ahead of the line and all the fish would see was a fly shadow alighting on the water. In addition to fishing, James liked to hunt, which is why he took my father out that day. He had promised he would take him during moose season, although it had to be a secret. My grandfather would not have allowed it. So the two boys set out with their father's rifle, thrilled with complicity and adventure. Before long, a moose was in sight, dappled in morning shadows, and the boys squeezed each other's shoulders and spoke in excited whispers. Then the rifle jammed and James thought he could fix it, but instead, he dropped it. A shot rang out and the moose ran off in terror. There was blood, then running and crying, then Smoothy Jackson, using wet cloths to wipe James's body, then putting him in a clean shirt.

But now, in the schoolhouse, my father didn't repeat the story. He didn't have to. It told itself in our collective memory, while the old wood beams creaked in the wind and gusts blew down where the stovepipe had been.

We took our time leaving the schoolhouse and rambled down the path toward the creek, which was marked along its course by swarms of mosquitoes. It was then I realized that we, too, were traveling a course, and the town, Perkins Camp, the wheat fields, the schoolhouse, and Saskatoon Creek were all part of it, and so was Smoothy Jackson, who was just downstream.

The next day we picked saskatoons by Beaver Lake. The small red berries were everywhere, clustered among the wild grasses and reeds that surrounded the water. We ate them as we went along. Some were sweet and some were sour and astringent. Accepting the nature of things, we felt obliged to eat them either way. Since the day was warm, the boys and I decided to wade into the lake, and rolled our pants up onto our thighs. We had swum in the chlorinated water of swimming pools and the salt water of the Pacific, but never in a lake. And so it must have been the excitement of first experience that kept us in the water so long, that numbed us to the dull pain grabbing at us. As I came out of the water, I reached down my leg, then let out a scream I would not have thought I was capable of; it hurt my ears. Both legs were covered with nightmarish things—long, black, slimy, cylindrical, and tightly fastened so they didn't budge even though by then I was madly stomping up and down. Jimmy and Alex pulled the leeches off their own legs then ran over to help me. By that time, many of the leeches had filled with blood and had fallen off, their bloated bodies writhing on the ground. I looked at our legs, covered with oozing puncture wounds, and started to cry.

"What a baby," Alex said.

"Yeah, just like a dumb girl," Jimmy agreed. They walked away, disgusted. Then I did feel ashamed and tried hard to suppress every hiccup. I didn't dare call them back. Slowly I staggered away and fainted in the tall grass.

The next thing I remember was my father's voice. "You're okay, Jorie," he was saying. He must have seen I was still a little woozy because he didn't try to get me up. We just sat on the ground for a moment with his arm around me and my head resting gratefully against his chest. The boys settled in the grass nearby, looking somewhat more sympathetic.

"You okay?" Alex asked. A faint sound eked out from my lips. I smiled bravely. I was actually feeling much better, but I wanted to get the most from the moment.

"Can we go to Smoothy's now, Dad?" I asked. I didn't feel like spending the rest of the day riding around on the bumpy roads or traipsing through monotonous fields, which had belonged to people in my father's memory, but not in ours.

"Please, Dad," I said, looking as pathetic as I possibly could. This was a new tack for me and it was not successful. Both the boys and my father burst out laughing. "Okay, Sarah Bernhardt," my father said. "Just promise you won't swoon when we get there."

Smoothy was everything I thought he would be. He was a big man, not tall, but well-muscled and sprawling, the kind of man that occupies more space than he actually takes up, a man who extends beyond his borders. When he looked at you, it was straight on. And when he asked you a question, he was intensely quiet until you answered; it was not as if you were ten years old. Within minutes of our arrival, he was showing us around. He didn't seem in the least put out by our unannounced visit, but apologized for having nothing to offer us except tinned soup and crackers. You could hardly see his eyes, covered as they were by festoons of skin, but when you looked closely, they were smiling.

"Canola!" Smoothy said to Jimmy as he pointed to acres of bright yellow that spread all the way to the road. "Of course your old man didn't recognize it; we planted it during the war, to make lubricating oil for ships. He was long gone by that time." Smoothy and Jimmy stood side by side, their arms around each other's waists, as if they were life-long pals.

"Now, canola's mostly used for varnish," he said. "Oh, and for margarine. No telling what they put in our bellies these days!"

"Good ol' Tom," Smoothy said to my father, pouring another Jack Daniels for each of them. "I knew you'd be back before they screw the lid down. You're a fine sight for these old eyes."

The whiskey overflowed onto the table. Neither man seemed to notice.

"I saw Father," my father said after emptying his glass. "He's softened."

"Age does wonders."

"Still, I don't think he'll ever understand—"

"Maybe not. Or maybe he just won't admit it. He must be the most stubborn man alive. Here, 'nother drink."

"I think he'd be happier if I'd failed. It would have proved him right."

"No, no you're wrong there, Tom. All these years, when some piece of news would find its way up here, he'd stick around to hear it. For Ewan Mackinnon, that's genuine interest. And he never passed a word of judgment." Smoothy continued to pour whiskey straight, no ice. As they lifted their glasses, the drinks spilled over their hands and down their arms. I had never seen men get really drunk before. It frightened me. I wished I could have stopped them, but I didn't know how. There was something compulsive in the filling and emptying, some shared determination to alter consciousness, to compress time until the thirty years was a snap of the fingers and presto, they were as they had been. I sat on the bear rug, looking at the smooth black lips pulled back from the fearsome teeth and imagined a time when this creature foraged in the woods, innocent and unsuspecting, until time stopped and he became forever something else, an object on the floor.

"Did you kill this bear?" Jimmy asked when Smoothy got up to get another bottle.

"Sure did," he answered. "Before he could kill me. Only two reasons I'd kill an animal—meat and self-defense. In this case, it was both."

My father did not look up from his glass. "I never hunted again," he said.

Smoothy poured out another drink; this time he didn't spill a drop. He sat down and looked at my father straight on. "After the accident, you mean?"

"Yes, after the accident . . . it was an accident."

"I know."

"It was an accident."

"I know."

"Only, it wasn't the way I said." My father looked down into his glass. "The rifle didn't jam. James wasn't even holding it." His hand gripped the glass tightly as he threw back his head and emptied it by half. "I talked James into letting me carry the rifle when I followed him on the trail. When he saw the moose, he was so excited. I was excited too. He wheeled around. His face was beaming. His face was so happy; I'll never forget the look in his eyes. I was following him so closely, that when he turned around, he bumped the gun barrel. I must have had my finger on the trigger." My father did not look up from his glass. He said, "I killed him."

"I know," Smoothy said. "It was an accident."

When I got up early the next morning, my father was already sitting at the table with a cup of coffee. He wasn't looking too good; I could see the blood vessels in his eyes. The Jack Daniels was taking its toll and Smoothy's sofa was not very comfortable, although it was better than the floor, which is where we children had slept. I was hesitant to approach him and wished the boys had gotten up first. A sweet, dusky odor lingered in the room, a blend of whiskey and cold ashes. Quietly, I opened the window, but not even the rush of a cool breeze would erase the evening's residue; it would linger long after the odor had blown away.

Jimmy walked in stretching out his arms and shaking his head. Alex shuffled in after him, rubbing his eyes, which were red-rimmed and puffy. "Are we going home soon, Dad?" he asked.

"Yes, Son. Pretty soon."

"Good," Jimmy said, "I've had about as much fun as I can stand."

When we went to the Rising Up Cafe later that day, my father ordered liver and spinach for everyone. Understanding that this was like medicine, we ate it without complaint, except for Alex who ordered extra bacon and onions so he could drown out the liver in every bite. "Anything for Hollywood boy," our waiter said. As before, the owner, Mr. Chow, came over calling his three-note greeting and spoke Chinese with my father for a few minutes. My father evidently told him about the leeches because he looked at us and nodded condolences.

"When we get home, remind me to ask Lou Costello to send an autographed picture to the Rising Up," my father said. At that moment, it was hard to even imagine being home; it seemed light years away, in a different galaxy.

"Are we really going home soon, Dad?" Alex asked. "Yes," he said as he rose from the table after paying the bill. "But we're going to say good-bye to your grandfather first."

When we arrived, Perkins Camp seemed even more forlorn than before. The wooden shacks took on a stony cast under the dark clouds that were gathering overhead. My grandfather walked outside and shut the door behind him. The boys and I took our places on the stoop and my father stood by the porch railing.

"You look a wee bit under the weather, Tom," he said. "I suppose you've been drinking with Smoothy."

"I'd forgotten what a small town this is," my father said in a voice too tired for surprise.

"I didn't say I'd heard it; I just supposed it, by the look of you . . . and look at these young ones here," he said, pointing at us. "They look a bit poohed out too."

"Leeches," I said, and showed him a bruised mark on my leg.

"Och, ay. I'll bet they don't have them in the city." With the pads of his fingers lifting my chin, he tilted his head and seemed to study my face. "You look a bit like my daughter, Eilean," he said. "A good girl she was too, a bonnie quean." I felt a tug at my chromosomes.

Then he looked at my father and said, "Sit. Sit down, Tom." Pulling over a three-legged stool, he motioned for my father to sit. Then he sat down close beside him. He said he'd had too much to drink himself the other night, and wondered why that had happened; he'd sworn off liquor years ago. He must have been fair disturbed. Yes, his son coming back after all these years, it caused a man to think. My father silently rocked back and forth on the stool.

My grandfather seemed to gather words from his silence. "I know why you've come back, Tom," he said. "You want to put your mind at rest." As the r's rolled from my grandfather's mouth, my father continued to rock, squinting in the sunlight that was coming and going between the clouds.

"But I can't forget that you turned away from your family, your God-given duty, not a care you had for us or the ground we worked with sweat and blood. And now you come back, fair prosperous, when all is lost. Och, but I'll not be your judge. Time will do that, time and your own conscience."

"I could not have stayed," my father said. "I'm not a farmer."

"Then you're no son of mine," my grandfather snapped back.

My father stood up and pulled the stool over to where it had been. "Good-bye, Father," he said.

My grandfather shook his head, then pushed the white hair away from his temple. "Och, you needn't go now, Tom. I'm none too well myself. We'll not leave it at this. You and James, you lads were filled with the devil. You were my curse and my hope at the same time."

"You blame me for what happened to James, don't you?"

"Ay, that I did. But not now, not any longer." There was not a trace of anger left in my grandfather's voice, only weariness. "It came to me the other night," he said, "when my mind was swimming in drink. I said to myself then, 'I cannot blame this Tom. The man who's come back is not the lad who left.'"

Then my father turned to him and said, "But what if I am the same Tom?"

My grandfather looked up to where the question was hanging, then stood up, as if he had answered it. Then we stood up too and brushed off the backs of our pants as if we had been dismissed. We all moved very slowly, even dreamily, the two men standing and turning, the boys and I starting down the path.

When I looked back, my father and grandfather stood facing each other, their long arms locked in a kind of embrace. Their hands gripped each other's elbows. Then my grandfather released his grip and with a pat on my father's shoulder, turned and went inside. The sun struck the closed door of the shack through a hole in the clouds. This is the final image of that summer. In my mind, my grandfather's door is finely etched on a wooden coat peg in an abandoned schoolhouse, in the northernmost prairie in the world.

*T*HE SEMESTER FOLLOWING OUR Canadian trip, when I was in the sixth grade, there was a boy who stalked me, glared at me, lurked around corners, and in general vexed me to the point of distraction. He was younger, a grade behind me, which is one reason his staring at me all the time seemed so strange. Other boys stared sometimes, but they were about my age, usually older. There was something different about this boy's stare. It had nothing to do with the first drips of hormone, demure glances, or breast buds. He looked at me as if he wanted to dig my heart out.

As we lined up in the school yard every morning after the bell, spacing ourselves before parading line by line into the building, I could feel his eyes burning into me. And if I tried to stare him down, he would boldly face me back, challenging. Aside from his steely blue, taunting eyes, there was something about the way he looked that was vaguely unnerving. Not that there was anything remarkable about his face: it hung pale and

ordinary under a mop of brown hair. I could not explain the
effect this face had on me. I learned from my classmate Millie
Rawlin's younger sister that his name was Andrew Haraty. He
was a good student; Millie's sister called him an egghead. I
didn't care what he was. I just wanted him to stop dogging me
like some clumsy private eye. Finally, one day I was irked
enough to overcome my shyness and I said to him, "Stop staring at me, Andrew Haraty."

"Why should I?" he answered.

"Because I can't stand your face," I said.

I asked Jimmy how to get a boy to stop staring at you. I
didn't ask Alex because he would have gone into a protective
rage and I didn't want the boy's head bashed in; I just wanted
him to cease and desist, as they say. Alex had been suspended
twice from junior high school for fighting and I didn't want to
add to his already disreputable record. Jimmy's answer about
what to do about a staring boy was "So what? Just ignore him."

I almost brought the subject up to my father when we were
inspecting the roses, something we did from time to time during the blooming season. Rose inspection involved a hike in
the foothills behind our house; we didn't have a rose garden.
His interest in roses, serious though it was, was limited to
climbers and ramblers, mostly of the old and wild varieties—
dog roses and prairie roses—and these he carefully planted
among the scrubby chaparral of the canyon and at the feet of
tall trees. Nothing would please him more than hiking up the
side of a hill to be greeted by a profusion of *Kiftsgate* clamber-
ing up into a eucalyptus. Or finding cascades of yellow
Mermaid among the poison oak. My father admired beauty
that cropped up under unlikely circumstances, as if the very
unlikeliness of it was the essence of its value.

My job was to keep a notebook, which I carried on the hike.
I was the rose scribe. As my father inspected each plant, he
would dictate notes on the rose's progress and habits as well as

odd thoughts that would occur to him on the way. Many did not survive, but those that did draped themselves in triumphant festoons among the native hillside shrubs.

"If someone stares at you and you don't know why—" I started to say.

"Look at this," he interrupted. "It must have grown eight feet since last year. Take this down: genus: *Rosa*; subgenus: Eurosa; section: Synstylae; species: *R. moschata nepalensis*. Vigorous growth, densely foliated, many hooked thorns—no, make that prickles—many hooked prickles, creamy white single flowers, in clusters. Blooms early spring."

"Dad, if someone keeps staring at you—"

"Just stare at this," he said, picking up the word unaware, like something on the bottom of his shoe. He had plucked a star-shaped blossom and was brushing the golden-brown stamens with his finger. "Originally, this rose was brought from the Himalayas," he said. "Its lineage is ancient. It grows from budwood . . ."

Grows from budwood, I wrote down.

"Ah, here's the prize," my father said as we headed up along the western slope. On the side of the trail was an Albertine in full flush. Its pink blooms covered a small, wide-branching tree.

"Write this down," he said. "Genus: *R. Wichuriana*, hybrid. Rambling habit, profuse blooms after slow start. Worth the wait. Has exceeded expected height."

"Is Albertine your favorite?" I asked.

"I really couldn't say," he said, reaching up to pluck a blossom from an overhanging branch. "They all have their strengths and weaknesses. I like Albertine because she not only survives, she flourishes. Look at that, fifteen feet in full bloom! Take this down: *Mu Hsiang*. It means 'woody fragrance rose.' In the last century Western botanists and collectors would filch a plant from a Chinese garden and then name the rose after themselves, like Fortune's Double Yellow. That rose had been cultivated a long time before Fortune showed up. That sneaky fellow. He probably smuggled opium too." My father glanced over as I was furiously writing in my notebook. "You can leave out the last part. Just speculation." He cleared a spot in the dry grass and sat down.

Close to where I was sitting, a column of ants was streaming out of a hole in the dry dirt. I scratched the dirt with a stick and watched the ants scatter and regroup. A warm breeze came up and I breathed in the rose's woody scent. "Oh, I wonder . . ." I said without preface, heaving a sigh.

"What?" My father strained to hear. "What did you say?"

"Nothing," I said. "Never mind."

"Never mind what?"

"Just, nothing."

"Then let's go," he said impatiently.

He brushed off the seat of his pants and pulled out several foxtails that had stuck to his socks. He glanced over at me just long enough to register his annoyance, then started down the trail. I felt as if I had ruined a perfectly good outing.

"All I want on my day off is peace and quiet," my father would say. "That's not too much to expect, is it?" From that we would infer that Sunday was to be free of problems, or at least any discussion of them. After all, didn't he listen to people's complaints all day long? Did we have to spoil his one day off by adding our burden of problems? *Constructive* is the word he used for the kind of conversation we should have. We could talk about the conjugation of blue-green algae or the refraction of light. Constructive conversation: That was the reason he would spend a day with us. But it's hard never to bring up personal issues that trouble you. It's hard never to spoil someone's day.

To avoid spoiling my father's day, Alex had taken to disappearing on Sundays. He would leave early in the morning with his hair greased back and a pack of Camels rolled up in the sleeve of his tee shirt. Occasionally I would venture a comment like, "Alex is gone a lot lately." My father would usually ignore this kind of comment, but once he put down his book and said, "I was on my own at his age and better off for it." Then he picked up the book and said to me, "You're becoming a mother hen. And I don't like it."

We hadn't had any kind of hen in the house for a long time, since we had given up on housekeepers. "More trouble than they're worth," my father said. I had my doubts about that since I was the only one who did the dishes and the laundry and made an attempt at cleaning the house when I couldn't stand the dust or dirty floors anymore. Since my father didn't believe in men doing housework, the three of them were no help at all.

I knew I was changing in ways my father didn't like. At times I didn't like these changes either; they made us both uneasy. Some of this had to do with my new Catholic school, where I was introduced to the concept of sin. I studied it; I embraced it. Sin was something I could get my teeth into. *La Petite Inquisitor* my father called me, without smiling. It was his way of telling me to keep my righteousness to myself.

My father never told me what to think and he expected the same courtesy from me. He had allowed me to transfer to St. Anthony's School in the fifth grade, without the slightest resistance, even though he regarded Catholicism as a lot of "mumbo jumbo." I had asked him about changing schools because I'd been told by a classmate that her parents were going to send her to parochial school so that she would have to work harder and she would end up with a better education. I liked that. Something about it must have appealed to him too, because he immediately sent his nurse to buy my uniforms, and by the next semester, I found myself gazing up at St. Anthony's bald pate, with a stack of homework under my arm, and a whole new view of the world.

By now, I had emerged from my early bewilderment about how other people lived to a state of semiconsciousness. I was learning just enough to believe I knew more. I watched "Ozzie and Harriet" and "Father Knows Best" and observed the mothers with their Pepsodent smiles waving their breakfast-fed children off to school before they cleaned their wash brighter than bright. I watched these idealized television families sitting down together at dinner, eating servings of the four basic food groups while the concerned parents gently prodded the children to talk about themselves. I believed this was the way other families lived. And I felt somehow that a mother would have known what to do about the boy who plagued me.

By now I had discovered that other children were taken shopping, were picked up and delivered to friends' homes, had swimming lessons and after-school activities and parties for various occasions, that their mothers were known by the teachers and by each other. Most of this information I learned from Millie Rawlins, whose mother was president of St. Anthony's PTA and school liaison with the parish Ladies' Sodality. At last I knew the secrets that had kept me as a young child in a dark and somewhat befuddled state. I knew now that other children were attended to in ways that we were not. But I didn't know why we weren't worthy of this attention, or worthy at least of some occasional help. And even though by now I rarely felt the need for help, the knowledge of its absence charged the air between me and my father and hovered there, an accusation. I blamed him for not helping my brothers either, especially Alex.

The last time Alex was suspended from school for throwing a wastebasket at a teacher, my father calmly told him that he was disappointed. Surely he could learn to exercise better control over his temper. Then he warned Alex about consequences, about having to sleep in the bed you make. He made it sound so logical, as if once Alex understood, he would never even think of making trouble again. It wouldn't be the intelligent thing to do. "It's just senseless," he added. "There's no reason for that behavior."

"Maybe he had a reason," I said under my breath. My father, being slightly hard of hearing, couldn't make out the words, but he could feel the current of judgment and looked at me coolly. That was another thing he always said about women: they constantly pass judgment on men—what men say, the things men do, the way men are. A woman will gnaw away at a man until she thinks he sees things the way she sees them, and even if he doesn't, he has to put down his paper and say, "Yes, dear." Women are like that; they can't help themselves.

I learned from my father that American women, in particular, adhere to their own version of *the way things should be* and do everything in their power to impose that version on men. When I was younger I felt a sense of outrage that a man like my father would not be free to do what he pleased, that a woman would dare to criticize or judge. I had heard him remark with obvious regret that my mother had started to become "Americanized." It occurred to me it was probably better she had died before she was completely ruined.

But now, my own womanhood was creeping in, like something sinister and foretold, but too early, before I could prepare my defenses. Now the creature was already inside me: growing, secreting, sprouting, and whispering her own version of *the way things should be.*

Sometimes I caught my father looking at me with an expression of loss, a look that said, "What a pity." I knew he missed the innocent child-skin I was shedding. I, too, missed it when I secretly struggled with the itch and scratch of puberty and tried to hide every dreaded "feminine" impulse and kept my monthly secret hidden like a sin.

At school the Haraty boy continued to haunt me on the

playground and in the hallway and even when I couldn't see him, his face rippled on the surface of my mind, a reflection of something I couldn't quite make out. And now my friends had noticed him too and would point him out.

"Your pet, Andrew, is waiting for you," Millie said in a sing-song voice.

"Why don't you give him a dog biscuit?" She pushed out her tongue and panted like a dog.

"He likes older women," said Pat in her knowing way. Then they burst into giggles. I giggled too, not because I thought it was funny.

"Why don't you just wave at him?" Millie said. "Or make a face. He might get embarrassed and go away." But I couldn't make a game of it. Something in his face prevented me, the way his eyes would settle on you for a lingering, butterfly moment before drifting off. My father had that look sometimes.

I never found the right moment to talk about the boy with my father. He didn't ask about what we did with friends. He rarely asked about school. I'd tried to please him by being a good student, but he wasn't especially interested in straight A report cards. In fact, he never commented about grades except the time that Jimmy got half A's and half F's, when he said in a laughing voice, "Shows what you're interested in, my boy." My father felt that schooling was only part of our education and didn't overemphasize it. Our education was for ourselves, not for him. "You have to learn your own lessons," he said. "No one can learn them for you." Part of these lessons we were to learn for ourselves was dealing with social or school matters; this included bothersome teachers or schoolmates. So I recognized that there would be no help forthcoming, that I would have to take the matter into my own hands.

"Do you have a problem?" This is what I finally said to Andrew Haraty. I had walked right up to him when he stationed himself at the side of the court where I was playing handball. I had decided enough was enough.

"No, do you?" he answered.

"Why do you watch me?"

He shrugged. "It's a free country."

"Well, it gives me the creeps and I want you to stop it." I tried to sound like I meant business.

"You can't make me," he said, his lips curled with contempt. "I don't have to do what you say. You think you're such a big deal?" When he said this, he stepped forward. I noticed that his feet were remarkably big like Jimmy's, but his shoelaces were clean. "You think you're so hot? You think you've got it made?"

"No I don't!" I tried to sound indignant although I didn't feel indignant. I felt puzzled and hurt. What had I done to him? He was the one who had been bothering me. "I do not!" I said. I tried to think of something else to say, but couldn't. I didn't know why I had to defend myself.

The boy was quite tall for his age, as tall as I, but more lanky. He moved his long legs and arms awkwardly, as if they had suddenly sprouted and he was still unaccustomed to them. He reminded me of an octopus, all loose appendages. His arms flailed in my direction as he spoke. "Just because you're rich and your father drives a fancy car—"

"What are you talking about? How do you know what kind of car my father drives?"

The conversation was so confusing. Rich? I had never thought of being rich. On the contrary, I knew for a fact that we had far fewer things than most of our schoolmates. My father didn't believe in heaping things on children; he believed it gave them the wrong impression. I hadn't thought about it before, but I now wondered if it was possible to be rich and poor at the same time.

"I saw the Mercedes when your father came to see

Monsignor Fitzhugh when he was sick," he continued in an accusing tone. "He parked it on the playground, with the top down."

"Monsignor Fitzhugh had a heart attack," I said. "It was an emergency."

"I don't care," he said. "My mother has an old Nash Rambler. And it's falling apart."

Now I had yet another reason for being uneasy. Through no fault of my own, I was somebody's enemy. It didn't seem reasonable that someone should hate me because his mother drove an old car. I had no control over what kind of car my father drove, or what we or anybody else had or didn't have. I had liked it better when I didn't know why he stared at me. I still didn't understand, really, but now I felt guilty. Feeling guilty didn't seem reasonable either, but I did.

For the next several Sundays, my father and I hiked in the hills to inspect the roses. This time we carried bags of fertilizer on our backs and tucked the spades into our waistbands. The surviving roses smeared themselves over the shrubs and trees and released their perfume into the warm air. "Take this down," he said. "*Guinee.* Deep crimson blossoms open flat, displaying gold anthers. Profuse, double flowers. Still, I'm not crazy about it."

"Dad, remember when I was little, you used to say that you were going to trade me in?" I said.

"Umm," he answered.

"Well?"

"Jorie, is this going to be one of those odd conversations you seem to be pressing for lately? I'm not in the mood."

"No, I was just wondering."

"Wondering what?"

"If you still feel the same way."

"No," he said, his bushy eyebrows sinking into a frown. "It's too late to trade you in." He poured the last bit of bonemeal around the base of the plant, crumpled up the empty sack and started down the path.

"Besides," he said over his shoulder, "in spite of your recent lapses, you're already trained."

A long time had passed since my father had threatened to trade me in. The current threat, mostly directed at my brothers, was to kick us out. The line was "I'm going to saw your end off the table." ("Yurrr end," he said, in a Scottish brogue.) This is what my father's father had said to him. And after having met my grandfather, we had no doubt that he had said this and that he would have done it, too. My father repeated it to be humorous, but we knew that he had left home at fourteen and to this day believed it was the best thing that ever happened to him. Fourteen was the age at which my father tumbled out of his home, into the wide world. So we knew that at fourteen a Mackinnon is on shaky ground.

Alex, now that age, must have felt that especially. And, like me, he was fighting a beast within himself. But his was not a whispering beast; it raged and spit and bit its own tail. It fed on itself. My beast was stealthy, a feminine creature with many voices and many wiles. Alex's beast was a clod. Alex couldn't hide his beast, since clods won't be hidden, so more and more Alex stayed away, never knowing when the clod would rise to humiliate him.

"Albertine is his favorite," I said to Hazel, my father's office nurse. "We went hiking last weekend and she was completely in bloom, even before we fed her."

Hazel picked up a stack of charts, tapped them on the desk, and pressed them against her starched bosom. There hardly seemed to be a body inside her stiff uniform. She was so thin, the starched white dress must have looked the same hanging on a hanger as it did hanging on Hazel. Back to front, side to side, she was straight as a yardstick. This was supposed to be the result of being a spinster. Or was it the cause? I wasn't sure.

"That's nice," she said flatly. She tolerated us in the office, but let it be known that we were in the way.

"Hazel, do you think we're rich?"

"Well, I don't know," she said, nervously shuffling the charts. The little blood vessels on her cheeks were like tangled pink threads on her pale skin.

"I mean, we're not like the rich people in the movies. We don't go to the French Riviera or anything."

"Your father takes a two-week vacation every year."

"I know. But we don't get to go with him. What is it then, he's rich and we're poor?" I was still trying to figure out what made Andrew Haraty think we were rich.

"I hardly think that's it," she said. "You're very fortunate. And your father works so hard. Here, why don't you file these and make yourself useful."

I took the charts and placed them in alphabetical order. I loved the alphabet; there was something cozy about it. Numbers, on the other hand, were not cozy; they were infinite and cold. The charts had case numbers too, but my father insisted that the names come first. "I could file charts all day long," I said to Hazel.

She looked at me blankly. "That's nice," she said.

I liked helping out in my father's office. There was always something I could do, like counting out pills from large stock bottles and dropping them into small bottles made of amber glass, or sharpening needles that soaked in a basin of alcohol. For these tasks my father always gave careful instructions: Wash your hands with soap and water for five minutes before dispensing pills. Do not talk while you count. Drag the needle across a cotton ball to see if it snags. After rubbing the needle against the sharpening stone at just this angle, check it again with the cotton ball. Hazel didn't think I should be doing these jobs, but my father told her firmly that I was quite capable; I was to do any job he assigned, according to his instructions. At first, she would peer over my shoulder, making little puffing sounds through her nose, but after a while she would let her glasses drop from the chain around her neck—a sign of resignation. She had other things to worry about, like "those female patients on the make." And she must have been right to worry because one day she left in tears, saying something like, "I give up," and didn't come back for a month.

Now, since the secretary was on vacation, a new job came my way. She had left a note with Hazel. I was to take the checkbook and copy the past month's check stubs into a check register, under Accounts Payable. I wrote with painstakingly careful penmanship: Western Linen Supply—lab coats, Bell Telephone—office, 2nd line, Pepe's Garage—new brakes, American Surgical—medical supplies, Levy Land Co.—rent, Marion Haraty—child support. I tested the word out loud. Haraty! The boy's face came to me as if in a mirror: my nose, my eyes, the same weak chin. And the boy must have known about me. He must have seen it too, the bitter resemblance.

Suddenly everything made sense: All this time my father must have had another life, another house, children, another family waiting for him. I remembered the photographs I'd accidentally come across a few years past. I didn't understand them at the time, but now I understood. An answer is obvious once you know it. And now I had written the answer with my own hand, the missing piece that filled the gap so perfectly, I couldn't doubt the truth of it. Then a storm of images swept through my mind, like insects on the rampage, a world war of ants and termites and wasps and whatever else pours forth in confusion and fury with great ripping jaws poised for defense. I imagined my father sitting with a strange woman, a strange child on his lap. I recalled myself at five years old, sitting alone in the dark driveway, waiting for him to come home. I imagined him tossing the infant Andrew into the air and laughing. And saw Jimmy bring morning coffee, as he had so often, to an empty room. All the times my father came home too late and left too early. Alex waiting, cracking his knuckles and tearing at his nails. It wasn't our fault after all. All this time, he had somewhere else to go. Gripping the pen between my thumb and forefinger, I pressed it until it snapped.

I had never seen my father amazed. But he was amazed. And I amazed myself, hearing my own voice so loud, so steady. Thick accretions of restraint had cracked and gave way under a streaming pressure of rage. I watched the disbelief in my father's face, the shock that flared in his eyes and temporarily left him speechless. He did not, I am sure, believe the force of a child's wrath. I had never dared to raise my voice to him and his face colored then paled under the barrage of my accusations. "I know about Andrew Haraty," I said. "How could you! Our mother was still alive; you had a family! You had us!"

"You don't understand," he said finally, with a forced calmness. His eyes narrowed, squeezed between his eyelashes, glowering gray. "This is not your business. It has nothing to do with you."

This I didn't want to understand. "Well it's my business now. The same school! How could you send him to the same school?"

"I didn't know where he went to school. It wasn't my decision. Sending the support checks is the only contact I have with Andrew."

"How can I believe you? Now I know why you're never home, why we've never had a regular life. We've never gone anywhere, we've never done things other kids do, we never get any help, with anything. Alex is having trouble and you don't even notice." The words poured out in a torrent. If I'd wanted to, I could not have stopped them. "You left us alone to be with them."

"You're exaggerating. And you're jumping to conclusions." He was talking faster now, but with a voice even softer. "Besides, who is *them?*"

"I don't know. Other people. People I don't even know."

"You know that's not true."

"I don't trust you anymore. I don't know what's true. And I don't care. I want him out! I want him out of my school!" My voice didn't falter. I could feel my father pushing back, trying to distance himself, cool himself, trying for reason. But my angry voice kept gaining on him.

"Think of it from Andrew's point of view," he said. "It's not fair to him. This is a new school for you; he was there first. Why should he have to leave?"

"Because," I said, "I can't stand looking at his face."

My father's ruddy hand rubbed against his mouth. He shook his head solemnly. "We'll see," he said.

But I had momentum and the words continued to spill out. "I want—"

My father raised his hand dismissively, palm flat as a stop sign. "Enough," he said. "Leave me alone."

Looking up at the flat of his hand and the sad glistening of his upper lip, I fell silent. By the power of his unraised voice, I was suddenly muted and exposed. I had unleashed my fury and it had come back to me, unrequited. What did I expect? An apology, a declaration of love? I could not have been that foolish. I felt myself shrivel in his eyes. He was so tall, tall and impervious as a skyscraper.

"I've taken care of my responsibilities," he said. "My life is my own and it's not for you to judge me. I've never imposed my authority on you; I've given you the freedom of your own life, so you should understand."

I listened for some defensiveness or arrogance in his

voice, or some anger that I could rally against, some justifica-
tion for my failure to control myself, my failure to understand.
But there was nothing in his voice except the cold note of reason. And by contrast, I could not help but feel that I had
become one of those detestable creatures, *hysterical women*,
and he, with ultimate patience, had to put up with it.

Calmly, he went on. "I don't have the time or the tempera-
ment to be both a mother and a father. But I've tried to be a
good father and I've taken care of you as best I can." He lowered his head and drew a deep breath. He was blinking slowly
as if recovering from a blow. "It's true that I've had outside
involvements and I have other children. But you are my only
family and this is my only home."

I didn't say anything because I couldn't. In the face of such
irrefutable truth, I found myself powerless and suddenly light-
headed. I sat down and lowered my head between my knees.

"Having said that," my father continued, "I think I can
trust you not to bring this up again. There's nothing to be
gained, only painful feelings. About Andrew, I will consider
what should be done."

I felt like crying, but didn't. I knew there would be no
comfort.

As I turned to leave, he raised his voice to call me back.
"Jorie—" he said.

"Yes, Dad?"

"You disappoint me."

That night I lay awake, the creature inside me stirring and
angry. I knew it was the creature because she was sharp-
tongued and accusing. Like a woman, she named names. Her
litany of charges droned on, loud and steady, but my father's
words also replayed in my mind, like a tolling bell: Disappoint.
Disappoint. Disappoint. I listened far into the night until I fell
asleep and dreamed I was still listening, as I took out the

pruning saw and tested its serrated blade against my finger. Dawn was just breaking over the city below, which stretched and blinked in a hazy pinkish light. The clucks and calls of quail rose up from the canyon and the wind blew in cold breaths as I carried the saw up the hillside. First I came to "Mermaid" looming phantasmal over the trail. Only the bottom of its gnarled trunk was visible under the canopy of bloom. From that vantage point I could see several spreading bushes including Albertine, glowing in the early morning rays.

"Cut them down," the creature whispered. "Cut them all."

"I shouldn't," I said to the creature. "He would be so hurt and angry."

"Why shouldn't you?" she answered. "What he did was far worse."

"I can't."

"You can."

I dreamed that I cut through the trunk, feeling the resistance as Albertine squealed against the saw. The branches didn't crash or settle, but stayed suspended just as they were, hanging like a skeleton in the tree. I saw the anguish in my father's face as he came upon the doomed Albertine, its blossoms withering and faded. It was the same look he had when I would daydream of my own funeral, a look of such sorrow and regret, it brought tears to my eyes. Filled with pity and satisfaction, I watched his face. A song played in the background, a single violin. I could read his mind: *If only I had let her know how much I loved her.* But it was too late. I was gone. And then in this dream, another look came across his face as he turned from the lifeless Albertine. His face was frozen in anger; his eyes were ice. I had died and he was glad.

"No," I said as I swung my arm in a wide arc, hurling the pruning saw down into the canyon. "Quiet," I said to the creature. "Be quiet."

•◆•◆•

The next time I saw Andrew Haraty I was surprised at how familiar he seemed: the way he leaned against the wall with his legs crossed, the way he cocked his head, his clowny feet. While I couldn't say I was used to him, I had come to expect his stalking me. Now I understood it and I also understood its limitation. For after the storm in my mind had settled, it occurred to me that I was in the better position. After all, I was legitimately, publicly, my father's child. I carried the status and validation of his profession, our name, our house, our car, and by extension, a promising future. What did Andrew Haraty have besides this wall to lean on? Whatever part of my father he shared, it was tainted and doomed to second place. I could almost feel sorry for him.

"Look, he's over there by the wall," Millie said. "Wait, he's looking over here. Don't look now."

"He's kind of cute," said Pat. "If he weren't so young—"

"Isn't he ever going to give up?" Millie said. "Tell him to stop it."

"Tell him to pick on someone his own age," Pat said.

"I'll tell him," I said, leaving Pat and Millie wide-eyed behind me.

Andrew pushed his back away from the wall when he saw me approaching and stood at his full height, awkwardly. I looked into his face for a long time, until he finally looked away. "What do YOU want?" he said.

I stood there, thinking. The confidence I had talked myself into had drained away. There was no first place and second place. There was only this boy, who was neither them nor us. And as far as I was concerned, there was no place for him.

"I want you gone," I said.

For the next few weeks Los Angeles was shrouded with low clouds and fog. Cars ran into each other in the mist, crashing like dominoes. At school I watched for Andrew Haraty, but suddenly, he was gone. I looked over my shoulder during morning assembly; he wasn't there. Again I looked at recess, then again at the lunch break. Millie tried to find him too, but couldn't. "You scared him away," she said. Once I thought I caught him in the corner of my eye, but it was just a shadow, my own.

I never told anyone about Andrew Haraty, not even the boys. I felt that silence was the price of having him out of my sight. My father and I never spoke of him again. Nor did we speak of any of his other outside involvements. There was nothing, it seemed, that could not be ignored. In an unspoken contract of silence, our life would continue as before. What mattered was that we were the only children with a true claim to my father and were thereby entitled to whatever security came with the Mackinnon name. Sometimes, when I allowed myself to think about it, I had a reluctant sympathy for Andrew, but I felt that my father didn't have enough time for his legitimate children, let alone for an interloper who, after all, had a mother to care for him. In that way, he was luckier than we were. He was certainly luckier than Alex. Shortly afterward, Alex was again suspended from school, this time for carrying a switchblade knife, then he was put back a semester for missing so much class time. It seemed that being legitimate gave Alex no advantage at all.

WHEN MY FATHER GAVE Alex the puppy I always wanted, I didn't begrudge him. Partly, it may have been the element of surprise that prevented me from working up a case of righteous envy. It was hard on the spur of the moment like that to come up with a calm, rational argument about the unfairness of it, about how it had always been my wish, not his. He had never said anything about wanting a dog, ever. Without warning, my wish had been usurped. But as it was, when my father placed the wriggling, tongue-flicking, wispy-eared furball into Alex's arms, I couldn't help but feel that some justice had been served, that Alex was being rightly compensated. This in addition to the savory satisfaction that I was being martyred for a greater cause.

"I'll call him Bill," Alex said. We got sick of hearing that name.

"Here, Bill. Come on, Bill. Let's go, boy." Alex wouldn't walk from one side of a room to the other without calling his dog. When he sat, he kept Bill in his lap, curled up under his shirt, the dewy nose sticking out between the buttons. He even kissed the pup when he thought no one was looking, and I had never seen Alex kiss anyone or anything. I didn't think he knew how.

When my father was home Alex was completely different with the dog. He issued commands and smacked him with newspaper when he sniffed and circled the floor. He was showing responsibility, which was what my father talked about when he gave him the puppy. Now that Alex had turned fifteen, he was becoming a man, my father said. It was past time he learned some responsibility.

As the weeks went on, you could almost see the puppy grow. Each day his legs seemed longer, his potbelly smoother, and big fangs emerged from his mottled gums. For a time he even had two sets of fangs; the new ones came in faster than the old ones came out. Soon he outgrew Alex's lap, but that didn't stop him from jumping into it anyway. He was turning into a frayed-looking creature, huge and shaggy like an Irish wolfhound, with a tan thumbprint over each eye—the only vestige of a Doberman ancestor. His testicles had grown to the size of baseballs; it was hard not to notice. *"Huevos grandes,"* Jimmy said, with arched eyebrows.

"Shut up," Alex said. He never joked about his dog. The best thing about Bill was his eyes: large, dark amber, rimmed with black. They seemed to know everything already, without ever having to ask or wonder. Even though he was still a puppy, he seemed to have grown up, grown old, grown young again. He seemed to have been here before. His only fault, if you could call it that, was an air of condescension, which he reserved for everyone except Alex. For Alex it was love, full-out and unabashed.

It was rainy that fall, real rain, not just the occasional sprinkle that barely washed the dust off the cars. The sky was thick with it; the gray slung low over the city. Welcome rain in L.A.

Because of it Alex and Jimmy stayed home more than usual and we tried to keep the dog inside, too, because when he was wet, he smelled dank as old rags. I liked to watch Bill sleep—something he did a lot. It had to do with his growing so fast. I wondered what the dream images were that caused his eyes to twitch and his tail to flutter like a butterfly. Was he seeing someone throw a stick? Sometimes he would make muffled barking sounds. Other times he would suddenly sit up, grumble a little, then lie back down. At first, we thought something woke him, but then it became apparent that he was still asleep. His eyes were open but not focused on anything. His face was expressionless. When we woke him by clapping our hands, a light would turn on in his eyes. When he progressed from just sitting up while sleeping to walking around the room, we were amazed.

"Somnambulism," my father said to Alex. "Look it up." Alex was sitting in a chair, pretending to read; he was also pretending not to hear.

"I'll do it," I said.

"No," my father said. "It's Alex's word."

Alex didn't move or even look up.

"Well?" my father said, "I'm talking to you."

Alex shifted his position and absently turned a page. "No," he said after a tense interval. "I don't want to play word games."

Silence burst in the room like sudden light. We sat there blinking. While Alex was known to challenge anyone he could, as often as he could, he never crossed the old man. It wasn't done. My father was silent for a moment. He looked at Alex like milk gone sour. "Then what game do you want to play?" he said at last. "Just what does interest you these days?"

Alex continued to look down into his lap. "Nothing," he said.

My father opened the newspaper in front of his face. "Well that's your loss," he said. "Why don't you take a walk, let off some steam. And take that sleepwalker with you. It might do you both good."

That was when Bill ceased to be Bill.

"Where's Sleepwalker?" Alex asked one day after school. "He wasn't waiting for me in the usual place."

"I don't know," I said. "He's probably somnambulating."

The trouble was I was right. At that very moment Sleepwalker was in a neighbor's atrium, having unwittingly cornered a rare gang-gang cockatoo. The bird, pacing on its perch of bleached driftwood, was screeching in terror at the sight of the great hairy beast, but it wasn't until it began to frantically flap its manicured wings that the light came on in Sleepwalker's eyes and he saw the wondrous thing suddenly in front of him: flapping, squawking, and smelling like fear. It was irresistible.

"Oh, thank God I was in time! Thank God!" the neighbor screeched. "My poor Tutu!"

"He wouldn't have hurt the bird," my father said, suppressing a smile. "He just wanted to play."

"Play, my foot! That dog's a monster. A killer. A horse!"

"A stallion," Jimmy said.

Alex stepped forward. "He's my dog and it won't happen again," he said.

"It better not. I'm warning you. If that dog comes near my house again, I'll take him to the glue factory myself!"

After she left, my father turned to Alex, who was patting Sleepwalker on the chest. "You hear that, Alex?" he said. "That dog is your responsibility."

"I said it won't happen again," Alex said sullenly.

"I'll hold you to that," my father said.

•◆•◆•

I still liked Sundays; I appreciated the fact that no matter what else was going on in my father's life, he usually managed to spend that one day with us. Jimmy still liked Sundays too, most of the time. He looked forward to spending the day with our father, even though he was usually put to work at gardening chores, mostly sweeping and weeding. It was better than nothing. Alex was getting restless on Sundays. Not that my father insisted on his staying home; he didn't, but there was a part of Alex that wanted to stay and another part that couldn't wait to take off.

"I'm going out," Alex said. He had obviously timed his entrance—a thinly veiled exit—for full impact. We were still sitting in the breakfast room, eating Shredded Wheat and reading the Sunday *Times.* His hair was slicked back on the sides and he was wearing a black leather jacket, without sleeves. High on his scrawny white, freckled arms the sleeves of his tee shirt were rolled up and I could tell they were about to roll down again and that his crinkly hair was about to spring out from the sides of his head and that if he didn't leave soon, the effect would be lost.

"Bye," my father said, hardly looking up from his paper.

"Gonna rumble?" Jimmy said, before he was hit dead center with my father's silencer look.

"Come on, boy," Alex said to Sleepwalker, rolling his shoulders and sounding cool, pretending he had somewhere to go. But Sleepwalker was full of enthusiasm. To him, out was as good as anyplace and they left looking like they had a purpose.

Alex should have known better. This might have worked on other parents, the kind who told their boys to stand up straight, tuck their shirts in, say please and thank you, use their napkins, but my father cared nothing about the civil arts or how my brothers presented themselves, so long as their hearts were brave and their minds were active. That applied to me too, of course, and even though I heard other children complain, I sometimes wished we had some rules, something you could get a grip on and throw when you were mad.

Later that day, after Alex had skulked back into the house, my father told us about somnambulism. "What happens is," he explained, "at least this is the theory, that if the spinal motor neurons are not inhibited during sleep by special cells in the brain stem, the sleeper may move, even walk around."

"Does he know where he's going?" I asked.

"Probably not. When you're asleep, you respond to internal brain stimuli, not to external stimuli. You're not aware of the world around you; that is, you're not conscious."

"Could he get lost?"

"Possibly."

"Or hit by a car?"

"Sleepwalker's not going to get hit by a car," Alex said, indignantly. I noticed that he was rubbing his thumb and forefinger together, a habit he had when he was nervous. He had been doing it a lot lately. He had also been sweating. "Rank!" Jimmy had said when he picked up the wrong shirt. I had noticed it too, when I collected their clothes to put in the washing machine. I supposed Alex was going through a metamorphosis (my word for the week). And with the red hair sprouting in his armpits, cigarettes hidden in his pockets, and his voice breaking into low notes, manhood could not be far off.

I had been covertly observing my own metamorphosis for some time, secretly buying provisions like deodorant and sanitary pads from my allowance and sneaking them into my room hidden under a pile of towels. As far as our metamorphosis into adulthood was concerned, I thought the boys had an advantage. At least they could learn from our father what it meant to be a man.

"Besides," Alex continued, "Sleepwalker can outgrow it; sometimes sleepwalkers do—at least, some children do and a puppy is like a child, isn't it?"

"It's interesting that you should know that, Alex," my father said. "You must have looked it up after all." He looked at him and waited. "Well, did you?"

"Sleepwalker is not a puppy anymore; he's a grown youth," Jimmy interjected. "No dog gets bigger than that!" Sleepwalker looked at him condescendingly.

Alex looked sideways at our father. "So what if I looked it up," he said.

Sleepwalker did not outgrow it. We found him in the most remarkable places. One time we found him wedged under the kitchen sink, his front leg looped around the drain pipe. Another time he was sitting on the low railing bordering the patio, three stories up; we were afraid to wake him. Alex crept up, put his arms around him, then we linked our arms around each other's waists like a chain and all pulled in, ending up in a pile of bodies telescoped on the floor, the dog on top.

That scared Alex; he was worried Sleepwalker might get hurt. "You gotta grow out of this," I heard him explaining to the dog. "I can't always be around to protect you." He had his arms around Sleepwalker's neck and Sleepwalker was looking at him with his resinous, knowing eyes and his tongue hanging down from the side of his mouth. "Do you understand, boy?" Sleepwalker slurped in his tongue and placed both massive paws on Alex's shoulders. Alex hugged him and looked like he was in the arms of a bear. There were other incidents, but they were not frequent. Usually the dog would just sleepwalk into a closet or climb into a bathtub. He never bothered Jetsam, who had already established her place as dowager in the family. She seemed to sense when he was sleepwalking and simply got out of reach. Alex tried tying a bell on the dog, but Sleepwalker could either get it off himself or he would run around making so much noise that the first person with frayed nerves and sharp scissors would cut it off.

One incident I kept to myself: It was on a cold November night when I woke to what sounded like rolling thunder. Drowsily, I looked up at my window and saw a clear, navy sky through the old square panes. I didn't want to move from my warm spot in the center of the bed, where I had folded my thin blanket in half. I watched the sky, hoping to see a flash of lightning, but there was none. Then I heard it again. I thought I might be dreaming, but as I turned over onto the sharp cold of the sheet I knew I was awake and that the sound was not only real but was getting louder. Lying there, I could feel the vibration of low rumblings. The sound was coming from inside the room. Then I was aware of another breath, warm and swampy in the cold air. And my eyes fell on the huge black silhouette, its white fangs bared in the moonlight. Tall and rigid he stood, facing nothing, looking at nothing, hackles up, saliva dripping from his retracted lips, growling deep and thunderous. I opened my mouth as if to scream but the sound was stillborn and I felt my arms and legs grow stiff and my heart pounding and my chest holding on to breath—cold breath, sucked in, held. Oh Sleepwalker, I thought. This is not good.

"Wake up, boy," I said, clapping my hands and slapping the bed. He startled. Then he was bounding toward the bed, tail wagging, his great mouth grinning out of the shadows. Wildly he licked my face and neck until I finally managed to push him down. "Go away," I said. But he settled down near the foot of the bed and both of us slept badly.

Sleeping badly had become commonplace in our household. I had always been a fitful and light sleeper, but now my father could often be found reading or pacing in the wee hours, and Alex's light was often on in his room, although he never ventured downstairs, except to let the dog out. Only Jimmy, recently moved into a room of his own, slept like the dead. Now with Sleepwalker in the house, there was yet another night wanderer to add to the creaking, rustling sounds of floor and stairs, doors and windows. And in the morning the house did not smell of a new day. I would open all the windows to let the morning air wash through, to take away the night that was spent with pacing and worry and bad dreams and whatever went on in Alex's room that took the place of sleep.

"I don't have time for this," my father said. Alex looked down at his shoes. The junior high school principal had called and wanted my father to come and get Alex personally. There had been a fight. Again.

"I barely touched him," Alex said.

"You broke his arm. In two places."

"He fell."

"You know better than to make excuses. A man owns up to his actions."

At the time I was sitting on the floor with my arms wrapped around Sleepwalker. I could feel the tension in his body, but he didn't move. I could feel his patience too. He was biding his time. The anger in my father's voice set my heart pounding even though it was not directed at me. This was not our familiar father, always calm and controlled, soft-voiced even in disapproval. Something in Alex was breaking through his anger threshold. I shuddered; I had always thought my father was unflappable.

Alex raised his eyes; I could see they were glistening. "I told you," he said. "The guy fell."

Now my father was pacing slowly like a lion, his eyes fixed on Alex's lowered head. "I expect more from you," he said. "You're turning into some two-bit punk. You know what a punk is? A punk is a coward. A punk is weak. He thinks he can hide his weakness by playing tough. He feels like a big shot if people are afraid of him. The principal tells me you think you're a *greaser*. Is that what you are?" Alex blinked and looked away. "Well, I don't want any greaser punks around here—and that includes you, if that's what you choose to be."

"This time it wasn't my fault—"

My father picked up his suit jacket from the back of a chair. "No excuses," he said. "I have patients waiting—sick people waiting in the office over two hours because of you. I had to come home to deal with this. People waiting to be discharged from the hospital, their families and the hospital staff inconvenienced because of you."

Alex just stood there, pale and diminished. His fists, his jaw, everything about him was clenched as the words strained through. Then he raised his eyes, defiant. "I don't care," he said.

"You'd better care, Alex," my father said, turning to leave. "You'd better care, or you can get out. If you don't care, I don't even want to know you."

Alex was put on probationary status at school. My father sent the injured boy to an orthopedic surgeon he knew, but insisted on paying full fee, of which Alex had to pay half, out of his allowance. A man pays his own way. My father said half was a concession.

Not long after that a neighbor's cat was missing, then another neighbor's screen door had been knocked in, but nothing had been taken, as far as he could tell. "The burglar must've been drunk," he told us. We didn't pay much attention.

Sleepwalker had stopped growing, but was filling out. He outweighed Alex by thirty pounds. He did everything a dog was supposed to do: come, heel, sit, stay, down, love without conditions. He accepted affection as his due, but also with a certain amount of gratitude. I forgave him for being Alex's dog.

At the start of spring semester Alex was still on probation at school. At home, he was usually unaccounted for. So when my father asked where he was that Sunday, we could only shrug. *"In absentia,"* Jimmy said.

"Exercising Sleepwalker," I suggested.

"I'm afraid we may have a problem with Sleepwalker," my father said gravely.

"No, Dad, there's no problem with Sleepwalker," Jimmy said.

"Sleepwalker's fine," I assured him, without looking at Jimmy.

My father took off his reading glasses and polished them on his shirt. He looked tired.

"I wanted to tell Alex," he said. "Dmitri's lost another cat."

"Cats always run away," I said.

"This one was not really lost," he said. "He was torn apart."

"Coyotes!" Jimmy said. "I saw one the other day, really, Dad."

"Some sculptures were knocked over in Dmitri's studio."

Jimmy thought for a moment. "Coincidental evidence."

"I hope you're right, son." I liked the way he said it, so gentle.

Later that afternoon I made oatmeal cookies that looked like cow patties. My father said they were delicious. Jimmy said they were terrible, but ate them anyway. Alex refused to try one, then changed his mind. "Just for you," he said.

"Thanks," I said and meant it.

The dog tried one too, then spat it out.

We were in the dining room. Jimmy was cutting pictures from *National Geographic* for a school assignment. Shards of paper floated to the floor, covering layers of sediment from earlier projects. I was sitting on a stack of encyclopedias, pressing wildflowers I had collected. I liked the purple-stained pages and would use the dried lupines to mark my favorite sections like the flora and fauna of New Guinea, with the picture of *paradisaeida*, the bird of paradise. My father was reading and surreptitiously watching Alex, who was milling around the periphery of the room. He was waiting for an opening.

"Have an interesting morning, Alex?" he asked, catching his eye.

"Okay, I guess," Alex said.

"How's the dog's training coming along?"

"Okay."

"He's learning everything?"

"Yeah, he knows everything."

"No problems?"

"No. He's smart."

My father slipped his reading glasses into their case and settled back into his chair. "Remember when I told you about the dog I had when I was just about your age, part wolf? Beautiful animal, smart, but—"

"I've heard the story, Dad."

"Want to hear it again?"

"No."

"Want to hear a new story?"

Alex licked his thumb, which was red and raw-looking. "No," he said. He didn't want to hear what he already knew. "I've gotta go," he said. At the snap of his fingers, Sleepwalker sat up, ears pulled forward, ready for the order.

"Hold on," my father said. "We have to talk about this."

"About what?" Alex said, putting on his sleeveless jacket over a yellow and blue striped shirt. He dropped his eyelids and curled his lips in an awkward, unpracticed way; he looked uncool. "There's nothing to talk about."

"Oh no?" my father said. He paused: an invitation to answer.

Alex said nothing.

"Tell you what, I'll help you build an enclosure for the dog, for when you're not here—"

"No," said Alex in a tone of alarm. "He wouldn't be happy. He'd be miserable. I don't want him cooped up like a prisoner. I'll take care of it."

"Now Alex—"

"I said I'll take care of it, Dad, I will."

My father waited until Alex looked up. "Don't just say it then; do it."

On Wednesday I went across the street to ask Dmitri about his cat. When I heard the familiar strains of Vivaldi, I knew he was working and let myself into his studio through the unlocked door, as I always had. He seemed surprised to see me. "Don't see you for long time," he said. He smiled and waved to indicate that I should come in. He was standing on a scaffold, bent over a large piece of stone, the curve of a forehead emerging under his hands.

It was true that I rarely came to visit him now, not like a few years earlier when I could often be found there, quietly listening to music and watching him work. "We got a dog," I said, by way of explanation.

"I know," he said, climbing down. "Nice big one. He visits me when you're at school."

"I heard about your cat. I'm sorry. Was it Sasha?"

"Yes, poor old Sasha," he said. He wiped his hand down the sides of his pants as he walked across the room. "But look, here is Sasha—from memory." And there in fresh clay was Dmitri's cat stretching as he did in life, toes fanned out, back arched, lips stretched into a smug Cheshire grin. "It is Sasha?"

I nodded.

"I think about dog," Dmitri said. His pale eyes were serious behind his splattered glasses. His white hair stood up in cottony tufts that didn't seem rooted, but looked as if they'd floated down on his head in a gentle breeze. "I know he's nice dog, but maybe he has dark side. You know, like Dr. Jekyll."

"He doesn't have a dark side," I protested. "He just walks in his sleep, that's all. He has somnambulism."

Dmitri shook his head in a dismissive but not unkind way. "Sign of times," he said. "Everything has big name. This *ism*, that *ism*—too many *isms*. But don't forget *real* life." I realized then how much I'd missed our visits—the long comfortable silences, the occasional harangue on what is "real life." He must have recalled it too. He smiled and continued: "About Sasha. I didn't say so to father, but I think he knows . . ." Dmitri's hand gently lifted my chin. "Good and evil," he said. "Is real life."

I couldn't accept that Sleepwalker had an evil side. Special cells in his brain were missing their orders, that's all. But what about us? When Dmitri said good and evil is real life, he didn't mean just the dog, but he must have meant all of us—Alex, Jimmy, my father, even me. I relished the idea; it gave me a new way of seeing the world. And the next time Alex came skulking in, I didn't see a boy struggling into manhood as I had been seeing, but I saw the dark Alex, overtaken by his shadow. The dark Alex raged and withdrew, failed tests, fell behind. Like Hyde, the evil Alex roamed the streets.

I was particularly interested in observing the exact moment of transition, when evil overtakes good, or vice versa. I looked for the dark side in Jimmy, too, and watched him closely. I stared at him to catch the moment the dark side appeared. Unlike Alex with his long, brooding moods, Jimmy would change quick as a flash. "Get outta here and stop staring at me!" the evil Jimmy would suddenly shout. "You give me the creeps!" Then I would leave, satisfied. Thinking in terms of good and evil sides made me feel strangely lighthearted; it simplified things.

Outside the rain began again and lost its welcome. It flooded intersections and saturated hillsides. Walls of mud crashed through sliding glass doors, killing people in their sleep and whole houses broke from their foundations and tumbled into the streets below. Raw sewage poured from storm drains onto public beaches. And the weatherman said the much-needed rain would relieve the parched southland and that would be good news for firefighters.

"Is this the Mackinnon residence?"

"Maybe," Jimmy answered.

The man at the door was wearing a tan uniform with creases ironed in the shirt. It had an insignia patch over the pocket. His pants were tight. He had a long smooth stick in a holster at his side. "I'm investigating a complaint," he said. "Is your mother home?"

"Nope," Jimmy said.

"When will she be back?"

"Never." We liked this answer. By now we had learned it had a certain shock value and used it whenever we had the opportunity. If someone asked, "Where is your mother?" we would answer, "Dead." This was often useful in averting trouble; it caught people off guard.

"Is your father home then?"

"Nope."

"Is anyone home?"

"Yup," Jimmy said with a taunting grin. Dumb question.

"Okay, kid," the man said patiently. "I want to talk to someone in charge."

"You're looking at him," Jimmy said. This was untrue. No one was in charge.

The man looked at him skeptically. "Tell your father to call this number, Department of Animal Regulation," he said, handing Jimmy a card. "Don't forget. It's important."

"I won't," Jimmy said in his best singsong voice.

As soon as the man was gone, Jimmy tore the card into little pieces. But we were worried. We thought we should warn

Alex, but we didn't know where he was. That was on Thursday. By Sunday, my father knew about the complaint. We didn't know how, but he did. He told us that Sleepwalker was found more than a mile away, in a house on Beachwood Drive. He had walked into a baby's room that had been left open to freshen the air. At the time, the baby was in the kitchen being fed. When the mother went to investigate the sounds of a commotion in the room, she found Sleepwalker growling and tearing apart what was left of the baby's mattress. Little pieces of cotton batting floated through the air. She screamed. The screaming woke the dog and by the time a neighbor came running, Sleepwalker was down on his haunches, wagging his tail.

"Whew! It's okay then; he didn't hurt anybody," Jimmy said. "I knew he'd never hurt anybody." Then he looked at my father's face and fell silent. Alex said nothing. The dog sat solemnly at his feet.

We knew then what had to happen. We knew because we had heard the story of my father's dog, part wolf, and had listened in horror when my father described how my grandfather handed him the rifle because it was his dog and a man has to do what he has to do. There was something wild in that dog that couldn't be tamed by patience or love or hope. There are some things beyond hope, like a wolf's natural impulse to kill or a brain's failure to block such an impulse when it arises during sleep.

My father looked at each of us as if he could read our minds. "It's merciful," he said. "Alex will hold him; that's the last thing he'll know."

We didn't cry. It would have been humiliating in each other's presence. Alex asked for just a few minutes alone with Sleepwalker. I could hear him crying from the other room. "I'm sorry, boy," he was saying. "It's my fault. I'm sorry."

But it was as unstoppable as a careening train. And we were on the train, with events clicking by in a blur on either side of us. We understood this train that we were on, that it started back at my father's boyhood farm and went forward to the next inevitable stop, so that when my father brought out his .22 rifle, Alex followed him outside in silent resignation with Sleepwalker beside him and he sat down and put his arms around the dog and the dog didn't move but just looked at him, knowing and accepting, and leaned away from Alex then dropped after one shot, heavy and dignified.

My father and Alex dug the grave and laid Sleepwalker into it. But my father said that Alex should be the one to bury him: to cover him with dirt, tamp it down, and place the marker, because when a man starts a job like that, he has to finish it.

Afterward, Alex wouldn't cry and he wouldn't look at my father either, or talk to him, but just walked away in a red haze, a red aura that shimmered all around him like dry heat and sizzled like something electric.

I realized this was about manhood and strength of character, that my father had proven himself to his father by just the same test, but I felt sorry for Alex. I thought of Sleepwalker lying dead and heavy in his arms and was glad not to be a man.

—————— • ◆ • ——————

THE GROUNDWATER OF THINGS UNSPOKEN

I KNEW FROM OBSERVING the girls around me that I was ahead of my time. At twelve, I was tall and had round breasts and a round bottom and in addition to all this round-ness, my head was filled with serious thoughts interspersed with gothic fantasies of sex. I already knew that men looked at me and I experienced this attention as something palpable. The most brief and casual encounter with a man could set off quivers in the pit of my body, leaving me with lingering feel-ings of fear, confusion, and a titillating sense of power.

Having become a Catholic, I had learned to pray. I prayed earnestly and often, going after school into the church next door and kneeling down in a hard wooden pew. I preferred the side altar of Saint Anthony to the ornate, vaulted main altar with the crucified Christ, gashed and bleeding. Saint Anthony, in his brown friar's robes, looked down benevolently onto his little covey of flickering candles. Saint Anthony is the saint in charge of lost things. I prayed for my mother, my father, Alex and Jimmy, Dmitri, Sleepwalker, everyone I cared about, living or dead. I prayed for myself, for the strength to resist the thoughts that drew me to a dark and unknown path. I was taught that a soul is something easily lost, a fact that made me question but also fear. Now, in the secret convection of my changing body, I sometimes imagined my soul melting away.

Every day Father Marconi walked along the garden path that surrounded the rectory, the tops of his shoes pushing forward under the long black cassock. As he walked, he held his breviary open with both hands, often shaping the words with his mouth as he read the Divine Office. I walked up the corridor between the church and the school and saw him pacing slowly, his breviary open. But he wasn't reading, he was looking sideways, scanning the schoolyard.

When I approached the garden, he lowered his eyes and began mumbling the words, turning to a section of path bordered by white chrysanthemums and a low brick wall.

"Good afternoon, Father," I said nonchalantly, pretending to almost not have noticed him.

"Hello, Jorie," he said. "Cold today."

"Yes, Father."

"Ready for Thanksgiving?"

"Not yet, Father," I said, as we started to walk along, side by side.

"Will you be cooking the turkey dinner by yourself?" he asked. He was interested in our life at home, and I sometimes caught him looking at me tentatively, as if I were a strange plant.

"Yes, Father. It's not hard; you just follow the directions in a cookbook."

"I'm sure it will be fine," he said. "Better than fine."

"No one complains. Well, my brothers make faces occasionally, but they always eat." Father Marconi smiled his small smile. I smiled mine. This was that certain point in every conversation, the point at which we either passed on with a wave or entered into our subject: my crisis in faith.

Sister Margaret Mary, alarmed by my skeptical comments on our religion test, had suggested that I speak with Father Marconi. "Take counsel with him" is what she said. Then she explained in a suitably awestruck voice that Jesuits were "broadly educated," so Father could answer all my questions. That was in September. With Sister's encouragement, we had talked often, but my faith was still on uncertain ground.

The reason was not as Sister Margaret Mary thought, that mine was a new faith with shallow roots not yet able to hold fast in the depths of my soul. The reason was that mine was a chosen faith and I took it seriously, far more seriously than my schoolmates who were raised Catholic and hardly gave it a thought. Having attended this Catholic school, I was attracted to the order and anchor of the Church's teachings and to the sheer beauty and power of its liturgy and music. And now, although I had not become a crusader, I had become a secret fanatic. I had no tolerance for classmates who whispered and giggled during Mass, or sneaked cookies during the three-hour fast before Communion. How could they knowingly offend God? They didn't believe as I believed. During the year I studied the precepts of the Church, I absorbed them into my heart; my every deed was weighed and guided by them. But it was not my deeds that troubled me, it was my thoughts. I had begun to question the objective truths that at first had attracted me, that seemed, at first, so full of sense and comfort. Now, I was relieved to have finally turned thirteen, having lied to Father Marconi for the last few months because I couldn't admit to being twelve. At thirteen, I had a right to serious doubts.

Our school uniform was a royal blue jumper with a white, short-sleeved blouse underneath. I liked wearing a uniform. It was easy to take care of, and it saved me the difficulty of acquiring clothes. I had always been outside the realm of whatever it was that enabled other kids to appear in proper order, but in my uniform I was as neat and correct as any other girl. Now, only my soul was in disarray.

"Father, I understand about Sanctifying Grace, but I don't think I can accept it."

"What exactly can't you accept?"

"That only those people with Sanctifying Grace at the moment of death will be saved. What about the person who lives a good life, but commits a mortal sin just before he gets killed in an accident? It's not fair that he's sentenced to hell forever."

Father Marconi closed his book and sighed. He was used to my questions, but he didn't give ready answers. He was careful; he took his time.

As I waited for his answer, the brick wall where I sat felt cold and hard beneath me, and I shifted my weight, uncrossing and recrossing my legs. Father Marconi stood close. I could feel the warmth of his legs against mine.

"God is merciful," he said.

Although Father Marconi was in his forties, his hair showed not a trace of gray. It was black and wavy like Persian lamb. His hands were large, long-fingered, and beautiful, with a scattering of dark hair that grew dense and disappeared under the cuff of his sleeve. I had watched these hands lift the Host during Mass, anoint foreheads, making the sign of the cross with his thumb. I had watched them turn gold-edged pages and write with bold strokes on the blackboard: *Agnus Dei*, Lamb of God, *qui tolis peccata mundi*, who takest away the sins of the world, *Miserere nobis*, Have mercy on us.

Recently I found myself thinking about Father Marconi's hands, how beautiful they were, how strong they would feel, how gentle. I would think of his hands outstretched during High Mass, the censer swinging like a pendulum from his fingers, the sweet smell of incense wafting up from his arms, his vestments gleaming with gold embroidery. I imagined his hands in candlelight, unbuttoning his white embroidered cuffs.

The next time I saw him he was standing beside the maple tree that had begun to shed its red-orange leaves on the rectory lawn. He stood in the warm afternoon light, a black silhouette; he was smiling. "And they say that Southern California doesn't have seasons! Just look at this," he said, laughing, dropping a bunch of crackling leaves into my hands. I was caught off-guard by this light and intimate mood and didn't quite know how to respond. The tone of our conversations had always been formal: teacher to student, adult to child, unequal. There was something comfortable in this formality, and safe. He must have sensed my uneasiness. "I guess we all welcome a change of season," he said, his face now self-conscious.

"Yes, Father," I said, letting some leaves fall from my hands.

"And what were you wondering about today, Jorie?" He was serious now and imposing in his black robes.

"Well," I said, "at home we've been reading about the Van Allen belts. You know, the bands of radiation that surround the earth."

"Yes I know," he said.

"Well the Church says the Virgin Mary was assumed into heaven, body and soul. How could she, without burning up? My father says it's impossible."

"Is that what he said?"

"Uh, not exactly. What he said was, 'She'd singe her tail feathers.'"

"Well, well," he said, laughing. "That sounds like him. You know, I met your father a few nights ago. A family had called me in to give the last rites to an old patient of his. Big family. Seems he takes care of them all."

"Did you talk to him?"

"Briefly. I don't think he liked me very much. He knows I'm your religion teacher. What puzzles me is why he allowed you to convert. He obviously doesn't believe in the Church. Why didn't he try to stop you—or did he?"

"No, he didn't try to stop me; he just said it was my decision."

"That's all?"

"And that I'd grow out of it."

"You think that is what's happening now, Jorie?" He placed his hand lightly on top of my head, as if checking my height. "You are growing," he said. "I've watched you."

I knew he watched me. I had known it for a long time.

"I want to believe, Father," I said. "It's just that I have questions."

It was true. I did want to believe. I wanted all the truths intact. I wanted the certainty of Truth. I felt if I could be certain of what sin was, I would not sin. If I knew for certain what I should do, I would do it. But my growing doubts gave me a freedom I didn't want; I had already had too much of it and knew its burden.

On the Wednesday before Thanksgiving I made a list: turkey, potatoes, onions, celery, cranberry sauce, canned peas, pumpkin pie. I had already gotten the bread from the Helm's truck, butter and whipping cream from the milkman. With the crisp twenty-dollar bills my father had given me, I walked the two miles to the market, then took a taxi back, loaded with groceries. I gave all the change I had to the taxi driver. It wasn't much.

When I got home the house was dark and empty. I turned on the lights and put on a record, Vivaldi's *Four Seasons*—mood music for Thanksgiving. I was used to spending afternoons and evenings alone. My father was seldom home. The fact of my father's separate life I had come to accept, and my brothers too were beginning to slip away into secret lives of their own. Jimmy came home first, usually after dark. Alex came home late, or he would stay out all night. We closed our eyes to Alex and opened them only when he acted "normal." Normal is what we required.

When our family was together, we were careful to stay on prescribed ground. This ground, its designation never acknowledged but understood, was sacred and essential. We talked about science and world events. My father talked about his patients. Some, like Elizabeth Bingham, we had known all our lives. What we didn't talk about was my faith (or crisis thereof), that I had chosen to become a Catholic, or what the boys were doing, in or out of school. We didn't talk about the fact that Alex no longer played the piano, except on rare occasions when we could coax him to play pieces for four hands. Jimmy had given up the piano gradually, as he started to dabble with other instruments—guitar and saxophone—but Alex had stopped playing suddenly. He had dropped it like something hot. We didn't talk about the times we found my father short of breath or stopping on the stairs, rubbing his shoulder, his lips dusky and wincing. "Pulled a muscle," he would say when we approached him. I believed him; it's what I wanted him to say. It even got to the point where I'd see my father stop to catch his breath and would walk right past him.

I understood this only years later, when I remembered a story my father told me. A patient had called him to make a house call to see her ill husband. She said her husband had vomited and was resting on the floor. When my father arrived, he saw that the man was dead. He had blown his brains out and the gun was still lying beside him.

"Didn't she see what happened?" I asked.

"No," my father said. "She couldn't see it, at least not at that moment."

• ◆ • ◆ •

On Thursday evening, we sat at the table, playing out a Thanksgiving dinner, as if there were nothing to talk about, nothing to notice. The table was decorated with red and gold leaves that I had picked up along the street. In the center of the table was a branch of pyracantha, laden with brilliant berries and crawling with little bugs I hadn't thought to wash off.

"Allow me, Senorita, on thees especial occasion," Jimmy said as he pulled out my chair. Only, as I started to sit, he pulled it out farther and watched with surprise when I slowly sank to the floor, without losing my balance.

"Good trick, Jorie," Alex said. It was good to see him smile.

Everything was normal: Pass the mashed potatoes. More turkey? Light or dark? We would not see my father slip a pill under his tongue. Alex did not smell of alcohol. And Jimmy did not make desperate jokes, one after the other. I cut the pumpkin pie into large wedges, topping them with overly whipped cream, almost butter. My father watched me as if I were a stranger, as if sizing me up. Then when the moment was right, he looked at me and said, "I met Friar Macaroni."

"I know. He told me," I said. I didn't mind that he was teasing about the name; that was normal.

"Did he tell you that I kicked him out of the room?"

"You did?"

"I had to. He almost scared poor ol' William to death. There I was trying to give William some encouragement, when Macaroni walks in, slaps down this big cross on the bed, then opens up his black kit. Ol' William's eyes almost popped out of his head! And then he started gasping for breath like it was his last. So, I kicked Macaroni out."

"And how's ol' William now?"

My father looked up from his pie with a satisfied smile. "Alive," he said.

Jimmy looked at my father, then at me. He had that canny look about him, his dimples all pulled in, his eyes squeezed into little mounds. "So Jorie's got a crush on Friar Macaroni," he said.

"Don't be ridiculous!"

"Then how come your face pops open when you hear his name?"

"It does not. And don't call him that. His name is not macaroni. It's Marconi, you know, like the inventor of the wireless."

"You have a crush on the inventor of the wireless?"

"I do not. And that's a terrible thing to say; he's a priest."

Putting down his fork, my father looked at me from under his bushy eyebrows. It was his Pay-attention-I'm-only-going-to-say-it-once look.

"A priest is a man, Jorie," he said. "Standard issue."

A week after Thanksgiving, it was record-breaking hot. Camellia buds failed to open and fell to the ground, brown as snails. Polar bear signs were hung outside the movie theaters—AIR COOLED, they said. The girls at school opened the top button of their uniform blouses. I opened two.

After school, Father Marconi and I walked along the side path where it was shady. Even in his black gabardine cassock, he always appeared cool. But on this day he pulled at his white collar and shook his shoulders now and then, as if his clothes were sticking to him.

"Father, do you really think Limbo is a place?" I asked.

"It could be a place, if you take the scripture literally," he said. His eyes were heavy on my chest, on the empty button holes. "Or," he continued in a halting voice, "it could be something like a state of mind, a plane of existence."

It was hard to reconcile what I had envisioned as a horde of empty-eyed souls, straining toward heaven, with a *plane of existence.* It was too hot to grasp anything like that. I focused instead on several chrysanthemums, weakened from the heat and lying face down on the path. I bent over to pick them up. I knew that Father Marconi was standing over me, looking down my blouse. I knew that he would before I bent down.

"Sister Margaret Mary says that the unbaptized go there—to Limbo," I said. "They just park there until Judgment Day."

Father Marconi reached over and softly slid the back of his hand along my neck. With his fingers pressing lightly against my skin, he slowly buttoned my blouse, starting at the top. I looked straight ahead, facing the black-covered chest and the chain with Christ on the cross.

I said, "That means that all the people who lived before Christ and most of the people who lived after him can't be with God. They just stay suspended."

"Jorie, why are you so concerned about Limbo?" he said, turning away.

"Alex and Jimmy aren't baptized and they don't want to be. Most of the people in the world aren't Christian. How can God reject them?"

For a long time we walked in silence, doubling back toward the shade when the sun beat from the west into our eyes. The only sound was the soft whoosh of his cassock. I loved the rhythm of it, a cadence of unearthly music. Several times he took a deep breath as if starting to say something, stopped, then continued on in silence. Our shadows grew long on the sidewalk. "I should go home, Father," I said.

"Yes," he said. "We can talk about this tomorrow."

I reminded him that we would have only a half day of school the next day because the nuns would be attending the funeral of their Mother General.

"I know," he said, sucking in another breath, letting it out. "I could come to your house in the afternoon, and we could talk." After a few steps, he stopped abruptly and pulled me over to the side of the path, keeping hold of my arm. His eyes were more intense than I had ever seen them. "You understand what I'm saying?"

"Yes."

"We'll be alone?"

"Yes."

"And you want me to come?"

"Yes."

The next day was still hot and it seemed the brief pause that was autumn had slipped by, leaving barely a mark in the year's cycle. The city smoldered under a layer of haze, making the Santa Clauses and giant snowflakes along Hollywood Boulevard seem incongruous and a lie. But the passage of days is relentless, even in Los Angeles, and we knew that winter was upon us, regardless of the temperature. To me, the problem of heat was immediate; I would have to run all the way home in the hot sun after school let out. I had to get there before he did.

At one o'clock the door bell rang. I was still breathing fast from running the three miles home, and from anticipation. The electricity of yesterday's touch had remained with me, as I had relived it over and over. With my hair still dripping from the shower, I ran down the stairs, pulling on a shirt and pants as I went.

"Hi," he said simply as I opened the door.

"Hello," I replied, barely able to get the word out, barely able to believe my eyes. This was all wrong! He wasn't wearing his black clothes, but stood there in garish plaid slacks and a V-neck shirt with one pearlized button in a loop. The shirt was not tucked in. The shoes he wore were brown and white with tassels, golfing shoes. In his hand, a little bunch of marguerites shyly wilted.

"Come in, Father," I said, unable to hide the surprise in my voice. It was not so much his clothes that shocked me; it was that he looked so ordinary. Here was a man you wouldn't look at twice on the street. He looked heavier and older, shorter and less substantial than the priest I walked with just the day before. This was not the man I had expected, certainly not the man I dreamed of. The man with whom I wanted my own secret life belonged with candlelight and the smell of beeswax, with his mystery cloaked in black cloth. Not this ordinary man. But now that he was there, what was I to do? Filled with dread, I led him into the living room and offered him a soft drink.

"Thank you, not now," he said. He smiled his small smile. I smiled mine. "Your father told me you play the piano."

"Yes," I said, backing up toward the piano bench.

"Will you play something for me?"

I nodded and sat down. A simple Bach came to my fingers, something from "The Well-Tempered Clavier." I could feel him behind me, the buckle of his belt hard against my back.

"Don't stop," he said when the piece was finished. I played something else while he lifted the hair away from my neck. "Beautiful," he said. "You love music, I can hear it in the way you play." He rested his hands on my back and neck, pressing himself between my shoulder blades.

"My mother was a musician," I said. "I inherited that from her, I guess."

"Music can be a sanctuary as well as a means of expression." His hands kneaded and gripped. "Do you feel that way?"

"Yes, Father."

"To me, music is a comfort," he said. "God gives us certain comforts . . ." Now we were walking slowly toward the couch and sat down. I felt his thigh against mine.

"You remember my question from yesterday, Father?" I asked lamely.

"Something about Limbo and baptism," he answered, his voice patient. "Do you want to talk about it?"

Yes I wanted to talk about it! I wanted to talk about anything—the weather, Christmas card sales, the miracle at

Lourdes—anything that would stall for time and allow me to escape. I could see the dark path before me and knew I wasn't ready to go.

"We don't have to interpret scripture literally," he said as he ran his cold hand along my cheek, my neck, and downward into my shirt. "Scholars disagree about the interpretation of the Gospels." I looked down at the tassels on his shoes, fighting back a nervous urge to laugh.

He moved closer, his arm raised to encircle.

"I have so many questions, Father," I said.

"Questions," he whispered.

"That noise—?"

"What?"

"The door—"

Just then, Jimmy came rattling through, closing the front door behind him with a bang. When he saw us sitting there, his jaw dropped straight down.

"What are you doing home!" he said.

"What are you doing home!" I answered, leaping to my feet. "I have the afternoon off."

Jimmy looked behind me, eyes blinking with surprise.

"Oh," I said. "This is Father Marconi. Father, this is my brother, Jimmy."

Jimmy's eyes fell on the blazing plaid slacks. "Hi ya," he said, staring shamelessly.

Only then did I notice a small figure eclipsed behind Jimmy's back. Slowly, she slid out from behind him, wide-eyed as a cornered cat. Her hair was in a "bubble," held back with a thin pink ribbon tied in the middle. One loop of the bow had come undone, and she was making little puffs with her lower lip, trying to blow it off her forehead. "Father?" she said in a tiny voice.

Trying to be matter-of-fact, but giving himself away with too many *uhs* and *ums*, Jimmy explained that I was his sister and that Father Marconi was my religion teacher.

"Oooh," she said.

"We can talk another time, Jorie," said Father Marconi as he walked toward the front door. His face was pale and his lips were drawn in as if he were chewing on them. I walked with him to the door and paused a moment before opening it. For the first time I saw him plainly, as someone with his own questions and doubts, and I felt his plight. I knew this was not just an embarrassment for him. He had come to the brink of a felony, as well as a mortal sin. I knew it was also my sin. And I had brought him to that brink and had said: Yes.

That night there was a cold front from the north and winds from the ocean swept over the city. We opened our windows to the crisp night air. Autumn had returned, unexpected. Jimmy didn't mention the incident with Father Marconi, nor did I. It merely seeped into the groundwater of things unspoken. But we had learned something about each other: Not only were we growing up, but also each of us was capable of a secret life that excluded the other.

For a while, Jimmy came home earlier. And like old times, we hiked in the hills behind our house and gathered pine cones sticky with resin. We went to see the reindeer in a corral on Wilshire Boulevard. That time together was reassuring and enough. Soon Jimmy returned to his other weekday life. "See you Sunday, old girl," he said.

"Okay," I said. "Gather ye rosebuds while ye may."

"Herrick," he said. "Now it is autumn and the falling fruit." Jimmy was standing now, his hand on his chest, projecting his voice: " . . . and the long journey towards oblivion . . ."

"Lawrence," I said. "Too dramatic. Not oblivion, good brother, if you take the Road to Mandalay. Come you back to Mandalay."

"Kipling," said Jimmy. "Mandalay! That's the place where memories stay."

"Who said that?"

"Me."

At three o'clock school let out. Disorderly lines of children spilled from the doors, a flood of little heads swirling in blue and white. Father Marconi stood close to the door and stepped out when he saw me. "I want to talk to you," he said. "Come walk with me." It was the first time we had spoken since that day at our house. Whether he had looked for me I didn't know, since I had been leaving right after school, trying to avoid him. But this meeting was not as awkward as I expected, and I followed him to the rectory path quite at ease.

The ground was bare along the flower borders, for the chrysanthemums had been cut to the ground, and nothing had been planted to replace them. As we walked around to the back of the garden, I listened to the whispering sound of his robe. Its rhythm was familiar and pleasant, as was his warmth beside me. Boldly, he took my hand in his. "I'm going away," he said.

"Where?"

"To a mission school we have in New Mexico. I asked to be transferred there."

I asked him when he would be leaving. "As soon as possible," he said. "The end of December."

I walked ahead of him for a while, then took his arm, knowing that we would never walk together again. At the gate, he held out his hand to say good-bye. It was an ordinary hand, a man's hand.

PART TWO

*A*LEX AND I SAT opposite each other in the small waiting room off the hospital corridor. I was tearing at the cuticle of my left middle finger and grinding my teeth. Alex was smoking. The ashtray was already filled with crushed and telescoped butts that gave off a musty carbon smell when he pushed another one into their midst. He hadn't spoken a word since he came back into the room. The doctor said we should go in one at a time. Alex had had his turn. Jimmy was with him now.

Jimmy was taking a long time and all I could think was that my father was going to die before I got to see him, before I could say good-bye, before he could tell me what I needed to know to make it through this. All I could think was that he was leaving us alone without instructions, without anyone to call, without the words I needed to hear, just once, to sustain me. I was fourteen years old and worried about myself.

I wasn't there when he clutched at his strangling heart, when his pulse turned violent and his lips darkened and he fell to the floor still holding the stethoscope he was carrying in such a hurry. He happened to be in this very hospital, making rounds. They said: Lucky for him.

Jimmy came into the room. His eyes were red, but dry in our company. "Two-fifteen," he said. "On the right."

The bed was cranked up so my father was almost sitting. An oxygen mask covered his face below his eyes, which blinked when I took his hand. He struggled to keep them open. A nurse came in to check the green oxygen tank by the bedside and told me I had to go, my father needed rest. I told her No I just got here and she looked at me as if I might kill him with my selfishness, so I left without saying good-bye. I said, "I'll be back when you've rested, Dad." I said this as a way of buying time.

Alex was sure my father was going to die. He was full of steely resignation. "We have to stick together," he said. Jimmy believed he could save him by sheer force of will. "He's going to be all right," he said. "I know he'll make it. He's going to pull through." Jimmy didn't want to hear about sticking together. He didn't want to think about what we would do if our father died; my asking this annoyed him. He said we didn't have to think about it. Dad's going to be fine. When Alex talked about getting jobs and renting part of the house, I sided with Jimmy. "Let's not worry about it yet," I said. Alex's plans were spinning ahead too fast and I didn't like them imposed on me. I knew he was preparing himself for the worst, but I saw this as an invitation for the fear to fulfill itself. I wanted to hold to the notion that hope would fulfill itself, if for no other reason than it makes the present bearable.

Visiting hours were over. I asked the nurse if I could see my father now. She said No, she had already made a concession once because I was underage. No more concessions. "You've already seen him once today," she said, as if she'd done me a favor. I glared at her. I knew I didn't feel as grateful as I should have.

After we waited two hours for him, Dr. Michaelman walked into the room pulling the stethoscope from his neck. He was a small man, compared to my father, and much younger. He wore round horn-rimmed glasses and a crumpled suit. His eyes were dark but not brown. He was uncomfortable when he saw me looking at him; he blushed. This was the first time I'd seen him up close, but I recognized his name from the card on his annual gift of Courvoisier: *Happy Holidays, Tom. Thanks for your confidence. Leonard Michaelman.*

"Well, kids," he said. "Your father is resting comfortably."

We looked at him incredulously for using that trite expression on us, for the condescension.

"Uh, well, kids," he started over, "it's too early to say for sure, but I think he's going to be okay. We don't know yet just how much damage there is to the heart muscle. But he's stable now and that's encouraging."

At home in my own bed I tried to imagine what my father felt like trying to sleep in a strange room, sitting up, the oxygen bubbling, footsteps clicking down the hallway, his heart beating uncertainly in his chest. The next day I found out. "I slept soundly," he said, barely able to articulate the *esses* with his thick tongue. "Best night's sleep I've had in years." I must have looked surprised. "Morphine," he explained. He told me not to worry and dozed off.

A high, plaintive sound came from far down the hall. It repeated and repeated until it seemed almost mechanical, but there was breath attached to it and a kind of disembodied pain. I didn't want to hear it, but it moved insistently down the hallway. When I got up to close the door, my father mumbled something into his oxygen mask. "What, Dad?" I said, touching his shoulder and bending close to his face. I coveted every word.

"Tomorrow," he said.

"Tomorrow? What about tomorrow?" Now I saw that his face was pale and his lips were dark beneath the mask. I shook his shoulder. "Dad, what about tomorrow?"

He took a sudden deep breath. "Oh! I'll call them. I'll take care of it tomorrow," he said.

I thought about Andrew Haraty and the other people in his life who we pretended didn't exist, and thought he might have wanted to call them. "Do you want me to call anyone for you, Dad?" He didn't answer.

The wailing sound from the hall had stopped. In its place a breeze was blowing, cooling the silence. I didn't want to disturb him, but his breathing didn't seem right. I shook his shoulder again. "Dad," I said, "what about tomorrow—you're going to take care of something?" I didn't really think he was trying to say something or that he was thinking about tomorrow. I just wanted to hear his voice and his breath, to be reassured that he was still there, hanging on.

Then he seemed suddenly awake and pulled the mask down, breaking the tubing. "The Wayward Wind," he said to me with no recognition in his eyes and violently pushed the side table away.

I reached over him and pulled the call light for help. "Hang on, Dad," I said. "Please, stay quiet. Stay. Please."

15

HOUSE ARREST

E CAME HOME ON a Tuesday. The sun was shining, birds sang, and great dumplings of clouds floated in a blue blue sky. Old Jetsam waited at the door with slowly blinking eyes, proving that cats have a special sense about these things—or so it seemed that day, when for the first time in three weeks, she pulled her old self up from her favorite pillow to wait for my father at the top of the steps.

They brought him home in an ambulance and carried him up to his room on a stretcher so he didn't have to climb all the stairs. I had prepared his room with extra pillows, a tray for water and medicines, a sprig of honeysuckle in a jelly jar, and a stack of medical journals I thought he'd like to catch up on. He had already agreed that I could stay home from school for as long as he needed me. Dr. Michaelman had issued strict orders that he could not work for six weeks and we were to make sure that he rested and didn't get into mischief. My father thought that was funny. Jimmy and I had a conference about how we could prevent him from getting restless. There had never been a time when my father had spent more than two days in a row at home, and even that was rare. Six weeks at home was almost unimaginable. We decided the best thing to do was to keep him entertained.

It wasn't hard at first. He wasn't strong and slept more than we thought he would. He took a lot of medicines, and my main concern was that in his drowsiness, he would bump into things. With the anticoagulant he was taking, there was danger of hemorrhage; already splotches of dark purple dappled his arms and legs. With each new splotch, I felt a small defeat. "Don't worry," he said to me one day, "I've stopped taking that stuff."

In keeping with our plan to keep my father entertained, Jimmy and I devised some kind of performance almost every day. I gave him a program early in the afternoon so he would have something to look forward to. One evening, for instance, we put on a "Beat" show. After dinner, he settled in his favorite chair with strong coffee and a bowl of black walnut ice cream, his favorite. To set the mood I dressed all in black and we played Ferlinghetti's recording of his poem, "Tentative Description of a Dinner to Promote the Impeachment of President Eisenhower" with Cal Tjader on drums. We talked Alex into playing a Thelonious Monk piece on the piano. After he was finished, I sat next to him, slumped, and stared at the floor. That was Jimmy's cue to make his entrance. He was dressed in a pullover sweater, baggy pants, and sandals. He stood between the piano bench and my father's chair and lowered his head pensively:

Jimmy: Fried umbrellas. Wear your carrots. Like nothing has meaning. Don't shoot the wombat.

Jorie: Like what do you want? Do what you want. Where is it?

(a dissonant chord, followed by a low B-flat)

Jimmy: Like isn't it obvious? Like the whole universe is a question, a sea of wondering, an ocean of why, and we're floating in solitude, like the essence of oneness, floating in pure forever—

(descending chromatic scale, ending in low G and C: d'dum. Jimmy picks up bongo drums, starts a syncopated beat.)

Jorie: . . . Drifting unborn, until you hit the waves and swells of time . . .

Jimmy: Hit the rolling, yawing swells and you puke into existence—

My father pressed his shoulders back into the chair and smiled. "That's so beautiful," he said.

"Beauty is," Jimmy called out.

"IS is," I said. (a minor chord with the soft pedal)

Jimmy sighed deeply, "Maybe. It depends."

"This is too deep for me," my father said. "I'm going to bed."

"Are you *beat?*" I asked. He laughed.

Jimmy said: "Groan."

After my father went up to his room, Jimmy and I looked at each other with silent congratulation. Another day to recovery. Another day without mischief.

I looked forward to the times Dr. Michaelman stopped in. His visits relieved the monotony of my father's workless days and seemed to cheer him up.

"You're taking good care of him, Jorie," Dr. Michaelman said. "Keep it up and he'll be just fine."

I liked it when he came in his casual clothes. He wore them more comfortably than a suit. On his free time, he wore a bomber-style jacket and khaki slacks. He wore crisp cotton shirts with the sleeves rolled up. I liked the way the hair lay flat and smooth over his forearm. I liked the darkness of the hair that peeked up from his open collar. My heart beat fast as I imagined how this hair on his chest might feel pressed against my own chest. Thinking of Dr. Michaelman brought on the same sensations that I'd experienced at first with Father Marconi, only now they were more specific and less dependent on the gothic atmosphere I'd associated with a priest. Now I didn't need the image of candlelight flickering on a rectory cell wall, or the unfastening of black robes. I thought about Dr. Michaelman's arms around me and kissed the back of my own hand, imagining his lips. I thought about him as I pressed my thighs together, until I was able to think of something else. I didn't think he was handsome, but I often found myself thinking about him with a tangible sense of yearning. I knew that he noticed me, too.

The best thing about my father's illness was his confinement to the house. *House arrest*, he called it. It meant that for the first time in my memory, we had a lot of time to talk. I served him lunch outside, then we stretched out on lounge chairs, basked in the sun, and chatted as if we were on vacation.

"So," he said, "have you thought about what you're going to do?"

"Oh Dad, you know Jimmy and I still want to be doctors. Only, I don't want to be a surgeon. I want to use my mind."

He laughed a little without opening his eyes. "Ah, the rivalry has begun," he said. My father's fair skin glowed in the sun. I thought I detected some color infusing it, the first hint of a suntan. I'd never seen him with some color in his skin.

"I meant I'd like to do research. I didn't mean—"

"No, you're absolutely right," he said. "Surgery is not the field for a woman."

"I know," I agreed, not knowing why, really, but feeling proud of myself for having made what he thought was the right decision.

My father had never looked so relaxed, as he sat with his feet up, his face to the sun. Nor had he ever seemed as accessible as he did then, sitting there with nothing to do and no place to go. There were so many things I wanted to ask about, things that had always run through our lives in a river of silence—my mother, his Chinese wife, his other women, his other children, the connections we didn't know about, the friends we never saw—but I didn't dare. It was important to keep his heart at peace.

"Don't dwell on the past," he said, as if he knew what was on my mind.

"Your life is ahead of you. Now's the time to look ahead, to think of the future." He didn't say the words, but I felt that he loved me at that moment. It wasn't the first time, or the only time I'd felt it, but it was rare. As we spent these particular days together, I felt his love almost tangibly, by a certain reverberation in the way he smiled when I fluffed his pillow, or complimented me on the food, or the respectful attention he gave me when I spoke.

"I was thinking I'd like to go away to college," I said.

"Where?" my father asked.

"I don't know, another country. I'd like to be somewhere completely different. I'd like to have an accent."

He opened his eyes and squinted at me in the bright light. "I would hope you'd have a better reason than that," he said. "Well, you can go wherever you want. I'll support you if you make the grades. You'll have all the education you can handle. But as far as deciding what you should do, you have plenty of time to think about it." He closed his eyes and turned his face into the sunlight and I did the same. I wanted to enjoy the warmth forever. I didn't want to open my eyes. I didn't want to see his swollen legs. I didn't want to hear his labored breath. Slowly my eyes blinked open and I stared at his doughy ankles with a blank mind.

A blank mind wouldn't work with Alex. Alex could not be ignored. One day he came home with an Apache haircut. It was the opposite of a Mohawk. A trough was shaved in the middle of the head, front to back, exactly where in a Mohawk the hair was retained and the rest of the head shaved. On Alex, it looked like a pink road in a red forest.

"Why do you have to pull this crap now?" Jimmy's voice was angry. "Dad's supposed to be recovering and he doesn't need aggravation. What're you trying to do?"

"Mind your own business," Alex said.

"You look like a fool."

"Who're you calling a fool!" I heard Alex shout, followed by the sound of a chair scraping the floor.

"Excuse me," Jimmy said. "I should've said CLOWN."

Their voices carried up the stairway; I was afraid if they got any louder my father would hear. "Hey, pipe down," I called down the stairs.

"You gonna throw that, tough guy?" Jimmy's voice was taunting. "Stupid punk."

"Who're you calling stupid!"

"Who else in this room looks like a tractor ran over his head—"

When I heard the sound of glass breaking, I ran downstairs to see what happened. Jimmy was standing in front of the shattered window, a shocked expression on his face. "You could've killed me," he said. "That bookend was solid bronze. You could've killed me!"

Alex's face went ghostly pale. Tears welled up in his eyes. Jimmy lunged at him, knocking him backwards, slamming him hard against the wall. Then they were rolling on the floor, white knuckles gripped below red faces. The air was thick with their violence. I started to cry, but held back my tears and pulled at their arms, trying to separate them.

"Stop it, stop it," I said, grabbing at Jimmy's shirt. But they continued to roll, kicking and straining to pry loose, banging each other's head against the floor or legs of furniture whenever they got the chance.

"Enough!" My father's voice came down on us like a clap of thunder. We pulled ourselves up from the floor. The boys panted for breath. Their faces, streaming with tears, were already swollen and discolored around their necks, lips, and cheek bones.

My father's face was pale; a moist film glistened above his mouth. "I told you boys to settle your differences with the gloves on. You know better than this." He glanced at Jimmy then turned to Alex and looked down and up his scrawny, disheveled form, ending with the gaping swath that separated one side of his head from the other. "Don't think that bothers me, Alex," he said. "Hair grows. What bothers me is that you waste yourself. I don't care if you shave your head or paint your face purple. I don't care about that. You understand?"

16

APOLOGIZED TO DR. Michaelman for not having any milk for his coffee. We had run out. He insisted on taking me to the market. "Is it okay, Dad?" I asked.

"That's sporting of you, Leonard," he said. "Since you're the one who won't let me drive."

My shopping list was divided by aisles. I knew how our market was organized and I prided myself in sweeping up and down each aisle in perfect efficiency, knowing what was there, never having to go back for anything. My father and the boys were impatient when we went shopping, so I'd learned to be quick. "That's what I call an organized girl," Dr. Michaelman said.

On the way home, he said I looked worried. Everything would be all right, he assured me. I told him about my brothers' fighting. I told him Alex wasn't really tough, but he was trying hard to come off that way. His teachers had called him a "delinquent." Jimmy didn't help; he just laughed it off. "You worry too much about the boys," Dr. Michaelman said as he helped me carry the boxes of groceries up the service stairs along the side of the house. "They'll be all right."

"But I'm afraid Dad won't stay home and recover," I said. "He doesn't like discordancy." He smiled back at me, his chin resting on a sack of potatoes.

"Discordancy? What kind of word is that?"

"I don't know, a Mackinnon kind of word, I guess. My father always gave us words when we were kids."

From the corner of his eye he looked at me, just from the corner. I could feel the pressure of his gaze on my face, my shoulders, the tee shirt I tied at the midriff to show off my waist. "When you were kids—that was a long time ago, I suppose . . ."

I hiked up the box with my knee, getting a better grip on it, and looked him full in the face. "Long enough," I said. "I'm not a kid anymore."

I worried about what effects the boys' fighting would have on my father's recovery. Certainly, it would upset him and raise his blood pressure, his adrenaline, and whatever else should not be raised when recovering from a heart attack. And, it would make him want to escape into work, a flight that would probably kill him. So Jimmy promised to avoid Alex or at least to restrain himself when they crossed paths, and we redoubled our efforts to be entertaining, a task that grew harder each day. Our repertory was wearing thin. Bach partitas put him to sleep, as did readings of poetry or novels. He liked charades, he liked Jimmy's impersonation of Elvis Presley and our José Greco routine (although it was hard on the dining room table), and the mixture of Jellos I made to look like stained glass, but now, more often than not, a pall of boredom covered his face and his pale gray eyes fixed longingly on the door.

"What's that?" I asked one afternoon, putting down a pitcher of lemonade.

My father closed the top of a brown metal file box. "Nothing," he said.

I knew what it was and I knew where it was from.

"You've been to your office."

"No," he said, "Hazel brought it."

"I didn't know she was here."

"Hmmm . . . Saturday. You weren't home." He was tapping the top of the box with his finger.

"Did Dr. Michaelman say you could work?"

"I don't need his permission," he said quietly. "Nor yours."

That afternoon he called his favorite patients. First Elizabeth Bingham, the elderly woman who had been with him since his training days at County Hospital, whom he treated for diabetes and hypertension: *Elizabeth? Dr. Mackinnon. Have you been checking your urine? What do you mean you're out of sticks, I gave you a bunch last time. . . . It's been that long? . . . Oh. . . . Yes, I'm much better, good as new. . . . When can you come in?* Then he called Mrs. Braun, who with arthritic hands baked him pfeffernusse every Christmas, and Mr. Chen, who was dying of stomach cancer. And he called Mr. Domlevski, a hypochondriac and translator of obscure Polish poets. Alphabetically, he picked out the most beloved and talked to each one and for the first time since he came home from the hospital, he seemed entirely himself.

It was not surprising then when he left for his office the next morning, three weeks ahead of schedule. And I returned to school, reassured by his proclamation of recovery (remarkable) and his promise (solemn) to start back slowly. I was taking all solid classes in my second semester at Our Lady of Lourdes High School and had a lot to catch up on. Only I couldn't really catch up; I had just enough time to cram for midterms and was soon overtaken by an exhilarating panic.

I remember bright days. I walked to school in dazzling sun and walked home westward into a white glare. Palm trees cast feathery shadows on the sidewalk and crows swooped down with palm fruit in their beaks, the sun reflecting blue off their wings. When I got home, I sat by a window to study and watched a bar of light slowly pass over my books to the floor and up the wall. My mind rattled with "The Rhyme of the Ancient Mariner," algebraic equations, French vocabulary, and the Magna Carta; I tried to fix them clearly in my brain. And prayed for multiple choice. Not literally. Although we prayed at school—our voices joined in rote incantations—for the past year I had prayed very little privately. More and more, praying seemed to me a futile exercise. When I watched Sister Germaine writing out the essay questions on the blackboard, I doubted whether praying would have helped. It was better to have studied, or at least, to have crammed.

That year, kids were enthusiastic about cramming of another sort. A record was set by cramming twenty-two college boys into a phone booth; forty students crammed into a Volkswagen bug. I didn't pay much attention. I didn't pay much attention either to the squealing hysteria over Elvis Presley, or civil disobedience in Alabama, or even to the new Russian intercontinental missile and the craze for home bomb shelters, except to learn the song: *When the air becomes uranious/ We will all go simultaneous/ Yes we all will go together when we go.* I sang this song without thinking. I sang it while washing dishes, I sang it while proving equations, I sang it until the words were drained of all but their rhythm and the rhythm had a way of driving everything to the periphery of my mind, leaving a space as blank as the eye of a hurricane.

Within a week my father was back to his usual routine: twelve hours a day, six days a week. Then there were the babies, which could strike at any time. It frightened me that he had gone back to work too early, but I tried not to think about it. I would hear his car pull into the garage when he got home and what seemed like a long time later, I would hear his key in the front door. He must have stopped several times on the stairs to catch his breath. For the first few days I waited, listening with a cocked ear for the sound of his key in the latch, but I didn't like how the waiting made my heart pound. Then, after a while, the long interval between garage and front door didn't seem so alarming; it simply became one more thing I didn't pay much attention to.

Alex shaved his whole head. In two weeks his head looked like a fuzzy cherry. I thought he looked cute. Girls were calling.

Jimmy won a statewide contest for a science project. He had successfully bred a line of nude mice. The appeal of a nude mouse, or *nu nu mouse,* is not only that it's hairless, but that it has congenital absence of the thymus gland. Fascinated by this and the mouse's other immune deficiencies, Jimmy had carefully written a detailed genetic record and analysis of the breeding program. He went to Sacramento to receive his award and stayed a few days. I don't think my father even noticed he was gone; nothing was said. When Jimmy came home, I wanted him to leave the award in the kitchen, in a place where my father would see it, but he just shrugged me off. "It would have been nice if he'd been there, but, it's history," he said. He sounded glib.

"I'm sure you're disappointed."

"Naw," he said. "You know, Dad's busy surviving."

"Still . . ." I wanted Jimmy to admit he was disappointed, or mad, or something. Anything. If he never admitted to feeling bad, never admitted to wanting or needing, then neither could I. We always had to act as if we understood, or didn't care.

Jimmy looked at me impatiently, like I was some sort of weakling. "You know what Dad always says: what we do in school is for ourselves, not for him." His voice wasn't so convincing, but I wouldn't push it.

I couldn't find Jetsam anywhere. Jimmy said she was out "catting around," but I knew something had happened to her. Since the first time my father had placed the tiny Jetsam in my hands, she had curled up in some corner of my day. Now, old as she was, she still came around every evening for a pet and a purr. Alex said she had gone away to die; she didn't want to bother anyone. Then Jimmy said, "Maybe coyotes." I looked for her every day for two weeks, scanning the whole neighborhood and the hill behind our house. I hated to think of her dying alone; I hoped she hadn't felt any pain.

I dreamed I was hiding from Dr. Michaelman. I was in a dark basement and could see the shadows of his feet moving against the line of light under the door. He rattled the door knob. I couldn't remember whether I had locked it. Then I reached up to hold the doorknob against his grip, to prevent it from turning. I tried to press the lock button, but the knob was turning hard, then the door started to push open. I woke up.

It was five o'clock in the afternoon when the phone rang. I wasn't thinking about my father because he never called or came home before seven-thirty. As I picked up the phone I was expecting a call for Jimmy or Alex. I was thinking of an excuse, in case it was a girl asking for Jimmy. He didn't like the girls who chased him. But then I remembered I didn't have to make an excuse; he wasn't home. Alex didn't like girls who phoned him either, but he took their calls anyway. I said hello in an unfriendly voice.

"Jorie," Dr. Michaelman said. "Jorie . . ." He seemed unable to continue.

I was gripped by a feeling of panic, but I held my breath until it passed. "It's Dad, isn't it?" I said.

"He hasn't regained consciousness," Dr. Michaelman said. "We're doing everything we can. You understand how it is—"

"Yes."

I didn't know where the boys were. I left them a note to meet me at the hospital and called a taxi.

For two hours I sat in the corner of his room, facing the window and watching the play of reflections in the dark glass. I could see the doorway behind me and the transparent figures passing by—people in groups of two or three with faces close together and linked arms, nurses pushing carts with squeaking wheels. Occasionally, white, legless forms would float through the reflected door over to the bedside and busy their arms in the dim light. Once, a large face appeared over my shoulder. I breathed on the glass and it disappeared in a fog.

Jimmy's reflection appeared in the doorway. I watched the blue plaid shirt float over to where my father lay in dark, bubbling stillness. "Dad? Dad," he said. He stood there for a long time before he noticed me. "Hey old girl," he said. "Did he wake up?"

"No."

"Not yet," he said. He reached into the pocket of his shirt and pulled out a Baby Ruth bar; it was slightly squashed. He tore open the top, gave me half, then walked over to the bed-side and sat down.

I stared into the dark glass, singing softly: *When the air becomes uranious/ We will all go simultaneous/ Yes we all will go together when we go. . . .* A blue reflection hung like a flag in the upper corner of the window. Jimmy's face was cupped in his hands and propped up by his elbows. Far into the night

I watched the plaid reflection next to the hospital bed and waited for my father's eyes to open.

It had stormed overnight and patches of clouds still hung over the city, some gray, some glaring white in the rain-washed air. On the streets and sidewalks, puddles glinted in the sun. Alleyways smelled sharply of mildew. I walked fast in the brisk afternoon and pushed through the hospital doors into the warm corridor. A janitor smiled a greeting as I passed, then returned to mopping shoe tracks from the polished floor. By the time I reached the hall to my father's room, I was warm again, but my hands had not lost their chill. From a distance I could see that someone was in his room. I couldn't see who it was, only a broad back in a tan coat.

The man was sitting beside my father's hospital bed and stood up when I entered the room. "Hello," he said, turning in my direction. "I'm sure you don't remember me."

It was impossible to answer at first; my breath had caught in my throat. I remembered him well. Long ago we'd called him *da Boss*. I hadn't seen him since I was just a small child, but I recognized him as if I'd seen him yesterday. And I felt the same ineffable sense of wonder and danger that I'd felt as I peered from behind the legs of Max, in the dark hall of our old rented house. I remembered the large-bellied body, the dark eyes slashed deep into the round, jovial face. His hair was gray now, and thinner, with a dome of skin shining at the top of his head, but he had the same wide smile that showed no teeth and the same eyes that belied the smile.

"I remember you," I said. "You're the man who sent me a doll."

"What a memory!" he laughed. His eyes passed over me, up and down and up again. "You've grown up to be a real looker."

I could feel the heat rise in my face, but I didn't want him to think he made me uneasy. I turned in the direction of my father's bed. "How are you feeling, Dad?" I said. Pretending to ignore the gangster's leering eye, I walked past him and stood beside the bed railing. My father was awake but drowsy. He nodded then closed his eyes.

The Boss leaned toward my ear and spoke softly, placing his smooth, manicured hand on my shoulder. "I've come to express my wishes for your father's good health," he said.

I didn't look at him. His hand, heavy and hot, moved away.

"Take care, Doc," he said. "We expect you to be up and around soon. Take a vacation when you feel better. Why don't you take this pretty little girl with you?" He was still looking at me as he picked up his hat and flicked the brim with his finger. He said, "It's Marjorie, isn't it?"

I nodded slightly and stared straight ahead, clutching the bed rail.

After that day, I dreaded running into the Boss when I visited my father. But I didn't see him again in the hospital room. Once I saw him from a distance in the hall and ducked into a doorway to avoid him. It seemed odd that he should surface now, after all this time. I wondered if he'd been part of my father's life all along, the other part, the larger part that had nothing to do with us. At one time, I would have been jealous and would have wanted to know who was the culprit who had stolen my father's time and attention and fidelity, which I laid claim to. But now, the revelations themselves were more threatening than my father's absence and I simply preferred not to know.

17

AS OFTEN AS I COULD

I SAW MY FATHER as often as I could after school and waited until six o'clock, when I knew there was a good chance of getting a ride home with Dr. Michaelman. After his office hours and after making rounds, he reserved the end of his day to visit with my father so they would have time to talk.

The first time I rode with him, it had been a week since my father's second heart attack and I knew Dr. Michaelman's schedule fairly well.

"Bye, Dad. See you soon," I said when I heard the sound of Dr. Michaelman's light, quick steps and gathered up my school books and sweater.

He smiled at me on his way in. "You don't have to leave on my account," he said. "You can wait outside for just a minute."

"It's okay. I was leaving anyway." I started to walk down the hallway at a pace so slow, one foot barely passed the other. I went to the ladies' room and combed my hair, then stopped by the little gift shop to buy a candy bar and browsed through the cards. I planned to be just about at the front reception desk when I would hear his steps again, hurrying in my direction.

"Jorie," Dr. Michaelman called out in a stifled voice. "Do you need a lift home?"

"Thank you," I said. As I had planned.

The inside of his car smelled of leather and pipe tobacco: sweet, male smells. Not the medicinal smells of my father's car. Not the perfume and popcorn smells of a car that transported women or children. A plastic mat covered the plush carpet under my feet. "Is this a new car?" I asked.

"Yes," he said, leaning forward and patting the dashboard. "It's actually my first new car. I got it to celebrate my fifth year in private practice. When I got this car, I felt I had finally arrived." The corners of his mouth kicked up in a satisfied way, as if the fact of his having arrived had just struck him. "Before this I had an old Pontiac, which I bought used. It had over a hundred thousand miles on it and I wondered if it would last until I could afford a new car. It was slow getting the practice started, but I'm pretty busy now. . . . Your dad's been a great help to me."

"He thinks you're a great cardiologist, especially since you pulled him through."

"Well, I'd like to take all the credit, but he's amazing. Most people wouldn't have made it, especially this last time. I had a case just last week—"

"Uh, excuse me—"

"You don't want to hear about it?"

"Sure," I said. "But you passed the turn. You were supposed to turn on that little street going up the hill, remember?" That would happen every time he drove me home; he'd get involved in what he was saying and miss the street. Dr. Michaelman talked more than any person I had ever met. He was the small, unsilent type.

When he pulled up in front of our house that first time we sat for a while as he recounted the details of his latest cases. I listened to the long strands of words, skeins of words, winding and interlocking. He wrapped himself in words; he covered himself. "You're easy to talk to," he said. "Most girls don't want to listen to shop talk." I didn't wonder. He had, in this long nonstop monologue, talked of nothing except arteriosclerosis, ventricular hypertrophy, Q-R-S complexes, and various acidotic effects, of which I understood nothing. But I listened intently and tried to follow as well as I could.

"Do you talk to a lot of girls?" I asked. His tie had slipped to the side and his shirt gaped between two buttons. I imagined putting my fingers there.

"Not very many," he said wistfully. "I guess I'm not much of a ladies' man. Besides, you know how it is, medicine doesn't allow much time for a private life. Most women can't understand that. They want your undivided attention. My ex-wife, for instance, she'd get upset when I was late for dinner—which I suppose was fairly often—and she was furious when I'd have to leave a movie or a concert or had to cancel weekend plans."

"Didn't she get used to it?"

"I guess not. After two years she got fed up."

"Then what happened?"

"She left." He reached out and stroked my arm. "You're a good listener, you know that?"

As I turned toward the door, I looked back into his glasses. Dots of light from the street lamp sparkled back at me; he kept his glasses that clean. "You're a good talker," I said. "Thank you for the ride."

My father's recovery was slower this time. The transitory haltings of his heart extended into congestive heart failure. His body raised havoc with its fluids, its electrolytes, its enzymes. He stayed in the hospital. I didn't see him every day; Jimmy and I tried to alternate our visits. Alex would go erratically, sometimes several days in a row, then not for a week. We never knew when he would show up but he always did, circling the parking lot on his Vespa motorscooter and parking in the ambulance entrance. He always walked up the exterior stairs, the fire escape near my father's room, hitting every step with his boots.

"Gestapo's coming," my father said.

"Alex," I said.

My father turned toward the door and smiled until the leather jacket appeared.

Alex said, "How're you feeling, Dad?" He paced around the room a few times.

My father answered, "Fine."

"You're okay then," Alex said, sticking his fingers into the Venetian blinds and looking out the window. "Yeah, well, I'm gonna split."

My father adjusted the pillow behind his back, shifting his position under the thin blanket. "Try the elevator," he said.

On the way home from visiting my father, Dr. Michaelman took me to Tiny Naylor's for a hamburger and deep-dish boysenberry pie. He ordered everything at once and asked the car hop for inside trays. We sat in the car with bulging cheeks and talked without stopping. He talked about the new methods of cardiac resuscitation, about drowning and respiratory arrest. I nodded appreciatively. "I like a girl with a good appetite," he said when I finished my chocolate malt and hamburger, the pickle, French fries, the parsley. I agreed to ice cream, even though it made the pie cold.

"Want anything else?" he asked when I'd finished that.

I shook my head. "I couldn't possibly."

"I feel so comfortable with you," he said. A serious look overtook his face and he reached over to push a lock of hair away from my cheek. His fingers tugged lightly as he tried to hook it behind my ear, but it kept springing out. I was embarrassed and didn't look up. Finally he let go and brushed my ear with his finger, his eyes and finger intently following its curve down and up. "A perfect ear," he said, then turned on the headlights for the car hop to collect our trays.

In the car, parked not far from our house, Dr. Michaelman continued talking.

I wondered why I'd thought at first he wasn't good looking. I didn't know his age exactly, but he wasn't all that old, thirty-five at most. His eyes were the deep green of the California coast. When he took off his glasses, you could see the curl of his eyelashes and a gleam that seemed to come from deep within the irises. And his straight, thinning hair wasn't so bad. Even when he wasn't smiling, his lips turned up at the corners, hinting of something pleasant going on in his mind. It took me a while to see what was attractive about him. I could still feel the rub of his finger along my ear.

"I feel comfortable with you, too," I said. It was true. I trusted him. He seemed unmysterious to me, and undangerous. Perhaps it was the forthright way in which he talked about everything, himself included. All the details of his daily work, which patients got better, which got worse, what he prescribed and why, his preparation for the cardiology board exams, his parents who had moved from Englewood, New Jersey, to Coral Gables, how they doted on him, his older brother, an oral surgeon with a wife and three children, how they teased him about being single. He wanted me to know all about him, everything.

"You think I talk too much, don't you?" he said, laughing. "I can tell by that little smile on your face. I can tell by that little grin in your eyes. I don't know, there's something about you. I don't usually talk this much, honestly." He slid from behind the steering wheel and faced me. "How old are you now?" he said.

"Almost seventeen," I lied, feeling childish for putting it that way. I waited for a laugh that didn't come.

"God help me," he said softly.

•◆•◆•

I was surprised to see Jimmy at the hospital on "my" day. He and my father stopped talking when I walked in. My father said he'd be discharged from the hospital soon. When I asked him when, he said he didn't know, but soon. "I'm glad," I said. "I'll take better care of you this time."

I didn't know how long Jimmy had been there, but he seemed intent on staying for as long as I stayed. And when Dr. Michaelman arrived, Jimmy announced that we were going on home and so we did. The next time I came to visit, Jimmy was there too. The time after that, Alex was there and drove me home on his Vespa. "What happened to alternating days?" I asked.

"Dad wants more company," Alex said. "He'll be breaking out soon, any day now, maybe any minute."

"I know he'll be coming home soon. Why are you making it such an issue?"

"You know," he said sternly. "Be prepared."

Another week passed, but my father was still not discharged. He continued to have pulmonary edema and chest pain on exertion. He said they didn't know how to juggle his medicines.

I wasn't sure if the boys were doing it on purpose, but I suspected they were. They must have sensed something, for without being overtly protective, they had successfully prevented me from getting a ride with Dr. Michaelman. So as I sat, Indian-style, behind an opened newspaper in the hospital lobby, I couldn't help but smile. I could smell my body, freshly bathed and doused with *4711*. I smelled of lemons. I was sitting at a perfect vantage point from the entrance: far enough back not to be noticed, close enough to spot Dr. Michaelman when he was leaving the hospital. A few minutes earlier I had surreptitiously watched Jimmy breeze past and now I watched his back as he pushed out the large glass door, letting a man on crutches pass in front of him. After he left, I stood near the reception desk and waited.

We ate hamburgers in the car. I hadn't known you could specially order a hamburger medium-rare, which was the way I liked it. The outside was dark and crusty and the inside was faintly pink. When I bit into it, juice ran through my fingers, down my arm, onto my sleeve. I ate the whole thing. Dr. Michaelman dipped a napkin into his water and dabbed at my sleeve until it was clean. He gave me some of his French fries, putting them into my mouth. He said he didn't want to wash my hands again and laughed. I ordered hot boysenberry pie and watched the steam rise from the golden crust. I gave him my ice cream, spooning it from the top of my pie onto a bread plate. He ate it slowly and licked the melted ice cream from his lips.

At some point between the ice cream and the check, within the span of a minute, his mood changed. The change made me feel suddenly alert, as if he had asked me something. At his temple an artery pulsed.

"Do you mind if we stop by my office on the way home?" he said, affecting a casual tone. "I have to check some records . . . just a lab report, really."

"I don't mind," I told him. "I'm not in a hurry."

As we stood in the hallway outside his office, his key stuck in the door. The whole door shook as he rattled the lock, until the plaque bearing his name fell off, until he finally extracted the key and bent down to pick up the plaque from the floor. We laughed nervously. "It always does that," he said, showing me the strips of double-faced tape on the back of the nameplate. "I have to get this fixed."

"Have you tried glue?"

"Yes, but it didn't stick. I guess it wasn't the right kind."

"Maybe if you fixed the lock—"

"Maybe," he laughed.

He had trouble getting the file cabinet open, too. At first he couldn't find the right key, then the lever wouldn't slide to open the drawer. His fingers were tense. He picked through the tabs on the folders, mumbling something staccato which I couldn't quite understand until I realized they were names he was reading, names he was stuffing into the silence until I asked him what name he was looking for. Freedland.

"Here," I said, lifting the chart from the file.

He glanced at a pink printed form, repeated something under his breath, then slipped the form back in the chart and put it away.

All the while he talked. But I had lost the thread of what he was saying. The words seemed so removed from the fact of our being there alone, from the emptiness of the place, from the fact of the night sky outside the window, from our reflections moving through it, from the fact of his sliding hand, his approaching face, the inevitability of it. He was still talking when he led me into the waiting room, when he slipped a cushion onto the floor. We sank to our knees then rolled, my hair falling down on him and—how did I dare—snuffed out his words with my mouth, extinguished them.

I thought he was crying that first time. Not knowing what to expect, I didn't know what to make of the moaning sounds, the shudder. I thought he must be filled with regret or shame or guilt or any of those rightful things I so readily assigned, but didn't at that moment feel. Until I heard his cries, I had forgotten to feel guilty. Guilt was the farthest thing from my mind; pain was closer. But I realized the next time that it was not the sound of crying after all. It was a different sort of sound, one that echoed silently in my own throat. I was glad I hadn't embarrassed myself by trying to console him.

Afterward he kissed me, light breathy kisses on my shoulders, arms, the palms of my hands, the pulse points of my wrists; tender nuzzling kisses along the small of my back, the backs of my knees. I watched him kissing me, picking up my head a little in order to see. It was not enough to feel it; my eyes also had to bear witness to this wonder. Would God be offended by this? Would He strike me down? I felt not quite there, like I was just emerging from a dream, the experience still real but fading.

"Are you happy?" Leonard said.

His voice startled me. I thought it was such an odd question; I wasn't even sure that he had actually said it. Perhaps it was just a voice from the dream.

"No," I answered.

Then I lay beside him, languorous, and wondered at the ease with which a soul slips away.

"I won't ask you where you've been," said Alex.

"To visit the queen," I said, looking past him.

"What?"

"The queen, I've been to see her." I knew my hair was a mess.

Alex looked puzzled and a little annoyed. "What the hell are you talking about?" he said.

Jimmy glanced up from his book and recited, disinterestedly: *Pussy cat, pussy cat, where have you been? I've been to London to visit the queen. Pussy cat, pussy cat, what did you there? I frightened a little mouse under her chair.*

"Bullshit," Alex said, sadly.

Jimmy shrugged. "No, Mother Goose, I think."

I just wanted to get to the shower.

My father was sitting in a chair beside the bed when I walked into his hospital room. For the first time I noticed how much weight he had lost. It seemed he had suddenly become spindly and old. His hands and ankles had returned to normal size, but were still pale and dry.

"Michaelman was here earlier," he said pointedly.

"How are you feeling, Dad?" I said in a tone that closed the subject of Michaelman.

"Better than you, apparently," he said. "In fact, good enough to go home."

"That's great," I said. I was ashamed that I was not entirely happy.

"This time it's going to be a whole different story. I'll start back gradually, then I'll cut down my hours—no more night call—and I'll cut out OB; these days it's mostly done by special-ists anyway. You'll see, it'll be a whole new program."

"I'll believe it when I see it, Dad. You didn't do such a good job of slowing down last time. Maybe you should stay here a little longer—"

"Absolutely not. I told Michaelman to spring me as soon as the tests clear, whenever that may be."

"I hope it's soon," I said.

I wasn't used to saying things I didn't mean. The words felt like something cold and heavy in my mouth. The truth was, I wished he'd stay in the hospital as long as possible because I didn't want anything to interfere with seeing Leonard. So far, we'd managed to spend some time together every day.

My mind was at war with itself. I thought of Leonard con-stantly, and also of my father's recovery and return home. I knew I couldn't have both, but wished for both nevertheless. Even if I would be able to get through the weekdays undiscov-ered, I knew that eventually my father would know about this affair. I knew that eventually he would sense it, he would see it in my face. It was strange: All my life I'd wished for more of my father's time and now I didn't want him around.

I KEPT LOOKING OUT the car window to hide my excitement. I didn't want Leonard to think it was my first dinner date, which it was. He was taking me to a small, out-of-the-way restaurant on La Brea. It was the first time we went out to eat, *out* meaning someplace other than a drive-in. In my nervousness, I became the talkative one and Leonard, nervous too, grew quiet. The restaurant was darkly lit, with booths along the walls and a few small tables with candles flickering in netted glass balls. On the way to our booth we stopped to look at a tank filled with tropical fish, which served as a room divider. On top of the tank were some dusty green plants. Cichlids, Danios, Characins, Loaches, Rainbow Fishes—I named them as they swam by, or stopped to face us popping their lips. "That's real Java Fern," I said. "Not plastic. The fern provides oxygen; that's good for them, you know."

"I imagine," Leonard said.

"I've never had tropical fish, but I like to go to pet stores. There's one on the way home from school."

He smiled, putting his arm around me.

"Uh oh, that one has hole-in-the-head disease," I said, pointing to a discus with small depressions in his sad-looking head.

Bending down to see the affected fish, Leonard adjusted his glasses on his nose.

"Oh yes," he said. "I recognize it."

The hostess who had been waiting patiently cleared her throat before repeating that we should follow her to our table. "One of your fish has hole-in-the-head disease," I told her as she handed me a menu. She looked at me as if waiting for a punch line. "It's a real disease," I said seriously. "It should be taken care of."

"I'm sure," she said. "Your waiter will be with you shortly."

Leonard looked at me with a bemused smile. I didn't know what it meant and fell quiet.

Our waiter took the orders without writing anything down. I ordered lobster, which I had never had, and a baked potato, which I had had, but not with sour cream and chives. We ordered Grand Marnier souffle in advance. I had never had that before either and I was feeling quite adventurous. The waiter served forks on a plate; I guessed right and took one. It was cold. Leonard stroked my knee under the table.

When we were alone, he couldn't stop touching me. Even while he was driving, his fingers sought and caressed me under my clothes. He liked pointing things out about me that were *perfect* as well as other things that were not perfect but that he loved anyway. It seemed so easy for him to use the word *love*. I was surprised. No one had ever spoken that word in relation to me, so it caused me a certain discomfort, as if some taboo were being broken. I could almost hear the crackle of thunder from on high. It was all so new and strange. I didn't know how it worked, this dance between a man and a woman. I sometimes found him watching me with an expectant look on his face. Was he waiting for me to say something? I wasn't sure. Most of the time I was uncertain about what he expected of me.

As we were finishing our souffle, Leonard ladling the last of the custard sauce over my spoon, two couples got up from the bar and followed the hostess who then seated them at the table next to us. He stiffened and moved away from me. "I know these people," he said under his breath.

"Well Leonard!"

I looked up into a burly face. A man extended his hand.

"Hi. Nice to see you," Leonard said, partially standing. "This is my niece—"

"I didn't know you had a niece."

"Removed," I said.

Two red faces turned toward me in perfect synchrony. One of the women coughed into her cocktail napkin.

On the way home Leonard was strangely quiet. "I'm sorry," he said finally. "It's not a good idea for us to be seen in public. I know too many people. It's hard to explain . . ."

The next time we went to dinner, he took me to his apartment, but on the way up in the elevator, we ran into a neighbor, a greasy-faced woman with see-through hair. "Well, who's this little lady?" she said.

"My niece," he said quickly. "Adelaide."

I looked at my knees. The three of us left the elevator together and turned in the same direction. "I'll run in and get the camera, Addie. Be right back," he said as he rattled the key in the lock and left me out in the hallway. The woman passed by me, bending her too pink lips into a smile—there was lipstick on her teeth—then looked back over her shoulder before disappearing into the next door down the hall.

"Sorry," he said as we rode down the elevator. "This wasn't a good idea." The camera case knocked against the door on the way out.

We weren't free to move around in the world. In spite of Leonard's efforts to lie low, we were frequently tripped up. We tried going to a movie once, going in and coming out separately, but we ran into a friend of his ex-wife's in the parking lot. "My niece," he said, quickly letting me into the car.

She glanced at Leonard, then at me, flashing us a sour smile. "Right," she said. She looked as if she wished me harm.

After that, he stopped trying to take me out. We did nothing together then, except to talk endlessly and make love, which we did in the car as a matter of urgency, or in motel rooms for long, marathon afternoons. Afterward, we would eat submarine sandwiches in bed. I sometimes felt like a bad habit, a private pleasure to be secretly indulged and publicly denied.

But when we were together, it didn't matter. It mattered only that for a few hours I was transported to a place unlike anything I'd ever known. I loved the warm pressure of his hands on my skin, and the thumping of his heart against my cheek. I loved the feel of his arms around me, his lips, gentle, on my neck. I loved the pleasure he gave me. He told me often that he adored my body, the lean softness of it, the suppleness, its unfinished bloom. Like satin, like silk, he said. Like velvet, like sable. Like a baby, like a woman. He had never made love to a body so young and it made him desperately excited and also afraid. I thought he was afraid of going to jail, but he said that wasn't it. He was afraid of needing me too much.

I didn't believe I was in love. Nothing in my life had prepared me for romantic expectations. *Love is just a word,* my father once told me. *An overused word at that,* he'd said. He meant to say that the word is cheap; it costs nothing to say it. He meant to say that it's only how you treat someone that counts, what you give. But because he withheld the word, it took on shimmering significance, as something too awesome to speak and, at the same time, something not to be trusted. But Leonard was wearing me down with his declarations of love and his constant affection. In his presence my armor weakened. I couldn't say the words, but I felt I loved him and in just a few weeks' time, I began to trust him in a way that I had never trusted or confided in anyone before. This man with dark green eyes, this unspeakable lover, had become my first real friend.

"Tell me what you're thinking," he said. "I want to know you." He whispered in my ear, "Talk to me, my darling love, talk to me."

I rolled over onto my back and looked into his expectant face. He'd become silent and fixed his gaze on me, and waited.

His eyelashes were dense and black and I loved to brush them with the tip of my finger. "What do you want to know?" I asked.

"Anything. Your hopes, your fears, what you wish for—"

"I wish I were twenty-five," I said. I thought he might laugh, but instead he looked puzzled and a little sad.

"Why? Why would you want to wish your life away?"

"Because then everything would be over. I mean settled." It was hard to find the right words. "Because I wouldn't have to worry all the time about what's going to happen."

He stroked my cheek as he thought about it. "No one ever knows what's going to happen. Nothing is for sure—"

"Yes," I said. "I know. But then I wouldn't have to depend on anyone. It's terrible to have to depend on someone who doesn't love you. I want to make my own life."

He continued stroking my face, his fingers tracing my eyebrows. "You're making your own life now, this minute."

"Yes," I said, suddenly feeling light and covering his face with soft kisses. "Let's do it again, and again, and again."

With my father in the hospital and the boys at home only for brief and sporadic stopovers, it was easy for me to be away in the late afternoons. And even in the evenings, I was not concerned about being missed. One night, one night only, we slept together in his apartment. I should say, *he* slept. I had never slept with someone else in the same bed and I spent the entire night wide-eyed, listening to him breathe. He'd fallen asleep so naturally, like a child, and stayed asleep until the room slowly filled with long-awaited light. By then, my excitement and nervousness had burned out and I got up, exhausted. As I sat at the kitchen table in Leonard's bathrobe, he gave me orange juice and a piece of toast. Then we had to rush to dress and get ready to leave. I imagined this is how my father had felt on the nights he'd spent away from us, waking up in the bed of a lover, rushing to get home. I'm just like him, I thought. Yes, it takes one to know one.

That afternoon, I came home to find Jimmy sitting in the semidark, his feet propped up on the table. He was listening to Muddy Waters. I was surprised he wasn't off somewhere because he didn't like being home alone.

"Hey, old girl," he said. "I've been waiting for you." I started to fumble with some explanation before he cut me off. "It doesn't matter. I don't care where you've been," he said. "Alex was arrested."

"What?"

"You heard me, Alex is in the hoosegow."

"What for?"

"Drinking on the beach, something like that. He was with some friends—"

"Does Dad know?"

"No, Alex called here from the police station. He had already told them that Dad was in the hospital and shouldn't be upset, for health reasons, but they're not going to let him go. I was hoping we could bail him out before Dad has to find out that he's there." Jimmy got up and flipped over the record. "Great harmonica," he said and settled back in the chair, his

feet coming down hard on the table. He seemed to be waiting
for me to suggest something. "Well?" he said.

"I don't know what to do."

He gave me a cautious look. "What about Michaelman?" he
said. "You think he could bail Alex out?" He must have seen
that the idea floored me. "After all," he added, "he's your
friend . . ."

There was an insinuation here, an insult, something I
couldn't quite put my finger on. I was furious that he should
even suggest that I call Leonard for help.

"If you're too shy, maybe I should ask him," Jimmy said.
With a lightning-fast sweep of the arms, I pushed Jimmy's feet
off the table.

"Over my dead body," I said.

Poor Alex, we left him in the hoosegow overnight. When
my father found out the following day, he called from the hospital to have him released, apparently with little difficulty.
Alex came home tired and bedraggled; he didn't look much
better after a shower and a night's sleep. I made him a sandwich and sat down, thinking he might talk about it. He ate
slowly, waiting a long time between bites, as if he had to make
a conscious effort to get it down. His eyes were sad and far
away.

"What're you staring at me for?" he said finally.

"I'm not staring," I said. Then I left him alone, which is
what I thought he wanted.

Leonard Michaelman and I were locked in the waiting room.
But we didn't know it until we were surprised by the sound of
the outer door rattling violently, someone's key stuck in the
lock. Our clothes lay in heaps somewhere inside the office.
Maybe they lay in trails, I don't remember. Hearing the rattling of the lock, he jumped up and ran for the door, for the

unyielding doorknob, which had locked behind us. Again the outside door rattled, this time followed by the sound of the nameplate crashing to the floor. Just as we heard the grinding extraction of the key, he called out in a threatening voice, "Who is it?" Answered by a man's voice: "Janitor!" Then from that pale, vulnerable body came the most intimidating sound. "Come back later!" Leonard bellowed. "I'm in a meeting!" After we heard the janitor's footsteps fade down the hallway, he pried open the sliding window and crawled through it onto the reception desk, pushing the telephone aside, the cleaved moon of him disappearing over the transom. "I'm too old for this," he said over his shoulder.

Later that night I caught him looking at me with something other than passion. He kissed my hand and pressed his cheek against it. I bent to kiss him, but he held me away, patting my hand and sighing.

"Good news," said Jimmy. "Dad's coming home on Saturday."

"That's great," I said. I was carefully pouring the last of one ketchup bottle into a newer one. "Why do we have two bottles open, anyway?"

Jimmy rolled his eyes. "You're nuts," he said. "A real obsessive-compulsive."

I really didn't care about the two bottles, but it was the kind of thing he expected from me and I did it to amuse him. "Well, don't get so caught up in ketchup that you miss a message from our sponsor—"

"What message?" I said. "What sponsor?"

"Just wait," Jimmy said. A few minutes after he left, strains of *South Pacific* floated in from the next room. I could hear the *rup!* of the record needle being picked up and put down: *There's nothing like a*—rup! *Some enchanted*—rup! *Bali*—rup! Jimmy sashayed past me, through the kitchen, and out the back door. Through the open window I could hear him singing, *I'm gonna wash that man da da di da da*—all the way down the back stairs.

The following day, as Leonard and I sat in his car, in our favorite parking spot with a view of the city, my hands went cold. He had just told me that my father was to be discharged from the hospital, and I was afraid of what he was going to say next. I could see the difficulty he was having. He started a few tentative sentences, all beginning with *I love you, but* . . . When he got to the but, the sentence would lose its footing and tumble over the edge, breaking up and falling, irretrievable. I didn't know how long I could sit there, fighting the pressure building behind my eyes. Perhaps I could help him with the words. The word *interlude* came into my mind. I had probably heard it in a movie. *Insurmountable. Untenable,* I thought, not a word he'd use. How about *but it's not fair to you* . . . I looked into his eyes, inky green and filled with distress, and knew I couldn't take hearing any of these words from him. It would have been too painful, too humiliating. I understood—yes, even then— that our relationship was untenable. But at the same time, I couldn't think of being without him. I had grown accustomed to the pleasure and to the attention he gave me. Now I watched him struggle with the words. The most talkative man I've ever met. How he struggled, rubbing his fingers together, gasping half-sentences. *I love you, but* . . . Just at the point of being unbearable, he sat up straight and looked at me, his eyes teary. He was going to say it. I sensed his resolve and on an impulse, seized it. "I'm sorry," I said quietly. "I can't see you after my father comes home."

Two days later my father was sitting across from me at the breakfast table. I couldn't eat. I couldn't even bring the toast to my mouth. I just wanted to touch it, to break it into little pieces. I knew by the way he was watching me that he knew something was wrong, but I also knew he wouldn't ask what it was. I poured coffee and pushed the sugar bowl within his reach. I poured orange juice, which he drank to wash down various pills. I tried some orange juice myself, but it didn't help with what I had to swallow.

"How's school?" he said.

"Fine," I said, thankful for having an unloaded subject. "Except Sister Charitas is going to be out for six weeks because she had an operation. And we have a substitute teacher whose eyes don't point in the same direction. You never know where she's looking." I didn't know where my father was looking either. It wasn't at me.

"She probably has a nystagmus," he said. "You'll get used to it."

"I don't want to get used to it," I said.

"But you will," he said, taking one last sip of coffee before standing up to leave.

THE DEALS

ITHIN A FEW WEEKS after my father had come home from the hospital, he returned to work and fired the capable Hazel, his longstanding office nurse. In her place he hired a young nurse's aide who had worked in a nearby convalescent home. She always misspelled patient's names and she spelled her name *Patsie*, with an *ie* and a little heart over the *i*. I was used to the starched and no-nonsense Hazel, so I was surprised that Patsie wore a false blond ponytail and plastic jewelry with a dingy uniform, but my father didn't seem to mind. Soon, he began to admit patients to a different hospital, complaining about some kind of confusion with admitting procedures. His work schedule changed too, beginning much later than in the past. Now I usually left before he did in the morning, softly tapping and saying good-bye to a closed door.

Something had shifted. My father's usual enthusiasm for his work had waned, and for the first time, he talked about business and money and deals, so that, except for the voice, the words could have come from a stranger.

It was now late spring and the end of the school year was upon us. Jimmy's grades had plummeted, but I was more worried about Alex. I tried to remember when I'd seen him last and wondered if he'd come home the night before. I'd planned to go into his room to change the sheets; then I would know if he'd slept there. I looked out my window and watched the city come to life and thought of my brother, waking up who knows where, mad at the new day. But there was nothing I could do about Alex. It seemed there was nothing I could do about anything, except to face final exams in a week. And I had term papers to finish, on which the grades were already ticking down with each overdue day. I got up at four-thirty. This time, this cold hour of dawn when the city lights still twinkled and the moon held the treetop in parenthesis, this was the only time my mind was clear enough to study. My concentration faded with the sky, breaking up into countless particles and drifting off. In the predawn, I could hear the sounds of my father's putterings carried up the stairs: drawers opening and closing, footsteps, the rattling slide of a window frame thick with paint. I didn't go downstairs, but sat at my desk and opened a history book with a feeling of dread.

I thought about Leonard Michaelman. For a long time, I had, deep down, expected him to call. At least, I had hoped. I was the first to run to the phone when it rang or to look out the window when a car slowed or parked by our house. I tried to accept that it was over, but still, I often dreamed of him, by day or night, and longed for him, so warm and solid beside me. I even missed listening to his constant chatter, which had seemed peculiar in the beginning because it was so unlike the quiet style of our family. But most of all I missed having someone to talk to, someone to listen. I wanted to ask him about the effects of heart disease and the effects of the medicines my father was taking. Perhaps he could reassure me about the perplexing changes in my father, about what we could expect during his recovery or perhaps he could suggest what we should do. But it was not our custom to ask for help. I wanted to call just for the comfort of Leonard's voice. Still, I couldn't bring myself to do it.

Before I went to school I had work to do that morning. Someone would be staying with us for a while, my father had said the night before. He said it casually, as if this were not the unprecedented event that it was. The guest's name was St. John. I didn't know who this St. John was or why my father was taking him in. He was going to help out with the new business ventures, my father explained. He was to stay in Jimmy's room, so I had to have the room ready before he got there. Jimmy had to move out; it didn't matter where. There were spare rooms in the house with no furniture; Jimmy could sleep in one of them. My father said he'd survive.

St. John arrived in the afternoon. "Which saint are you named after?" I asked, trying to sound hospitable. The skin of his face was fractured by the sun; cracks radiated around his eyes and intersected over sunken cheeks. He was shorter than the men in my family, with a small chest that curved in like a spoon. He wasn't old, but looked like someone who'd been mummified in his youth.

He looked at me with a brazen smirk. "Saint?" he said.

"You know, St. John Chrysostom? St. John the Apostle? Or John the Baptist?"

St. John tapped a soft pack against the edge of the table and withdrew a cigarette with his pale lips. He flicked the lighter and sucked in. He exhaled slowly and picked a fleck of tobacco off his tongue. "I was named after an island," he said.

He followed me with his eyes as I cleared yesterday's paper from the table and turned on the floor lamp in the corner. I couldn't remember where we had an ashtray, but in the meantime placed a saucer near his hand. He looked from me to the saucer then back to me. "I guess you don't smoke," he said.

I shook my head.

"Wanna puff?" he said, lifting the cigarette as if making a toast.

"No, thank you." I didn't know what I was supposed to do. I thought I should treat him as a guest, but just being in the same room with him made my palms sweat. "Dad's going to be home early," I said.

"Yeah?"

"That's what he said . . . about six . . . for him, that's early."

St. John picked at his tongue and rolled his wet fingers together. "Whoopdedoo," he said.

When my father came home from work, he put down his bag on the landing, as usual. St. John stood up. "Good to see you, sir," he said, extending his hand. "Nice house you have here."

"Hello, St. John," my father said, shaking his hand. "Are you settled in? Is your room all right?"

"Everything's fine, sir. I appreciate the accommodations. Hope I'm not putting anybody out."

"No. Of course not," my father said.

"Just my brother," I said out of my father's hearing range, and smiled.

A few days later, Jimmy came home after eleven and headed straight for the refrigerator. "I'm starved," he said. "Is the guy here? San Juan?"

"Yes, he's here," I said, rolling my eyes.

"What's he like?"

"He gives me the creeps. He's so phony with Dad, you wouldn't believe it. And Dad falls for it! I wish you'd come home early. I can't stand being in the house with him."

"Look, I've got finals coming up, basketball, and I'm trying to put this car together so it'll run. And I'm sleeping on the damn floor in a sleeping bag, locked out of my room and I can't get to my stuff. There's some books in there I need—"

"Why can't you get your stuff?"

"Because San Juan locked the door. I checked."

"Did you knock?"

"Yeah, he's not answering. Anyway, old girl, under the circumstances, I'm sure not going to come home early. Believe it or not, I'm beginning to think Alex has the right idea by staying away."

"Don't say that. It's just temporary."

"You know what bothers me, Dad didn't even ask if this guy could use my room. It was just: You're out. The stranger's in."

"Jimmy, this guy is bad news. There's something about him—"

"Nothing we can do about it," Jimmy said. "It's up to Dad."

I didn't see Jimmy much after that night. He didn't like sleeping on the floor of an empty room. He went to stay with his friend, Paul Kremmel. Sometimes he would stop by on Sunday, when my father and St. John were out. Once he tried to pick the lock to his room, but St. John had installed a dead bolt so we couldn't get in. Then we stood outside the door, not talking, just staring down at the bent hairpin, useless in Jimmy's hand.

"How's Dad?" Jimmy asked as he was leaving.

"Okay, I guess. You know, he's working. He's tired when he comes home and he doesn't sleep well. I guess that's a lot of the problem. We don't talk much. St. John's usually here in the evening, and I stay in my room mostly."

I didn't tell Jimmy I had begun to lock my door at night.

At school, end-of-semester jubilation was in the air. We ate our lunch out on the rolling lawn; some girls sat on the steps and swung their knees over to let people pass. The subjects of conversation during lunch were boys, movies and music, school activities, parents, curfews, vacations, clothes, other girls. I might as well have been on the moon. I didn't bring any lunch. Most often I pretended I wasn't hungry. The decline in communications with my father had affected my income. I had never asked him for money. He usually gave me a monthly household allowance and a small personal allowance, which was the same as the boys'. Recently, however, the household allowance was reduced and always late; my own allowance had stopped altogether. Now, on the rare times I could talk to my father alone, he looked distracted and pale. I didn't want to trouble him with the subject of money. To get the money I needed, I found a job in a little gift shop not far from school, sometimes waiting on customers, but mostly dusting shelves and glass figurines. I worked on Saturdays and three after-noons a week after school. I did our washing and ironing on my free afternoons and all the other housework on Sunday. Woman's work.

I began to oversleep and had to force myself out of bed in the morning. I was finding it more and more difficult to fall asleep at night, sometimes lying awake until just before the alarm clock rang. I could hear St. John in the room next to mine, coughing, playing country music. Sometimes he tapped on the wall. Sometimes he tapped on my door. I could hear my father's footsteps on the stairs, his door closing and locking; then I'd hear him come out again, then the sound of his hand sliding heavily along the bannister. The sound I welcomed was the put-put of Alex's Vespa chugging up the road. But on the days Alex came home, he slept late, so I rarely saw him. St. John slept late. And now my father slept late too. I left for school from a silent house.

One Sunday morning, about two months after St. John had moved in, the boys and I sat in the breakfast room quietly peeling oranges as we waited for our father. We had scattered the Sunday *Times* all over the table and Jimmy and Alex put their sizable feet up on the adjacent chairs, leaned back and looked settled in. St. John slouched in the kitchen doorway and drank his coffee standing up. When my father came in he stood up straight and took the smirk off his face. "Good morning, sir," he said.

"All present and accounted for?" my father said.

"Morning, Dad," I said, handing him a cup of coffee.

Alex lifted his feet off the chair. "We're ready to go," he said.

"Is *he* going?" Jimmy said as he lifted his eyes to St. John.

"Everybody's going," my father said, spilling some coffee over the rim of his cup. I thought he must have burned his fingers, but he didn't seem to notice. "This is something I want all of you to see. It's a great deal. St. John's worked hard to set it up."

Alex looked St. John up and down. "He set up a great deal?"

"Him?" Jimmy said.

I had never seen anyone change his face like St. John did at that moment: his sharp blue eyes took on a vapid hue and the ravages of his cheeks seemed to melt away. He seemed suddenly so innocent and self-effacing. It was as if he had somehow slipped out of his skin, which gave me the strange feeling that he was in another part of the room.

"Don't mind the kids," my father said. "It'll take a little doing to win them over."

St. John let out a feeble chuckle. "I don't mind, sir. I know how happy they'll be when these deals work out. Then you can retire."

We were silent on the road to Tehachapi. St. John rode up front with my father, trying to read the Thomas map that flapped wildly in his hands. The three of us sat low in the back, the boys' long legs folded at uncomfortable angles. My father took a few wrong turns, but undaunted, he drove on, forgiving St. John for bad directions along the way. He had put the top down and I felt the wind and sun hard against my face. I tried not to feel anything else. Alex and Jimmy watched opposite sides of the road as we drove through canyon passes and rolling hills and dried-up riverbeds severed by the highway. As we came into the high desert, we could see huge boulders, perched recklessly atop the hills as if they were about to tumble. The scenery was bleak: a lot of dirt of the light-brown kind, in which nothing will grow except small, ragged, gray-leafed plants that cringe in the midday sun. And not even these could be seen for long stretches beside the highway, where there was nothing except the rocks with their slanted shadows and occasionally the tracks of a sidewinder embossed on the bare ground. And the silence. The silence was everywhere—in the cloudless sky, on the pallid ground, in the car. I watched the sun beat down on the back of St. John's neck, its crevices glistening and growing redder by the mile.

"Nobody's curious?" my father said, looking into the rearview mirror. The boys continued to look to their sides, right and left. I closed my eyes against the sun.

"I guess we'll see soon enough," Jimmy said after a long pause.

"This deal's going to be big," St. John said.

Alex turned toward St. John and glared. "Yeah? Who says so?"

St. John looked back over his shoulder. "Let's not get hot under the collar, son."

"Don't call me *son*, asshole," Alex said, leaning forward, his hand grasping the back of the seat. A crosswind whipped around the inside of the car, then died down.

"This is it. Coming up," St. John suddenly announced, jolting us out of the tense quiet. "Redrock Canyon."

My father made a right turn at the sign onto a narrow two-lane road. A gathering of small greenish buildings appeared in the distance, an outcropping of desert life. As we approached the gate, I could see a man leaning out of a pickup truck. The truck was completely rusted. I had seen cars like this in junkyards, or abandoned in places off the road, but never with people in them. When we parked, the man spilled out of the driver's seat, slamming the door behind him. He had a bronze, chiseled face and shoulder-length black hair pulled back with a leather cord. His plaid shirt was open and stopped short at the waist. I was used to tall men, but this man was a giant. Alex and Jimmy together could have fit inside his shadow. He walked over to St. John and shook his hand. "I was waitin' for you, man," he said. He shifted his weight from side to side as if his feet were giving him trouble. "What took you so long?"

St. John looked him over, his eyes showing some concern. He reached up and patted him on the arm. "Okay, man," he said. "I want to introduce you—" He turned to my father. "This is Raymond Tall Horse. He and his brother Herman own the property. Ray, this is Dr. Mackinnon." Ray's eyes flitted from side to side; he couldn't seem to get them to settle on anything. St. John moved in to face him, to get his attention. "You know," he said. "The investor."

"Excuse me," my father said, as he took St. John aside. "We have something to discuss." They walked a short way up the road then stopped in animated conversation, St. John obscured by my father's long back.

Ray didn't seem to mind that my father and St. John left him standing alone. I thought he was just going to wait there until he turned his massive neck in my direction and headed slowly for our car. "Some car, man," he said. "Bitchin' Mercedes." He went around the front and pulled up on the hood. It didn't open. The whole car rocked as he pulled up again and again. "Hold on. Wait a minute," Jimmy said. "Let me release the latch."

Still holding the front end of the car, he lifted his face up. The car bounced when he dropped the front. "Oh," he said meekly, then started to laugh. Soon he was doubled over laughing, actually making the sound: hee hee hee, pounding on the front fender. "What's the matter with him?" I whispered.

"He's stoned out of his mind," Alex said.

I couldn't see him after he propped the hood up, but the car leaned and bounced under his weight and his tinkering fat hands sent vibrations through the car.

"Start 'er up!" he yelled.

Jimmy walked over to the side of the car. "We don't have the key," he said.

"Oh!" came the voice under the hood. "Hee hee. No key. Bitchin', man. Hee hee hee. I know a way." Still laughing, he swung out from under the hood and started for the door when he saw me sitting in the back. "Howdy," he said as he reached in the car and grabbed my hand. "I'm Ray Tall Horse." Then he stopped laughing, as if he'd suddenly forgotten what was so funny.

"Hi," I said. "I'm Jorie."

He leaned toward me, swaying a little, squeezing his brows to get his eyes in focus, all the while keeping a tight grip on my hand. Someone once told me that Indians have an extraordinary sense of smell. I was afraid that Ray Tall Horse could smell my fear.

"I'm Ray," he repeated, letting go of my hand. He shook his head and blinked several times as if clearing his thoughts. "Me and my brother Herman are selling this farm. It's worth big bucks." He looked over at St. John and my father as they headed back toward the car. "Your daddy?" he said.

"Yes."

"Well now," he said. "We'll make him a real good deal."

There were rows of them. In each row were about a dozen cages; each cage housing a single chinchilla, silver-gray and round as a pom-pom. Order: *Rodentia*; Family: *Chinchillidae*; Species: *laniger*. A quadrupedal, placental mammal, native to the celestial Andes, given to scampering, burrowing, nesting, and denning. But not these. The cages were raised about four feet off the ground on wooden tables, so as I walked by I could see the despair in their bead-black eyes.

"Softer than mink," my father said as he picked up a chinchilla by the scruff of its neck.

"Yessir, softer and warmer. Careful there, Doc, he might bite." Herman reached over my father's hand to grasp the chinchilla and place it back in the cage, but not before the creature had laid a bunch of dark pellets along his bare arm. Jimmy and I tried not to look at each other, but burst out laughing anyway. Herman didn't laugh. Without looking up he walked to a coiled hose at the table's end and washed off his arm. Herman was as tall and bronze as his brother Ray, but was older and thinner and stooped over. He walked with grim determination, stiff and slow. I didn't like Herman. I didn't like his sour face or his dragging walk, or the way he handled the chinchillas as if they were already dead. And I didn't understand why my father wanted to do business with him and his brother. I didn't understand why he would want a chinchilla farm in the first place. He had never done anything except practice medicine, but recently he'd said he was going to broaden his horizons, to try his hand at some free enterprise.

Then my father took us on a round of inspection, just the boys and me. I knew it was our chance to talk to him. I don't know if they saw the opportunity, but I saw it. I remember struggling with the questions, none of the words fitting together. I couldn't come up with anything resembling a question, or at least resembling the thing in my mind that needed to be answered.

"See there," my father said, pointing to a chinchilla. "Watch the way he's gnawing on that stick. Gnawing is the primary behavioral innovation of rodents. You know, their incisors grow continuously. And they have enamel only on the anterior surface of the tooth, so they gnaw to keep a sharp chisel edge."

"Speaking of the varmints, Doc—" Herman's voice came from behind us. "I was just about to dress some pelts. I thought you might like to see how it's done."

"That would be interesting, Herman," my father said. "We don't have much time, but maybe we could watch you get started."

I begged off.

"S'matter, girl, you squeamish?" Herman said with a note of disdain.

"No," I said. "I just don't feel like it. I'm going to stretch my legs."

I walked between the buildings, toward a clearing in the back that curved upward into a soft slope. In the sunlight beyond the buildings, drifts of orange poppies dappled the hillside. I was thinking how nice it would be to gather some poppies to take home and how they would look in a blue ceramic bowl and whether they would last all day in the car, or maybe I should just press a few. A foot blocked my way. When I stopped, St. John withdrew his brown boot, scraping a line in the dirt. "Hey, chickee, chickee," he said. He was sitting against the side of the building with his knees pulled up, holding a small bottle of whiskey. Then he put one hand on the ground and pushed himself up. He wiped the hand on the front of his pants. "Want some?"

I started to leave, but he reached out. I shook his hand off my shoulder.

"Don't touch me," I said. "You're drunk."

"I am drinking, but I am not drunk." he said. "Can't you tell the difference? You need some experience, little chickadee. I could teach you a few things, hm?"

"Don't talk to me."

"Ah, don't be like that. I have to tell you something."

"What?"

"Just, something."

"Okay, what?"

"I just want to say that you—have a great ass."

I turned quickly, not wanting to show my burning face.

"Don't go," he said.

"I'm going."

"I have to ask you a question."

"No."

"Come on, one little question."

Stopping, I looked back over my shoulder. St. John upended the bottle into his mouth, the whiskey bubbling under his hand. He replaced the cap and wiped his mouth on his sleeve.

"What is it?"

He smiled. "Why don't you unlock your door tonight?"

Inside the chinchilla house, I sat on a bench to catch my breath. I could hear Jimmy calling me. As I got up to leave, one cage caught my attention. The chinchilla was lying flat on the bottom. When I got closer I could see that it was dead, its eyes open and lifeless. It was spread its full length as if its final breath had come in the middle of a good stretch. It looked something like a rabbit, a dead rabbit with short ears. I opened the cage and removed the corpse. Its fur was indescribably soft. I thought of dandelions. I held the dead chinchilla against my chest, stroking its fine stiff back with a kind of consolation and felt the tears uncontrollably spill out over my hands.

"Are you crying?" Jimmy was staring at me, concerned and amazed. In our family, it wasn't done. "What are you crying about?"

"I don't know," I said, sniffling. "I don't even like chinchillas."

When we returned to the car, St. John and Ray Tall Horse were standing beside the pickup. It was then I noticed the three children, the same rust color as the truck, sitting in the back. I wondered how I hadn't seen them before. They all had long black hair and runny noses; their upper lips glistened.

"Daddy," the smallest one said, rubbing her eyes.

"Later," Ray said.

The children jumped out of the truck and came close to stare at us. They were very small, the oldest not more than six or seven. I gave each of the children a Lifesaver, which they received in their upturned palms. The smallest offered hers to my father, a little green circle in the middle of her sticky hand. "Thank you, but that's for you," he said. She closed her fist and frowned.

Then a sound rose up from the valley floor. Crackling, like the crackling of cellophane. It seemed to come from every direction, surrounding us. For the first time, Ray stood still. "Cicadas," he said. "They're coming out."

"Cicadas," my father repeated, awe in his voice.

"Big money in chinchillas," St. John interrupted.

"Shhh," my father said. "Forget that, just listen."

My father squatted and gathered the children to him. "Listen," he told them. "We may never hear this again. At this exact moment thousands of cicadas are emerging from years of sleep, right now, while we listen."

"Did we wake them up?" a child asked.

"No, something inside them says that it's time to break through their chitin casing. Then nothing can stop them."

"Then what do they do?"

"They fill the sky," he said. "After years of waiting, they try out their new bodies. But they live only about a week. If we're lucky, we may see them."

Imitating my father, alight with his enthusiasm, the children cocked their ears and looked into the sky. He cupped his ear and smiled. For a moment, he reminded me of the father I once knew.

*T*DREAMED ABOUT THE cicadas. In my sleep I could hear the chirruping. It seemed to come from a distant chorus singing out in a cycle of crackling crescendos, slowing ascending, notes floating upward, growing fainter and fainter as they dispersed. I didn't actually see the cicadas in my dream, but only heard the echo of their voiceless noise and I could feel them unfold into wakefulness, stretching out their untried wings. The vibrations of their bodies oscillated the air, so I awoke with a tingling as if I'd been shaken then suddenly stilled. The cicada awakening was silenced. And I was glad I hadn't seen them, that I woke up before I had to witness the inevitable fields of death.

Still shaken and clearing my head from a night of dreams, I didn't notice at first that the door to St. John's room was open. I had already started down the stairs before I saw the morning light streaming from the bedroom window onto the wall of the upper landing. No light had come from that room since Jimmy was there. I listened for sounds before I went in. St. John was gone.

Jimmy's room was never much of a showplace, but now it looked like the back room of a blighted flophouse. Stains were spattered on the bed and on the carpet; I didn't want to know from what. And the walls were riveted with nail holes and patches of missing paint, where he had pulled down everything he had put up while he was there. I could picture him doing this: his dirty fingernails scraping the wall, the still-glowing ash from his cigarette falling to the floor as he yanked—pictures, posters, photographs? Who knows what he liked to surround himself with. Cigarette burns were everywhere; they covered the furniture like scabs.

"You mean he just flew the coop?" Jimmy said, later that day, as he stood in the middle of his room appraising the wreckage.

"Yes," I said. "When I got up, he was gone." I looked around the room, not knowing where to start, not wanting to touch anything. It seemed to me that everything there had been contaminated. I wished we could have burned it—set a great bonfire of purification, then swept up the ashes from an aseptic floor. "Maybe we could burn it?" I thought aloud.

Jimmy looked at me quizzically. "Burn what? All we have to do is clean it up, maybe some fresh paint—"

"That wouldn't be enough for me."

"That's because you're too *fathtidious*," he said, imitating Elmer Fudd.

It was a weak laugh, but the first we'd had in a while. He opened the windows and closed the door, leaving the ruins of his room behind.

"I don't understand it," I said. "What's going on with Dad? The chinchilla farm, this thing with St. John, firing Hazel—"

"Tip of the iceberg, I'll bet," Jimmy said. "But what can we do about it? It's not our business to interfere with him." He looked at me briefly then looked intently at a spot on the wall. "No one interferes with you."

I followed him from the kitchen into the dining room and back into the kitchen. He couldn't seem to make up his mind where he wanted to be. "I don't want to interfere," I said. "I just want him to be himself, to be okay."

"He's not okay."

"I know he's not," I said. I was hoping that Jimmy understood what was happening, that he might know something I didn't know. There were too many things I couldn't explain—anonymous phone calls, strange cars parked in front of our house or slowly cruising by. "Have you been getting hangups?" I asked.

"Yeah, some hang-ups, but sometimes it's a woman asking for him."

"Yes, then as soon as I say he's not here, she hangs up. Who do you think it is?"

Jimmy shrugged. "I don't know. You know he's got outside friends, people who depend on him. It's really no surprise."

I wondered how much he knew. Before now, we had never discussed my father's outside friends, or the possibility of his having another life that excluded us, but it seemed an opportune moment to ask. "Do you know we have a younger brother?" I asked.

"Sure," he said, almost nonchalantly. "Do you know about the older boy, Donald, and our little sister?"

"What, a sister?"

"That's right, a sister. I ran into her in Dad's office about three years ago. She was very sick, pneumonia or something. She lives with her grandmother. Of course, Dad said mum's the word."

So Jimmy knew about the other families all along. A flash of recognition passed between us. We both had taken my father's lesson to heart: A good man keeps his own counsel.

"Do you think there are more children?" I asked. "Good God, was he trying to populate the planet?"

Suddenly we were laughing, Jimmy's mouth pulled out into a grimace, his breath coming in and out in short sucks. We bent over, holding our stomachs, as if our guts would come out in big belly laughs. Tears rolled down our cheeks as we shrieked with laughter and pounded our fists, until we leaned against the kitchen counter, moaning and gasping for breath.

We wiped our eyes with the back of our hands and coughed. Jimmy was still for a moment, then blew out a long sigh. "You know why the natives are restless," he said, noisily inhaling. "Because there's no money coming in. Dad was off for a long time. If he doesn't work, no one eats."

"But he's working now, isn't he?"

"Not like he used to."

"Nothing is like it used to be before he got sick."

"So, don't tell me you're longing for the good ol' days? Well, there weren't any, in case you didn't notice."

"That's not true," I said. "Don't be so cynical."

Jimmy sniffled and wiped a tear left over from laughing. "Okay, it's not entirely true. There were some good ol' days." He put his arm around me playfully. "Cheer up, old girl," he said, squeezing my shoulder. "Maybe things will get better—"

"You really think so?"

"To be honest," he said, "I don't."

I decided to make a special dinner that night and asked Jimmy to stay for it. For me, it was cause for celebration, although I didn't put it that way to my father when he came home. He looked pretty miserable. I just said, "Dinner's served, Dad." He seemed to know St. John was gone, even though he hadn't seen the room and we hadn't said anything. He didn't look for another place setting or make any reference to our absent guest. He hesitated over soup as a separate course—a fleeting recognition of something out of the ordinary—but then resumed his head-down posture with a barely audible *hmm.* He seemed to be fighting to stay awake. I didn't know the circumstances of St. John's departure, but I felt that with his absence something had been regained. So even though my father was downcast, I couldn't help but feel a little happy.

Jimmy seemed to be making undue noise with his soup. I shot him a glance. "So," he said when he got my attention, "a horse walks into a bar and the bartender says to him, 'Why the long face?'"

"Dumb," I said.

"Okay," Jimmy said. "How about a moron joke."

My father's eyes were sliding closed. I thought he was dozing off, but then he surprised me by suddenly raising his head. "Morons aren't a joke," he said.

We got through dinner without mention of St. John, but my relief at having him out of the house was hard to suppress. I could tell that Jimmy too was holding it down. "Best canned peas I ever ate," he said. "You sure know how to heat'em up."

"Why, thank you—my own secret recipe," I said, trying to catch my father's eye. "What did you think, Dad?"

He stood up, letting the napkin fall from his lap. "Very good, Jorie," he said without looking at me. The napkin clung to his shoe as he pushed the chair aside; he seemed too weary to retrieve it. He turned and kicked it aside, then went upstairs and closed his door.

Jimmy offered to help with the dishes. "You? Help with the dishes?" I asked, exaggerating my surprise. "S'matter, you sick?"

"Just hand me the towel," he said. "This is a one-time offer."

"So, Mrs. Kremmel made you and Paul do the dishes, huh?"

"How did you know?" he said. "It was positively grueling."

"I figured you must've learned something about domestic chores when you were staying with the Kremmels. I knew you'd be back, where the livin' is easy."

Jimmy expertly dried both sides of a plate then broke out in one of our old favorites: *Don't let the stars get in your eyes, don't let the moon get in your ears.*

Passing him a dripping soup bowl, I sang, *Stars shine at night, by day they ain't so bright.*

"Yee haw!"

When your teeth fall out, remember they are mine.

"Yip yip!"

I don't know how long Alex had been standing there behind us; he seemed to have materialized out of thin air. We stopped singing.

"St. John's gone," I explained. "We're celebrating."

Alex didn't look surprised. "It doesn't make any difference," he said.

"Not to you, maybe," Jimmy said. "But I get my room back."

"What difference does it make? If it's not St. John, it'll just be another creep, then another—any con guy with a scheme. Dad doesn't give a damn about your room; he doesn't even know what he's doing anymore."

Alex's words flashed true. For an instant I could see how bad things were. But in the next instant, I dismissed it. Jimmy started to sing again with a too-cheerful voice. "Your chorus, senorita!" Then he picked up the tune, faster than before.

For a time, I continued to think of St. John's presence in our life as a kind of glitch, as my father's heart failure had been a glitch. Something temporary, something interrupting the normal flow of things. Now, I wanted to believe we could get back to the way things were. We had plans to make, the boys and I. Alex was a senior in high school; Jimmy was a junior; I was a year behind him. It was time to think about the next stage. We were on our marks, ready to go, but my father didn't notice. His concerns were elsewhere.

His office hours had become erratic. Patients waited a long time, got angry, left. He lost many patients during this time, even some who had been loyal to him for years. And several times he was put on probation for surgical privileges; word was spreading that he was unreliable, even dangerous. Sometimes he would come home angry, railing at bureaucrats, turncoats, or ignoramuses—all of which I assumed to be the result of the changes that were beginning to occur in the practice of medicine. I'd heard about the introduction of third-party payment and the emergence of bureaucracy-run medicine, but I didn't know how this was affecting my father's practice, if at all. I didn't know if he was really under siege as he claimed to be. I knew only that nothing in his professional life was as it used to be.

Even more unusual was the fact that he didn't appear to care about events in the wider world. While the situation in Southeast Asia was intensifying, it seemed to hold surprisingly little interest for him—surprising because my father had always been fascinated with all current events in the Far East. He had visited French Indochina during the time he was living in Shanghai in the '30s, and had closely followed the civil war since the French defeat at Dien Bien Phu. Occasionally he would get hold of Chinese newspapers to get a different slant on the situation and to brush up on his Chinese. When President Kennedy started sending U.S. troops to Viet Nam, we thought he'd get riled up, we thought he'd say "Stupid Ngo Dinh Diem! Damned Ho Chi Minh!" We thought he'd get current Chinese newspapers. We thought he'd say, "Listen to this. This is what's really going on—" But he said none of this. He twisted the outdated Chinese newspapers and placed them under stacked logs in the fireplace. And fell asleep as the columns of tortured black characters unwound and melted into flames.

Within weeks of St. John's sudden departure, it was like he had never been in the house. Jimmy and I managed to clean up the room. We shampooed the carpet and even patched and painted the walls. Jimmy rearranged the furniture and moved back in. Alex could be heard coming and going on his Vespa, never staying for long, never saying more than a few words. We presumed he went to school but we didn't know for sure. I could tell when he'd been home by the smell of smoke. Jimmy and Alex were still at odds, so I wasn't surprised the day I heard them arguing in the next room.

"We'll manage—" Jimmy was saying, in a defensive voice.

"Oh yeah?" said Alex. "How? How do you go to school with no money? Just tell me that."

I walked into the room thinking I would save the day. I could tell him. I thought he knew that my father had kept separate college funds for each of us. I had always known that, ever since I could remember. "Even if something happens to me," my father had told me, "you'll always have your own money, for as much education as you can stand." Then I'd say, "I can stand a lot." That made him smile.

"Don't you know we have our own accounts for our education?" I said to Alex. "Dad's been paying into them for years." He gave me the briefest, impenetrable look, then turned away. Jimmy looked out the window.

"Really, they have our names on them," I continued. The boys' silence was palpable. "I saw the little blue books—"

Jimmy reached for a side chair and sat on it backwards, pulling the back against his chest, resting his arms on the top, and heaved a sigh.

"That's funny, you didn't know we have bank accounts?"

Jimmy looked at me solemnly. "Not anymore."

Now Alex was looking out the window. "Dad blew it," he said.

"He just borrowed it," Jimmy snapped.

"Yeah, with no chance of paying it back. Some loan."

I couldn't believe it. I looked from one to the other. "What did he borrow it for?"

"Remember the Tall Horse brothers?" Jimmy said.

I nodded.

"Well, the chinchilla farm was just the beginning. Ray Tall Horse, with the help of his pal, St. John, sold Dad a peachy-keen oil well on a prime piece of real estate in the middle of a desert where even cactus won't grow. And if that's not enough, it turns out that while Tall Horse's family owns the land, they don't own what's under it. The mineral rights belong to the reservation. Which means, of course, that even if that well ever produces a drop of oil, Dad won't get the money. And, he'll probably never be able to sell the land."

"No sane person would buy it," Alex said.

"You mean he used all our money on a chinchilla farm and a worthless hole in the ground?"

"It wasn't really our money, when you think about it," Jimmy said. "We didn't actually earn it. It was Dad's money; he earned it."

My eyes stung with tears, but I turned my face away so as not to shame myself. I ground my teeth together. At that moment I realized that you can't count on anything, that any hope you may hold for the future can be swept away, behind your back, and you are powerless to retrieve it.

Alex looked at me; I swallowed hard and hoped he couldn't see my panic. The words tumbled from my lips, calm and false: "Easy come, easy go."

•◆•◆•

I would like to remember something Alex said before he left, some words that I could nestle in my brain, some downy memory. But he said nothing. I could tell from the things he took, and also from the things he left behind, that he wasn't coming back. He took the army surplus duffel bag that had always lain crushed in the bottom of the linen closet, and exactly a duffel bag-full of things: his newest underwear, socks without holes, shirts, one jacket, one sweater, one towel, unopened toiletries from the cupboard, a package of graham crackers, a photograph of our mother in a tarnished frame. On the kitchen counter he left twelve dollars and fifty cents—exactly the amount he owed me.

I didn't expect a speech, certainly not an explanation, maybe not even a good-bye—that would have been too difficult. But we could have played a scene: He could have pretended that he just wanted to get away for a while, to figure things out, to decide what he wanted to do with his life. He could have pretended that he had a plan, a place to stay, that he would be in touch as soon as he was settled. He could have said, *Don't worry, I'll be fine. I'll check in occasionally to see how you are,* and I could have pretended to believe him. I could have jokingly handed him a stamped, self-addressed postcard and pretended I expected him to send it. We could have agreed that he'd come home for Christmas. He could have left me those little lies. He could have left that much.

21

ALL THOSE WHO LOVE LIFE, RAISE YOUR HANDS

*A*FTER ALEX LEFT I gave up expecting our life to return to the way things were. My father didn't talk about Alex, except to say that when a fledgling is ready to leave the nest, he leaves. That's nature for you.

Now I knew my father's illness was not merely a glitch in our normal life's progress. It had become the locus around which everything seemed to deteriorate. I knew there was no going back, there was only bracing for the next thing to happen, there was only keeping your wits about you and holding on.

One Sunday we again headed north on Highway 14 to the chinchilla farm. To my relief, my father let Jimmy drive. He drove too fast, but at least he didn't doze off or drift out of his lane as my father was prone to do.

The sky was not blue that day, but an ashy white, the color of sky in an overexposed photograph. Dirt blew into drifts and dust devils twirled among the Joshua trees. Red-tailed hawks circled overhead. On the ground two buzzards fought over the carcass of a jackrabbit. A suspension of dust floated heavy around us, so when we turned onto the unpaved road, I felt like pushing the air aside like a net, in order to see the flat-top buildings of the chinchilla farm come into view. I wondered if my father had called ahead because there was no sign of Herman, no scrawny silhouette waiting at the gate.

As soon as we got out of the car, something told us. The way the gate creaked on its hinges, the banging of a screen door in the wind, the carious smell whispering from the open windows, skittering and sliding along the ground: the sounds of the desert reclaiming itself. We knew as we walked into the abandoned building. Most of the tables were empty, some knocked over, a few with cages still sitting on top, chinchillas desiccated and rotting inside them. We hardly breathed.

On the way home, the silence. My father's shoulders lifted with each inspiration, followed by a faint whistle escaping from his throat. He didn't talk about St. John, or the oil well, or the lien against the house, which we had just learned about. And I knew he wouldn't speak of this either, that this also would weep into the ground and disappear.

The following Saturday, at about eight o'clock in the morning, a construction crew arrived. I saw them down in the street, looking upward and swearing at the stairs. One of the younger men, well tanned, had a red calico scarf tied across his forehead. "Holy shit!" he said. His voice splashed against the long white wall. "This place must have four floors. It's a goddamn tower." Jimmy had already left for his weekend job at the service garage and I was just leaving for my new job at the bookstore. I didn't know what this construction gang was going to do to our house, but when I recognized Dan Castro, a patient of my father's, pointing and giving directions, I presumed it must be okay, at least to the extent that anything that had gone on recently was okay. It was beyond my knowing and understanding and control, but it was okay nonetheless because after all, I was not the captain of this boat. I was just a gob, a polliwog, less than that—a rat with no view of the horizon, a flea.

I walked down the stairs that morning, past the calico scarf, the tanned faces, the half smiles, the beer bellies, the tattoos; I almost didn't ask what the lumber was for, or the saws, or the sledge hammers. "Not that it matters," I said to Dan Castro, the contractor, as I passed him, "but what are you going to do here?"

He made a visor with his hand and looked upward toward the top corner of the house. "We're gonna close in that sun porch," he said, "and knock out a few walls. Your dad wants to build a big suite up there. It's gonna be real nice."

I had fond memories of that sun porch. I remembered Kitty sunbathing up there, and Sleepwalker, tall enough to hang his paws over the wall, barking when Alex came up the street, and the boys and I playing the hybrid game of billiards and marbles we invented. We used the porch floor like a pool table, and occasionally lost some marbles down the corner drain spout. I looked at Dan Castro. "Real nice," I said.

The crew got a lot done that day. By the time I got home, the door leading to Alex's room from the upstairs corridor had been plastered over. And the west wall of the room had been knocked out so it was now open to the sun porch. Some headers were placed to start the framing of the upper wall and ceiling. Two-by-fours were neatly stacked against the wall. On the opposite side, a hole had been knocked through the bottom of the wall into my closet for access to the plumbing. Some of my clothes had been knocked off the hangers. My shoes were full of plaster dust.

"Where is he?" the head nurse wanted to know. She was calling from the hospital at eleven o'clock one Saturday morning. "The patient is waiting to be discharged. Her family has come to take her home." I put down the phone and looked up the stairs at the closed door. I told her my father wasn't here; he must be on his way. At times like this, I was glad he had changed hospitals. Unlike the old hospital where I knew every-one, here I couldn't put a face to a voice, which spared me con-siderable embarrassment. "He's on his way," I lied. It had become my stock answer.

My father's upstairs suite had been completed; he opened the door with a key. Once a week he would leave the door open, so I could go in to clean and tidy up. During the time I was there, he would wander in and out of the room, asking questions or seeming to look for things. "Don't touch this. Don't touch that," he'd say.

One day when I went in, he was sleeping, fully dressed, on the bed. The covers were pulled up beneath him, but the pil-lows were out, stacked three high, white. He was breathing deeply. I turned to leave until his voice came softly, like a tap on the shoulder. "Jorie," he said.

"I'll come back later, Dad."

"No, you can come in." His hand lay heavily on his chest, pale and puffy. A spot of blood was on his shirt sleeve. His nail beds were slightly blue. I sat down on the bed beside him. "You don't look well, Dad. Can I get you something?"

"No," he said. "Thank you." He could barely keep his eyes open. His skin was gray and mottled. "It's not easy these days," he murmured. "I suspect it's not easy for you, or the boys, but life is hard sometimes, it surprises us. I don't know what will happen . . ." His voice started to waver.

I couldn't stay there any longer. "I'll be back later, Dad," I said. "You should rest now."

Without opening his eyes, he turned his head toward me when I stood up. "I tried to be a good father," he said. "Maybe I've failed lately, but I have tried—"

"I know."

"Jorie, it's funny, I liked you most when you were four years old, just after your mother died. You were so sweet, so lost."

"Yes, Dad."

Jimmy and I agreed that we would try to get my father to see a doctor. For some months now he had steadfastly refused, saying he was doing fine, a doctor couldn't tell him anything he didn't already know. But it was obvious that whatever he thought he already knew wasn't helping him. Once meticulous about his clothes, he now looked disheveled, his shirts stained at the cuffs, his expensive Italian slacks wrinkled and sagging, hiked up by a mismatched, tired-looking belt. At the table, his eyes closed between bites and the fork slipped from his hand as he nodded off. I wasn't surprised when his operating privileges were rescinded. He was furious when that happened. He called it a conspiracy. He would resign from staff, change hospitals again, they'd be sorry.

For Sunday breakfast I made buckwheat pancakes, the way he used to make them in the old days, big. But mine were lighter and I got maple syrup for Jimmy and me because we couldn't stomach my father's molasses. I made the coffee strong and the bacon crisp and blotted it on paper towels. Jimmy announced that he was going to stay around the house that day to do some gardening. I played a jazzy version of "The Yellow Rose of Texas," a song my father liked. We wanted him to be in a receptive mood. Jimmy started off.

"Hey, it just occurred to me when I looked at the calendar—"

"What calendar?" my father interrupted.

"You know, the calendar with the Vargas girl. Anyway, it occurred to me that it's about time for you to get a check-up—"

"Which girl was that?" my father said.

"Dad, you should get checked out."

"Is that the one with a black see-through thing covering her backside?"

Jimmy caught the middle of his lower lip with his teeth and blew out on both sides. "Come on, Dad," he said. "Why don't you see Dr. Michaelman. He took good care of you before."

"That quack."

"How about Dr. Gruenfeld. You trust him, don't you?"

"Gruenfeld is a butcher. I wouldn't trust him with a dog."

"Come on, Dad."

"An old dog."

"Okay, okay," Jimmy said. "But you're not even taking care of yourself. You're supposed to be walking and following the special diet. And at least you should be taking the medicine Dr. Michaelman prescribed."

My father clanked his cup hard into the saucer. "Snake oil," he said.

Jimmy and I looked at each other. We were obviously getting nowhere.

"Now, if you two are finished ganging up on me, I've got things to do." He reached into his pocket and pulled out the key to his room. We didn't look up as he left the table, tripping a little over the leg of his chair. Jimmy looked straight ahead as I speared a piece of bacon and let it drop on the plate.

The following week Elizabeth Bingham died. Elizabeth of the vanilla-scented hands and peppermint breath, Elizabeth of the soft, abundant body and long brown arms that held you close and swept the hair from your forehead, Elizabeth of the sleepy Mississippi voice that said: "Come over here, Jorie girl. Gimme some sugar." My father would say: "That's the only sugar you're allowed, Elizabeth." Then she'd laugh. "I knows that, Dr. Tom," she'd say. "I don't want no trouble from you."

They met while my father was an intern. Elizabeth came on the bus to his Wilshire Boulevard office; she was his first private patient. I hadn't seen her in a long time, but I knew her diabetes was bad. She was almost blind and she had lost her right foot and part of the left. Until my father's last heart attack, he still would make house calls to the South-Central neighborhood where she lived. Her son and grandchildren would guard the car while he was there.

On the day of her funeral, Jimmy and I paced at the bottom of the stairs, waiting for my father. "We're going to be late, Dad!" I shouted up the staircase. I turned to Jimmy. "Can't you go hurry him up? We'll never make it on time." Finally, Jimmy went up and pushed through the door when my father didn't answer. In a few minutes, he came back down, alone. "What is he—" I started to say until I saw Jimmy's bloodless face.

"Just don't say anything," he said, looking away. "We're going without him."

On the way to the funeral, my mind railed with silent questions: Why didn't he come? What was he doing? What's wrong with him? What made Jimmy's hands shake, even as he held the steering wheel? I knew I couldn't ask, or even make a sound. I knew that we were barely afloat. One question could sink us, one word.

"We're sorry," we said to Elizabeth's family. "But he's too sick. He wanted to come. He sends his condolences. He's very sad."

That evening Jimmy and I sat at the dining room table. My father was still upstairs, locked in his room. Jimmy pushed up from his chair several times, paced the floor and sat back down. He wanted to talk but seemed unable to start. I wanted to help him but I was no better at it than he was. So much of what we shared between us we'd always left unsaid, so it was difficult to approach a troubling subject directly. We didn't have enough practice. I looked down in my lap, then out the window. The sun had just set, leaving a faint orange streak in the sky. Following a warm beam of light that stretched across the room, I stared at my sun-colored fingers as they ran up and down the ridges in the Coke bottle. Finally, I had to break the silence. "You were going to tell me about Dad," I said.

Jimmy's voice trembled. "He was shooting up," he said, taking a deep breath. "That's what he was doing when I went upstairs to get him. He didn't even know I was there."

"What did you say?"

"I knew he couldn't come to the funeral, so I didn't say anything. I just left." We were silent for a moment. His elbows on the table, Jimmy held his head in his hands.

"My God" was all I could say. "My God." I started to swallow tears, but I managed to control it. Tears clung to the back of my throat, then went dry. "What are we going to do?"

Jimmy glanced up at me hesitantly, but seeing that I wasn't going to cry, he seemed to gather strength. "Just swallow it, like everything else."

"I can't," I said.

"Then we have to do something to help him," he said. "We have to find a way."

It took three days to gather enough courage to call Leonard Michaelman, but I had no one else to call. I was afraid my voice would give me away, that he would be able to hear my desperation. It took three days to stuff it all down—the need to talk to someone, the need to cry. I narrowed it down to one favor. I would allow myself to ask just this. My hands shook as I dialed his number. "I'm glad you called, Jorie," he said in a voice so kind it put me at ease. "But your dad won't come in to see me. I've asked, but I can't force him."

"I know," I said. "But can't you drop by the house? Pretend you were just in the neighborhood?"

He laughed. "Right," he said. I remembered that laugh: lilting, abbreviated. He laughed again; it pressed down in me like a deep ache.

I tried to explain some of what was going on with my father, that he seemed disengaged and ill and was medicating himself. I didn't explain it very well because most of it I didn't understand. "I don't know," I said to most of Leonard's questions. "I don't know." I told him about some of the business deals gone bad, the chinchilla farm, the oil well with no mineral rights. I tried to make it sound funny, like these were just crazy, off-beat schemes: joke material.

He didn't laugh. "I'll be there Sunday," he said.

When Sunday came I wanted to escape or hide somewhere. My father was up in his room and Leonard Michaelman was at the front door, two solid objects on a collision course, thanks to me. Somehow I had to let happen what I had caused to happen, but now that the time had arrived, I had cold feet.

With Leonard behind me, I knocked on my father's door. Then he was standing there in front of us, towering and red-faced. "Dad, Dr. Michaelman's here to see you," I said.

Leonard extended his hand. "Sorry to barge in on you, Tom," he said. "It's time for Mohammed to come to the mountain. How are you feeling?"

My father hesitated for a moment, then with obvious pique shook his hand. "We'll go down to the library," he said coolly, almost brushing Leonard aside.

But I could see Leonard watching him, taking him in. "I thought we could have a chat, like old times, maybe talk about a few cases," he said to my father's back as he followed him down the stairs. "And I wanted to see if you've been taking care of yourself."

My father glanced back over his shoulder. "I'll bet," he said.

I brought them coffee on a tray. As I set out the cream and sugar I stole a look at my father. He looked like a cornered animal, a bear. He was breathing heavily. I didn't dare look at Leonard before I left the room in a hurry.

Pacing nervously from one side of the kitchen to the other,

I stopped to wipe the tile, then I decided to make more coffee. I measured coffee into the basket of the electric percolator, poured in the water and plugged it in. "Good to the last drop" it said on the label. I remembered how my father always used to say, "What's wrong with the last drop?" or "Don't give me the last drop; it's not good." He was a stickler for words. Had been. What was he now? I didn't know.

I carried the coffeepot to the dining room, which was not too far from the library where my father was talking with Leonard Michaelman. It seemed they were in there a long time. Maybe not. Perhaps because I didn't hear the small outbursts of laughter that had always punctuated their conversations—the long trail of their voices was unrelieved by the usual peaks and valleys—I felt the perverse resistance of time to move forward. Not so much that I wanted it to go fast; what I wanted was to get this over with. I vacillated between hope and dread, at times feeling both at once, in equal measure. Maybe Leonard would recognize right away what the problem was, maybe he'd suggest some quick and easy therapy. If my father wouldn't accept treatment, we could get past him by subterfuge, the way he used to give me penicillin shots when I needed them. I imagined that after this treatment he would recover; then he would forgive us for ganging up on him. Or, it occurred to me, what would I do if now my father was acting convincingly normal? It could happen. Some days my father seemed perfectly fine. If this was one of those days, Leonard would come out wondering what was *my* problem. Then I'd have to face both of them, guilty.

After a while, I went back into the room under the pretext of bringing fresh coffee. They were standing, unmatched figures, in front of the fireplace, Leonard backing away but I could see him calculating the limits of the senior man's power. My father's voice was charged with anger, but it wasn't anger I saw in his face, it was fear.

"So, you're in on it too," he said. "I suppose they sent you—"

"Now Tom, nobody's out to get you," Leonard said. "You need help. I want you to get it—"

"What is this—some kind of kangaroo court?" The question was punctuated with a short, contemptuous outburst of air. "Liars. Jackals. And you're one of them, the worst, an ungrateful backstabber. Do you realize what this means? If I lose hospital privileges, I'm through. Ruined—even if it is a pack of lies. They don't even have to prove I'm guilty; just making the charge is enough to destroy my reputation. You're on that committee; I know you are."

"That's not true," Leonard said, looking anxiously into my father's face but holding his ground. "But there are suspicions. You should know that some men are pushing for a review, to get you booted off staff. I've tried to plead your case, but I'm only one voice. Tom, you can avoid all this. Take a leave of absence. Get off this stuff. Get well. Think of your kids. Jorie—"

"Interesting that you should bring her up." My father's voice took on a slightly different tone, angry still, but ascendant. "I know about your involvement with my daughter, Leonard. Did you believe I wouldn't know?" Now he glanced in my direction, bristling with accusation. Then he turned back to face Leonard. "Yes. I know what's been going on. Do you think I'm stupid? How do you think I felt, a prisoner in that hospital bed, watching you go off with my teenage daughter every night? Do you think I'm blind? Well, if you think you're going to ruin me, think again. Jorie is underage. There's a name for that. How do you think your kangaroo committee will feel about statutory rape?"

I felt myself turn liquid and drew a slow wet breath. "You never said anything before," I said. "If you knew, why didn't you say something?"

"You know I never liked to interfere with you—"

"No," I said, gasping. "That's not why." My father stood

before me in an expanding bubble of light. "You didn't say anything because you really didn't care. Did you? That's what women are for, isn't it? You didn't mind if I went off with Leonard every night. You never said anything until it affected you. Until you could use it against him." My voice shook but I had to go on. "I want you to know that he never forced me. I knew exactly what I was doing. Yes. I wanted it to happen. I wanted him to love me."

My father flinched at the unspeakable word.

"Yes, LOVE," I repeated. "He's the only one who ever expressed any affection for me. He loved me. He made me feel wanted." Swallowing hard, I tried to keep the tears from rising up. "Until we, until he—"

"You mean to say until he was finished with you?" My father's voice was a stone. "*Love,* as you call it, must not have much staying power."

Silence. Then Leonard's voice punctured through. "Tom," he said. "You know you don't mean this. Neither of you mean this . . ." He looked at us, one to the other, his face alarmed and sad. It was the kind of helpless expression one has at the scene of a drowning. He straightened to his full height and turned to my father. "Tom, you know I wouldn't rape your daughter."

Stepping closer, my father glared down on Leonard's face, his eyes searing under level eyebrows. "And you know I'm not on drugs," he said. "We have an understanding then. I would like to leave it at that."

Watching Sister Charitas polish her glasses on a white handkerchief, I thought of the whiteness of Leonard Michaelman's face when he left that day. Even his voice had a pallor. It seemed old-fashioned for her to use a handkerchief, something an elderly person would do; a young woman would use a tissue.

"There!" Sister Charitas said, putting her glasses back on. "You all look brighter now." A few chuckles broke out from the front row.

As I sat there in class, I relived the afternoon we confronted my father. I remembered catching Leonard at the front door, just as he strode out. "I'm sorry," he'd said. "I tried. But I can't do more."

"Now the surprise," Sister Charitas said. "Cardinal McIntyre is coming to give the May Day address. He's asked to speak to some representatives from each class, nothing formal, but we should be prepared."

I remembered how Leonard kissed my cheek and looked at me with such directness I could not look away. I knew I couldn't pretend with him. "What is it?" I said.

"I don't know for sure, but I think he's addicted to morphine. That's what he was taking for chest pain. It may be more than that now." He pressed my shoulder, which was now as tall as his. "He didn't mean what he said to you in there. And he probably won't even remember saying it. You know he's not himself. It's not easy, but try to be understanding."

I knew my father wasn't himself, that he hadn't been for a long time, but I also felt the splinters of truth that had surfaced then and I knew that neither he nor I were likely to forget them.

I recalled how cold I had felt, how embarrassed I was, shaking like that under Leonard's hand. "I miss you so much," he'd said so softly I could hardly hear him, and left.

"Jorie. Jorie!" Sister Charitas's voice swooped down. "You're not paying attention." With that, she turned her back and walked to the other side of the room. I watched the folds of her black veil overlap into perfect triangles down her back and the black scapular fall straight to the heels of her shoes. I looked around the room, at the faces of the other girls. At that moment they all looked exactly like Sister Charitas, even Sally

Matsumoto, even Maria Chaca who was Guatemalan Indian. All their faces mirrored her face, glowed with her skin, looked expectantly with her eyes, smiled with her modest mouth.

"Sing praises to the Lord," she said. "Be glad and rejoice in Him. The psalm says: 'Make a joyful noise unto the Lord, all ye lands. Serve the Lord with gladness: come before his presence with singing.'" Her eyes lowering earthward, Sister Charitas clasped her hands. "We all celebrate life, don't we?" Then, raising her hand, she said: "All those who love life raise your hands!" Hands shot up.

Sister Charitas stood in front of me, her hand high overhead. Her pale eyes wouldn't leave me alone. First they were puzzled, then cross, then encouraging as with a baby's first step, then hurt. Why was I doing this to her? Everyone should love life. Why didn't I love life? My arm was heavy. I pulled it up from my side to the top of the desk chair. I tried to raise it, but it wouldn't go up. The more I tried, the heavier it got. Her eyes glimmered with the question. My arm was no longer mine to command; I strained to raise it from the shoulder. Then, as if lifted by some heavenly puppeteer, my arm bent at the elbow and my hand lifted up, not high, but straight to the ceiling.

May Day came and went. Blue and white banners brushed with chancery lettering, too pretty to throw away, were displayed outside the chapel for an extra week. Sister Philomena informed us that the properties of light would be on the final exam.

Needing more money for living expenses, I took a new job with more hours. Every afternoon and all day Saturday I sorted mail at Prudential, breaking down the huge bins of incoming envelopes into stacks for Divisions, Departments, Suite numbers, Executive titles, a secretary named Wendy. I collected a paycheck every other week, which spared me from having to ask my father for funds. The times I didn't receive the meager household allowance from my father's office, Jimmy and I pitched in to pay the gas and electric. We didn't keep much food in the house; what there was was cheap and filling, mostly bread. My father seemed hardly to eat at all. I gave up on preparing dinner. No one showed up. Jimmy worked as a car mechanic in the afternoon. At night, he raced stock cars on Riverside Drive, for bets. His fearlessness earned him extra income. My father kept odd hours. Mostly he locked himself in his upstairs suite, the former sun porch and Alex's bedroom that by now were fading into memory.

So our days continued. I got up in the morning and brushed my teeth, went to class, went to work, did my job. My father and I didn't speak. I avoided him when I heard his steps and I believe he avoided me. We could not admit the knowledge that had surfaced, nor could we face the conflict that had passed between us. I didn't call Leonard Michaelman again; I was too mortified. And I didn't want to make trouble for him. I knew that my father's charges could have serious consequences. I knew that they could, in fact, ruin his life. Besides, Leonard had said there was nothing he could do, under the circumstances. He said that you can't help someone who refuses help.

Meanwhile, Jimmy brought some friends over. We ate spaghetti with meatballs and played charades. We found some striped ribbon candy left over from Christmas and divided it among us. I played two of Mendelssohn's *Lieder ohne Worte* on the piano. Jimmy and I did our rendition of the Okefenokee Swamp dance. We did our washboard and kazoo rendition of Ravel's *Bolero.* They all clapped.

22

NO ANSWER

I REMEMBER WHAT THE sky was like that day. There were fast-moving clouds. At first they glided sideways in clusters, then were followed by swirling bands of froth. The bands quickly coalesced until the whole sky was opaque, all this happening fast as I waited for the sirens in the withdrawing light. In a few minutes a fire truck wound its way up the hill with its sirens blaring. A few moments later I watched my father's locked door give way under the fireman's crowbar, the gnawing sound intensifying to a ripping crack.

If Jimmy had been there, he would have picked the lock, or forced it, or broken down the door himself. I couldn't have done any of those things. The fact is, I didn't even try. There was something about the insistent ringing of the phone. It was ringing as I came home from work, passed my father's car in the garage, climbed the front stairs, opened the front door. I can't explain how I knew it had been ringing for a long time before I got there, or that it would continue to ring until I picked it up. It was Patsie, from my father's office. "He didn't show up today," she said. "Everything's a mess. He had a lot of appointments this afternoon. Some people left, but the waiting room is still full—can you believe it—everybody's mad. The hospital's been calling . . ."

I remembered seeing my father's car still in the garage and suddenly my mouth went so dry it was hard to swallow, hard to loosen my tongue enough to form words. "Send them all home," I said finally, my hand dropping to my side, the *but anana nana nanana nana* of Patsie's voice still droning through the receiver as I held it over the cradle and let it drop.

Beyond the fireman's back my father's body was slumped over, a bloody glass syringe at his foot. I pushed to go inside and saw his face pressed cheek-down against the bed, his eyes abandoned, his legs dangling, a sockless foot gray-white and marked with blood. Someone spoke to me but I didn't answer. The voice seemed like part of an elaborate hallucination: the flash of the camera, the inspector licking the end of his pencil, jotting notes as if he were tallying a score, the inspector flipping his notebook closed, saying, "Well, that's it for here!"

Only my father's body was real. It was the only thing I believed completely. The voices, the circling presence of men in the room—all was a blur, except for the body of my father, which was absolutely real and still.

As I watched the sheet being pulled up, I felt myself go numb, as if my circuits had died, as if I had become disconnected. I stood there, silent, all cut wires. From the top of the stairs, I watched with unblinking eyes as the stretcher descended. It was bouncing, its full length filled, the stretcher bearers sweating from their burden in the day's heat, panting as they reached the bottom of the stairs, then wiping their hands and foreheads before sliding the sheet-covered mound into the coroner's car.

Jimmy didn't ask any questions when I told him. He just stood there, nodding like he already knew. At that point we were beyond asking questions, beyond searching for answers. It no longer mattered. There were no answers that could have unshattered us.

We had no idea where Alex was. He never called. Wherever he was, I presumed he didn't read obituaries. I had heard of people sitting up, startled, in the middle of the night, having been awakened by some ghostly messenger—perhaps the loved one himself—then knowing with absolute certainty that the person has died. I wondered if this could happen to Alex, or if it required a mystic sensitivity, or perhaps a profound spiritual connection between the persons involved. But then I thought no, it was unlikely that Alex would have been jarred out of sleep by a passing spirit, that wherever he was, for this day at least, he was spared the pain of another leave-taking.

The days that followed were obscured by a kind of haze, an auditory haze that made everything muffled. Conversations sounded like they were under water. When Patsie called, she was close to hysterical and didn't know what to do or say. We told her to cancel all the appointments and call the regular patients to inform them of my father's death. She was to say that he was suddenly taken ill, that's all. Most people knew he had a bad heart. We couldn't see beyond simple tasks. Jimmy and I numbly made the arrangements, mostly just by answering questions on the telephone, not by any particular plan. Do you want your father to be cremated? Yes. Is there to be a memorial service? No. We wouldn't have known how to go about it. Where is he to be buried? Next to our mother. We found out that my father had purchased adjacent grave sites for all of us, in the event of an accident, I suppose. I thought about that at night, our graves, side by side, empty and waiting.

When Leonard Michaelman called, I was still feeling numb. He was so sorry, he said. If there was anything he could do . . . I said we were fine, we'd manage. He told me he knew now that I was only fifteen. "Almost sixteen," I said.

He laughed at that. "You know it's impossible," he said.

"Don't you think I know that?" I said. "I'm not asking for anything."

What I thought about most during the days after my father's death was my mother. Not the shadowy mother of my memory, what I couldn't stop thinking about was her absence. I wondered how different our lives would have been had she lived, and whether we would have turned out to be different people. I thought about the fact that no one, except Leonard, called us when my father died. We were that isolated in the world. I thought if my mother had lived, we might have had friends to consult, or to comfort us.

When I thought about my father, waves of anger swept over me. I blamed him for becoming addicted, for being estranged from us, for always leaving us when we needed him, for leaving us with nothing. I blamed him for dying. Then the anger would give way to unshakable sadness, knowing that I had loved him and he had loved us in his way, and now we would never be reconciled.

I sat down to write Alex a letter, even though I didn't have his address. *Dear Alex*, I wrote, then stared at the page, wondering what to say next. *I'm sad to tell you that Dad has died. I'm writing this because I don't want you to find out by accident, or to be told by a stranger, to be surprised that way. I would like to explain what happened.* The image of my father's slumped body flashed back to me, but I tried to push it from my mind. Thinking back, I tried to retrieve earlier images, good images—my father walking on the beach next to an edge of receding foam, the wet sand reflecting red in the day's last light, the boys' feet slapping along next to him. I wanted to remember better times.

But I can only tell you what happened at the end. I know what happened. I don't know why. Sometimes my father would swim with one of the boys on his back. Alex didn't like the water in his face.

They think it was an accidental overdose. So you see, it wasn't really his fault. He wasn't in control.

I recalled the cool of my father's neck as he carried me sick and feverish to recover in the privilege of his room. So long ago.

Remember, Alex, when you were carsick? Dad always let you sit in the front seat, with a wet towel blowing in the window. And remember how he always gave you first choice of every-thing? It wasn't just because you were the oldest. I'm sure it was his way of showing that he loved you.

Images slipped from my mind as fast as they arose; I couldn't hold on to them. Always the intrusion of his still, gray face.

He had so many responsibilities, so many people depended on him, probably even more than we knew about. You must know we were just a small part of his world. No wonder he pushed himself to keep working, even when he wasn't well. No wonder everything came apart.

In my memory Alex and my father put down their shovels, then stomp on Sleepwalker's grave, compacting the dirt with their feet. Alex's jaw is taut as he covers his footprints in silence. *I know what you're thinking, Alex. And maybe you're right. Maybe there is no excuse. I don't understand about the drugs, except that they took him insidiously. I guess he was a man who thought he would never lose control.*

I didn't know what more to say. The word *forgive* came to mind. Forgive. I wrote it down.

23

A DIFFERENT KIND OF FREEDOM

RADUALLY I REALIZED I was not shattered. After the headline: PROMINENT DOCTOR FOUND DEAD OF OVER-DOSE after the coroner's inquest, after the FBI, the IRS, the DA, the property assessor, the bank investigator, and a parade of attorneys representing people I had never even heard of, after everyone who claimed to have any vesting in my father's affairs had elbowed their way into a long and intertwining line, I stepped outside and found myself whole.

I hiked in the foothills behind our house, retracing the familiar trails in the long day's light. Wild mustard splattered itself along the flank of the hill, just as I had always remembered it. A mockingbird, beak opened on a dark berry, quickly flew past me into a tree, to a flash of yellow mouth. I could see the roof of our house in the distance: curved red tiles in a euca-lyptus frame. When the sun began to sink, its rays stretched over the red distance, I turned toward home, thinking: This place will always be mine. I ran across one of the roses that my father had planted years ago, now feral and draping carelessly over a dead shrub. Some of the canes crawled along the ground like thorny snakes. Just a few ragged flowers gave off an intense fragrance. I held one to my nose and smelled my whole life.

Jimmy and I promised ourselves that we would hold things together until he graduated from high school and I finished my junior year. It was only a few weeks.

"Piece of cake," Jimmy said. Pooling our income, we were able to stay in the house under minimal conditions—essential phone calls only, wartime frugality. "Mooch when possible," Jimmy said.

Tyrone Bingham, Elizabeth's son, called to ask if there was something he could do. "Yes," I said. "You can take my mother's piano; it's the only thing I want to save."

"I'll keep it safe," he said. And he did.

The day after Jimmy's graduation, he surprised me by enlisting in the Army. "May as well," he said. "With Nam heating up and no college deferment, they'd draft me anyway. This way at least I'll have some choice." He went to Fort Bragg to train for the Special Forces. He said he was learning to be an airborne jungle guerrilla. I had this image of large acrobatic primates wearing green berets. He liked the songs in training camp, but not the drills, he wrote.

"What is it about, the war?" I asked on the phone.

"Eisenhower had a theory about dominoes," he said. "And that's related to the doctrine of containment. Containment of communism: that's what it's about." But that wasn't what it was about for him. He liked jumping out of planes. It clears your head.

Meanwhile I stayed in the house, not opening the second notices, the third notices, the red-lettered final notices, watching them pile up. Every morning when I got up, I wondered if the lights would go on or if the stove would light. So far, so good. I put all my belongings in two boxes and two large shopping bags, light enough to carry when the time came. I swept the floors and dusted and washed the windows and arranged fresh flowers and placed things just as I liked them, preparing the house for its abandonment, composing a memory.

A pair of crows nested in the spruce that grew up along the side of the house. Outside my bedroom window, the rustle of black wings.

It was about seven o'clock on a balmy summer evening, not yet dark, when I saw the black Cadillac parked in front of our house. I could see a man sitting in the driver's seat, smoking. I walked up the stairs and opened the front door to find da Boss waiting inside. He was wearing a well-starched light blue shirt and linen trousers. As I walked in and closed the door, he stepped forward and reached out to embrace me, but I withdrew.

"I didn't mean to scare you," he said, backing away. "But the door was unlocked. So I came in."

"I'm not scared, not at all," I said, trying hard to sound convincing.

He laughed, not taking his eyes off me. "No?" he said, waiting a moment as if giving me time to reconsider. Silently, I returned his gaze. "Moxie—that's what you got," he said. "I like that in a girl." He gave me a hesitant and almost curious look. "I think we can be friends, don't you?" I didn't answer. "By the way, I feel like I've known you all your life, but we've never been formally introduced. My name is Joseph Gold. Call me Joe." The mitt of his hand wrapped warmly around mine, some seconds longer than was comfortable.

"You don't know me," I said. "You only know my name," I said.

"I know you don't like to be called Marjorie, correct?" I didn't answer. "Well, Jorie," he continued, "I'm sorry what happened to your father. When he died, I lost a good friend and I feel really bad about that. I wanted to tell you how sorry I am."

When I didn't reply, he nodded almost imperceptibly, his double chin bouncing a little against the starched blue collar. "Look," he said. "Can we sit down for a minute? I just want to talk to you. I just want to know how you're getting along."

"Fine," I said, motioning to the sofa. I sat on an adjacent chair. "We're getting along fine."

"I can see that," he said. "You are one healthy-looking girl. But you said 'we' and by that you're playing with the truth. I know your brothers are gone." He hiked up his trousers then straightened the pleat, his eyes still fixed on my face. "So you see, I know that you're alone now." He smiled at what must have been alarm in my face and waited a while before speaking again. "Look, don't misunderstand me, I wouldn't take advantage. Oh, I know you're independent. The last time I talked to your father, I told him he had to look out for a pretty girl like you. And you know what he said? He said he raised you to look out for yourself. But I came to make you a sincere offer. I want to help you, no strings attached. Just friends, okay? I can make sure you finish school, you know, all the way through college. Your dad told me you're a smart girl. And you won't have to work at Prudential Insurance; I can give you living expenses."

For a moment I'd hoped to make up some lies about my situation, but then I realized that he knew exactly what my situation was. There would be no point in lying. "Why do you want to help me?" I asked. "I don't even know who you are."

"I think you do," he said. He didn't blink. "Even though you may not want to admit it. You know your father was my doctor and my friend. He saved my life, more than once. He took care of my associates and my family. And he never betrayed my trust. That's why I want to help you."

"What about his other children, are you helping them?"

He laughed out loud. "You're no fool," he said, his eyes level, but still chuckling to himself. "The others are taken care of, at least, the ones I know. But don't be angry, Jorie. He loved you best. You and the boys, you were his number one family."

He was right about my reaction. It's true that I had felt a momentary sense of anger, of bitterness really, but it passed just as quickly as it came. Joe Gold had said just the words I had always needed to hear: that my father loved us, that we were number one.

Then I no longer saw him as a shadow in consort with my father's shadow. I still didn't see him as a friend, but by saying those words, he'd become an unwitting and unexpected liberator. And as a result, I felt as if an overwhelming weight had been lifted. From that moment on, I knew I would make it on my own.

As if he sensed the infusion of strength I'd experienced, he said, "Be smart about this. You may not look it, but you're just a kid. What are you gonna do? There's taxes owed and big debts. This house and all that's in it, your father's car and properties, everything will be taken away. You'll have nothing to fall back on. Nothing."

I stood up and started to walk toward the front door. "I'll manage," I said. "Thank you, Mr. Gold—Joe—but I don't need your help. I can take care of myself."

It didn't matter to me if his offer was earnest. I didn't want his friendship or his money, whether or not he would at some point, as I assumed he would, call in the debt. I didn't want his help under any circumstances; it was a point of pride.

"I can make it easier for you—" he started to say.

"No," I said. "If you were really my father's friend, you will let me be who he raised me to be."

Joe Gold did not press me anymore. As he slowly walked through the doorway, his face remained impassive. Then he turned to me, neither jovial nor concerned, and cupped his hand around the side of my neck. "I wouldn't force you," he said. "You can call me."

Toward the end of the summer, an attorney tracked me down at work. He said I would have a court-appointed guardian. "You've got to be kidding," I said. "Who said so?"

I went downtown to talk to the judge; we sat in his chambers.

Afterward, he signed a paper officially declaring that I was what I was: an emancipated minor. I folded the paper and asked for an envelope to put it in, to keep it clean. I knew I would be needing it; I didn't have a driver's license yet. Jimmy had left me his peacock blue '49 Dodge with scavengers, four-barrel carburetors, glass packs, and Tijuana-special tuck 'n roll upholstery. I drove it with a learner's permit and counted on my luck to hold out. Several times police officers had pulled up beside me. They looked at the car and me in it. They watched it shake and listened to the noisy loping of the engine, smiled, and moved on.

My luck held. Every day I expected to come home to an eviction notice, or a house without gas or water. The telephone was all I paid for. Either by some mysterious benevolence or bureaucratic inefficiency, I was able to stay on while I looked for a cheap apartment. I planned to move before school started.

Jimmy got his orders. He waited in line for an hour to call me the night before they shipped out for Viet Nam. It was hard to believe he was really going. I prattled on about whether he had everything he needed—socks, insect repellent, writing paper. He told me not to worry, they provide everything. Then I went on about wearing ear protectors, and keeping his feet dry, about using antifungal powder. Watch out for mosquitoes, watch out for vipers, watch out for *Trichophyton mentagrophytes*. I pulled the words out as fast as they would come, hoping for the right ones to appear, knowing they wouldn't. I couldn't stop myself: "Drink lots of water, not *their* water, careful you don't get *onychomycosis*; remember what Dad said . . ." I didn't finish.

There was silence on the line. But I could hear Jimmy's breath as if he were standing next to me. "Good-bye, old girl," he said.

Weeks later I received Jimmy's letter, written from a troop carrier, somewhere between Guam and the South China Sea. He said he liked to stand on the fantail and look out over the water. Once there were Portuguese men-of-war as far as the eye could see, floating on the water like blossoms, like offerings on the Ganges. On dark nights he watched a trail of phosphorescent plankton turned up by the ship's screw, a glowing froth in the black water. In the black night, an arbor of stars. He had learned the Latin names for the southern constellations: Canis Major, Circinus, Corvus, Antlia. "You know what Antlia is?" he wrote. "An air pump!" But the best was when the moon was full. It turned the sea metallic, the water tricky and sleek as mercury.

"Remember," Jimmy wrote, *"Don't let the moon get in your ears . . ."*

I could hear the country twang in his voice. I touched the words on the page, and sang back: *"When your teeth fall out, remember they are mine . . ."*

On the night before I left the house, I turned on all the lights and wandered from room to room as in a dream. I opened drawers and cupboards, doors and closets: spaces of dreams. I spent a long time in each room, listening to the voices coming from chairs and through the thresholds of doors, strains of Rachmaninoff under Alex's fingers, the crackle of my father's newspaper. I walked into my room with the audacious red carpet and smiled at what I had been. Leaving the upstairs alight, I went down and stood for a moment at the top of a wooden stairway before pulling the light chain, then went down into the basement.

On the far side of the raw brick wall there was a shelf,

empty except for a cardboard box encased in yellowed paper and a dense blue smell. It was the box that contained souvenirs of my mother, the only tangible things that remained of her. It had been years since I visited this box, but I remembered each item well. In it were books of music, a filigree and garnet necklace in a satin-lined box, a leather-bound photograph album. Each photograph was both familiar and remote; I looked them over as I would have recollected a book, refamiliarizing myself with the characters, enjoying again a favorite scene: On the first black page, fastened in black corner brackets, is a picture of my mother as a small child, chubby in a white linen dress, a wreath of flowers across her forehead. In another picture she and her mother stand side by side on wooden skis, with the Alps white and jagged behind them. I can see something of the boys and myself in both their faces. In the Austrian passport, her face glows fresh under a schoolgirl's beret. This is someone who is easy to remember.

Under the photograph album, stacked to one side, are some cards made by a child's hand. All are inscribed to *Mutter* or *Vater*. One of the cards is rendered in bright pastels, a square house with many windows, symmetrically placed and outlined in blue. The top right window is filled with brilliant yellow. Printed above the house, like a banner in the sky, reads: *O Licht im schlafenden haus!* (O light in the sleeping house!)

After removing all the cards, I saw something lying flat on the bottom of the box that I hadn't noticed before. The paper covering was the same cardboard brown as the box. It was a phonograph record in a plain paper slipcover. When I pulled it out, I was surprised at how thick and heavy it was. It was a home recording disc, with two holes, one in the middle, the other about an inch to the side of it. There was a blue and white label, with the title handwritten, "Alex's 1st Birthday."

I carried the record upstairs, then cleaned it with a camel's hair brush before placing it on the turntable. First, the sound of a piano—the classical composition of "Twinkle, Twinkle, Little Star"—Blam! Blam! a baby slamming his palms on the keys. Laughter. "Oh, very good!" My mother's voice. "Do you play again?" Bam Bam Bam! *Wunderbar,* my golden boy . . . Give Mummy a kiss—" More laughter. "Is today your birthday?" A baby's sound: Da. Again, laughter. I listened to the record several times through, trying to picture each moment as it was revealed by the voices, until I had a vivid image, a birthday frozen in sound.

Then I imagined Alex and Jimmy, not as they were as children, but as they were then: Alex playing "Magnetic Rag" in a dimly lit bar in downtown Vancouver. His hair is long and bushy and he's grown a beard that flames onto his cheeks. The bar is busy almost as soon as it opens; he's got a following. Alex is unaware that the same people come back every evening to listen to his music. He plays with his eyes closed. Jimmy wiping mud off an M16, singing softly to himself. He's shared the spice cake I sent with his buddies, but the citronella candle he keeps for himself. It's supposed to ward off bugs, but of course he can't light it. He smiles at my naivete. But he carries it anyway, maybe there's something else it might ward off. Jimmy casts his song out on the river, a tributary of the Mekong, which flows eastward through scorched valleys and empties into the sea.

I imagined my mother, too. I felt her there, by my shoulder. Her face was impossibly young. Not the schoolgirl face in the photograph, but the distant face I vaguely remember, the face on a white pillow, reflected in a mirror. I told her that I wasn't afraid to leave, in fact, I was excited. I was used to freedom, but it had been the kind of freedom that bears down on you, that drives you into small rooms with doors. But this was a different kind of freedom and I was buoyant. I showed her the photographs of my father and brothers, picking them out of my packed suitcase. She took her time, looking carefully at each one. I thought she looked bewildered.

"Don't be surprised," I said to her. "This is who we have become in your absence."

The next morning I loaded my things into the car. At that moment the sum of my possessions could be contained within the souped-up body of an old blue Dodge. It started with a roar, blowing black soot from the dual exhaust pipes. The car rocked from side to side as I revved up the engine. The morning was clear and warm after a night of gusty winds. The air was ripe with summer and dry leaves crackled along the sides of the road. Tall eucalyptus leaned into the street and dropped blue shadows onto the car's long hood. Popping the clutch as I started down the hill, I turned on the radio and took one last glance at the abandoned house before it disappeared behind me. I tapped on the steering wheel, keeping time to the music, the voice of Elvis: *Tutti-frutti! All-rutti! Tutti-frutti! All-rutti!* I rolled fast down the hill toward the city, singing with Elvis, taking each familiar curve with ease. Funny, the songs you remember.

*Y*esterday Alex flew in from New York, where he's been doing studio work and playing at a nightclub in SoHo. He's shaved his beard, but his hair is wild, a tumbleweed on fire. Jimmy didn't have far to come since he moved back to L.A. after Viet Nam and medical school. We've decided to meet at the La Brea tar pits, where as children we came to see the bones. Gases still bubble up from ponds of shimmering tar, while nearby, the replica of a doomed mastodon silently trumpets into the pungent air. Now the bones have been neatly labeled and arranged in glass cases: saber-tooth tigers, giant sloths, Dire wolves. But when we were here, there was no museum yet, only the tar ponds and excavation sites, where you could peer down into a pit studded with skulls and ribcages and long bones, all muddled together. Now there are walls mounted with bones—all sorted out—and dioramas and a gift shop, where I buy a book on the Pleistocene and a brightly colored puzzle for my little girl, who waits expectantly at my side.

I've brought my daughter to meet her uncles for the first time. Her hair is the color of new pennies and she is very small, even for a four-year-old, so we call her Thumbelina, which she doesn't seem to mind. After we wander through all the exhibits, she's getting restless, so we go out to the surrounding lawn to let her run. We sit down on the grass and leisurely scan the park, Jimmy reclining back on his elbows, Alex sitting forward with his arms on his knees. We look out to where some boys are playing with kites and mothers with small children sit on blankets and peel fruit. We look one to the other, exchanging half smiles and reciprocal sighs in an atmosphere filled with words unsaid. And for this moment we are content, watching Thumbelina chase pigeons, clapping her hands to make them fly. Then she runs up and throws her arms around me, holding me at arm's length, pushing her face forward and squeezing her eyes. "I can tell that you love me," she says. I mimic her expression, squeezing my eyes back at her, and kiss her nose. Laughing, she runs away. We watch as she plucks a dandelion from the grass and blows it into the wind.

Why do I tell you this? So you know that for her, things will be different.